Only Make-Believe

Clarissa Ross

LET THE ORGY BEGIN!

Nita followed the other actors onto a set representing a banquet hall with a huge table at which nearly a hundred people could be seated. Cameramen were located at all corners of the studio, and two assistant directors were busily seating everyone. Von Eltz rose as waiters appeared to fill their wine glasses, and announced, "We will eat, drink and be merry!"

As the banquet progressed, Nita soon found that her head was reeling. A girl had leaped from her seat and, climbing onto the table itself, had torn off her dress and was now dancing in her filmy underthings. Men rose and toasted her with champagne, as Von Eltz watched it all with cynical detatchment. More frightening to Nita than the noise, drunken laughter, and blatantly erotic actions going on around her was the relaxing of her own inhibitions. Feelings coursed through her which she had known before only in the most thrilling moments of passion. Like the other, she was no longer in control of her emotions. In her last few seconds of coherent thought she realized dimly what had happened. Von Eltz had put a strong aphrodisiac in the wine, turning all the actors into his puppets. This was the secret of his great success as a director of powerfully erotic films. Nita laughed raucously at a suggestive remark from the man across the table from her, and found herself eagerly returning a stranger's lascivious kiss.

ONLY
MAKE-BELIEVE

Clarissa Ross

LEISURE BOOKS ❧ **NEW YORK CITY**

To my long-time staunch friends,
Ruth and Peter Bertolami

A LEISURE BOOK

Published by

Nordon Publications, Inc.
Two Park Avenue
New York, N.Y. 10016

Chapter One

It was an evening in April, 1920, in Lynn, Massachusetts, and the Nolans were having a party.

Not that this was anything out of the ordinary. The big, noisy Nolan family were always throwing parties. But this late Saturday night was a very special celebration, in honor of the third youngest son of the family of twelve, who had just finished playing a week in the vaudeville show being offered at the local motion picture emporium, the Orpheum. All the Nolans were there along with many of their friends. Marty Nolan, the star of the event, a gangling red-haired youth with a freckled face and winning smile, danced and mugged his way about the lower rooms of the modest frame house in which his family lived.

For one of his guests, pretty, black-haired Anita O'Hara, eldest daughter of butcher Ned O'Hara and his wife, Mollie, who lived next door, it was the most exciting evening of her life. For Anita was hopelessly, foolishly in love with Marty Nolan.

From the time she was eleven or twelve she had spent endless hours in movie houses and vaudeville theatres. Despite her father's growled warnings that all actors were little better than tramps, she was enthralled by the images of Mary Pickford, Douglas Fairbanks, Valentino and too many others to enumerate. The vaudeville stage shows accompanying the movies seemed just as magical to her. The tackiest of staging, the shabbiest costumes and the second-rate talents of the weekly parade of vaudevillians who appeared at the local theatre, were all transformed into glowing, glamorous mystery in her eyes.

Dan Nolan, Marty's proud father, was a member of the Lynn Fire Department. He was a huge man with a lilting tenor voice of which he was proud. His wife, overweight and jolly Rosie, played the piano with great gusto entirely by ear. And if the ancient upright rescued from some long-ago restaurant at a bargain price was a little out of tune, no one noticed it as Dan Nolan sang and his son, Marty, the star of the evening, did a soft shoe.

The place was filled with Irish faces and Irish laughter. There were a few "foreigners" in the group—like Louis Grimaldi, the Italian boy from down the street who had been Marty's friend since early school days. Louis now had an uncle in Revere who was making excellent gin for the Prohibition trade, and it was he who had supplied the alcoholic refreshments for the affair.

As the dancing and·singing went on, Louis came up to Anita with a glow of sheer happiness on his olive-skinned, pleasant face and said, "What do you think of Marty now?"

Admiration gleamed in Anita's lovely green eyes as she told the young man, "I think he's wonderful!"

"So's your old man!" Louis teased her in the latest slang.

"No, I really mean it!" she enthused. "Every minute I could get away from the restaurant this week I've been at the theatre watching him! He's the best on the bill! And one of the most popular acts we've had here in weeks!''

Louis said, "Well, he's a local. And then he's Marty! I always did like the kid!''

"Kid!'' she exclaimed in reproach. "He's at least as old as you! He has to be twenty-two! He's four years older than me!''

Louis enjoyed teasing her. "So now I know your age! You're sweet eighteen and never been kissed!''

She blushed. "You know that's not true! You've kissed me yourself!''

"And I'd like to kiss you more, in a lot of different places," he said with a knowing smile.

Anita turned away from him quickly. Louis had the reputation of being fast with the girls in the neighborhood. They all agreed that anybody who went out with him had to be careful. She wanted none of that. She was saving herself for someone like Marty, and for a stage career for herself. Working as a waitress at O'Reilly's was only temporary. She had no intention of remaining there. When she had enough money saved she was taking a train to New York and then straight to Hollywood.

Dan Nolan was now leading a sing-along of "Rosie O'Grady" and his boozy friends were joining in with drunken sentimentality. Marty stopped dancing and talked and shook hands with some friends. Then he headed straight for Anita, a purposeful look in his blue eyes.

He came up close and taking her hand in his said, "Let's go out to the back hall!''

The dark back hall was the only place not filled with guests. Marty embraced her hungrily and she thrilled to his multitude of kisses. She begged laughingly, "Let me breathe!''

Marty, still holding her, looked down into her face

7

and smiled. "I'm leaving after midnight on the night train," he said. "I open in upper New York State on Monday."

"You're so wonderful, Marty," she whispered huskily. "I just know you're going to be a great star!"

"Sure I am," he replied with Irish bravado. "I've got weeks of work ahead. And one of these days I'm going to join my pal, Billy Bowers, in Hollywood!"

She gasped at the name of the two-reel comedy star who had gained widespread fame as a bashful, awkward young man always struggling to win the lady of his choice. She said, "You actually *know* Billy Bowers?"

"Uh-huh," he nodded. "We played vaudeville together. But he's had all the lucky breaks."

"You'll be as big a star as he is, I know! I've been to the theatre almost every performance this week."

"The owner told me," Marty said. "And I told him it was because you had good taste!"

"Oh, Marty, I do love you so!"

"You mean it, kid?"

"You know I do," she said.

"Then come away with me tonight," the red-haired youth said as in the other room his father switched to singing, "It's a long way to Tipperary," and the gang in the front of the house raucously joined in.

She at once felt a thrill of excitement along with some apprehension. "I couldn't! What would my folks say?"

"That you were lucky to catch yourself a star!"

"My father hates actors! He calls them bums!" she worried.

"He better not let me hear him say that. I'll show him who's a bum!" Marty said with some anger.

"He doesn't really mean it," Anita told the young man as he held her close to him. "He's just afraid I

8

might marry some actor and go away. He knows how I love the movies and the vaudeville shows."

Marty said, "You want to go on the stage? Marry me and I'll take you into my act!"

"I'd never be able to," she protested. "I wouldn't be any good. I don't know how to sing or dance well enough!"

"I can show you," Marty said, and kissed her again. "In fact, I can show you a lot of things!"

She was trembling now, afraid of her own emotions. She truly cared for the red-haired young man and being in his arms had stirred up feelings which she wished she could ignore. Nervously, she asked, "Shouldn't we go back and join the others?"

Marty's smile was mocking. "They've never even noticed we're not there. Listen to Dad murdering 'I'm Just Wild About Harry!' They'll be singing that for the next ten minutes or so. When they get a favorite number they keep going over it!"

"Please, Marty, someone might come here and find us like this!"

"Is it a crime to hug and kiss? If so, I ought to be put in jail, kiddo!" And he laughed.

"Let me know where I can write you," she said.

"Come with me and you won't have to write," he told her.

"I couldn't! They'd never forgive me!"

"Listen, forget about them. Think about us! I love you, Nita. You're the only girl I'd ever ask to marry me. I get the others without any strings."

She was trembling and in a troubled voice, she asked, "But Marty, are you sure you truly love me?"

Marty's blue eyes were fixed on her in a most peculiar way. His voice suddenly became low and taut and he said, "I'll prove it to you!" And he took her by the hand and started to lead her up the dark back stairway.

She pulled back. "We can't go up there!"

"Don't be a ninny!" he said, almost harshly as he literally dragged her up the steep back stairs to the upper floor of the house where the bedrooms were. He halted before a door, opened it and then manipulated her inside. "This is Jenny's room," he said. "She won't be up here and she wouldn't snitch on us anyway!"

Anita stared at him in the near darkness, bewildered. "Marty, what is it? Why did you bring me up here?"

He took her firmly by the arms and pushed her back onto the bed and whispered, "You asked me to prove that I love you! I'm going to do it!"

And to her added shock he lifted up her skirt and pulled at her scanty underthings. He unbuttoned his trousers and within a matter of a few seconds she felt the pain of his hard sexual organ penetrating her. She gave a tiny whimper of pain and would have cried out had not he placed a hand over her mouth and told her to be silent. Anita had barely gotten over the first discomfort when Marty's probing came to a throbbing end.

Now the enormity of what had passed betwen them in that tiny cubicle of a dark room struck her. She began to sob and said, "I've always been decent!"

Marty was buttoning himself up. "You're decent now!" he told her.

"No!" she wailed. "I've disgraced myself and I've disgraced my family!"

"Holy Mother!" Marty cried, placing his hand over her mouth again. "Not so loud! Next thing you'll be asking me to bring Father Pat up here for a special confession!"

"I couldn't tell Father Pat," she wailed. "I can't tell anyone!"

"Listen," he said earnestly, bending over her, "You've not a thing to cry about! I told you we'd be married, didn't I? All you've got to do is come away with me tonight."

She considered it and knew that now she had no alternative. If she refused to marry him she might find herself alone with a baby in Lynn in nine months! And she knew what her father would have to say about that! Her mother as well!

In a panic, she said, "Where will I meet you?"

"I'll wait for you out back of your place. I'll go to the station first and get our tickets and check my baggage. Then I'll come back for you and your bag. Don't bring more than one!"

"I only have one," she said sorrowfully. "And I haven't enough good clothes to fill that. Can I bring my doll with me?"

"Your *doll*?" Marty said incredulously. "What kind of a bride am I getting?"

"It's my good luck charm," she told him. "My grandfather gave it to me. It always brings me luck!"

"Okay!" Marty said with disdain. "So bring it along! And do you have any money?"

She nodded. "Almost forty dollars. I've been keeping it under my mattress. To take me to Hollywood one day."

"Bring the money with you," he said, rising. "We may need it—it costs money to be married. And I'll take you to Hollywood!"

"All right, Marty," she said, halting her tears and beginning to shamefacedly arrange her clothes. As she covered her nudity it occurred to her she was probably the only girl who had ever lost her virtue to

11

the rousing melody of "Barney Google," which Dan Nolan was roaring out in the room below them.

"We'd better get back to the party," Marty said smoothing back his hair. "I've got some drinking to finish." His urge to return to the party was in direct contrast to his lack of interest in it before.

"I hope I look all right " she worried as she stood up fumbling with her skirt.

"No one will know," he promised her. "There's no special look on you after a little tumble in the hay. The girls in the shows often do a trick and then go straight onstage singing and dancing and no one ever guesses."

"I hope you're right," she said. "My face feels red still!"

"It wasn't your face that was involved," Marty jeered at her. "Let's get going."

"When do we meet?" she wanted to know.

"One-thirty," he told her. "The train leaves at two. And be sure you get out of the house without anyone hearing you."

"I'll do my best," she promised. "I can't believe we're going to run off together and get married!"

"That's life, kid," Marty told her somewhat impatiently. "You just happen to be a lucky girl."

They went back down to the riotous party and it was true that no one seemed to have noticed they'd been away. But when Marty's sister, Jenny, smiled at her, Anita turned beet red at the thought of the way they'd rumpled her bed.

The singing went on and by enthusiastic request Marty did another tap dance. After that he amazed her by the amount of gin he downed within a short time. She hoped that he wouldn't get so drunk that he'd forget all about meeting her. The singing went on with

12

Dan Nolan and Molly doing a duet of "Mr. Gallagher and Mr. Shean," which was very well received.

"Where were you and Marty?" It was the Italian youth, Louis back again, smiling at her in a wise fashion.

"Nowhere!" she stammered.

"I'll bet you had lots of fun there," Louis teased her. "Your dress is all wrinkled in the back.

"Don't talk that way to me!" she protested indignantly, looking for Marty to come to her aid. But Marty was having another gin.

"You needn't worry about me, kid, I can keep a secret," Louis said with another of his teasing smiles and then went on to join the group where Marty was holding forth.

Anita decided the party was over as far as she was concerned. She edged her way to the front door and then let herself out into the cool night. She hurried across to her house, a shabby frame structure like the Nolans'. All the rest of the family were at the party so she was able to go straight up to her room, turn on the solitary light and by its soft glow drag her battered cardboard suitcase out and place it on her bed. She quickly transferred all her scant supply of clothing to the suitcase and then put in her make-up, and lastly her beloved doll with real brown hair and eyes which opened and closed, depending on how it was tilted. At least she wasn't venturing out into the world without an old friend. She arranged the doll amid her clothes and tilted its legs so that it fitted into the suitcase neatly. Then she snapped the suitcase closed, sat it on the floor and began the vigil until one-thirty.

A little after midnight she heard the rest of the family come home. The younger members went dutifully to their rooms and then her father and mother came upstairs, laughing and talking as they often did when they were more than a little drunk. They went into their room and closed their door with a slam. She felt a great moment of relief. They had not noticed she was missing.

She placed her forty dollars in her pocketbook and then warily made her way downstairs with her suitcase in hand. She let herself out the back door, which her father had carefully locked on the inside. Then she stood shivering in the shadows waiting for her love.

Marty was late in coming and she was beginning to have moments of real despair when she heard an uneven footstep and saw him approaching. He bowed to her drunkenly and, swaying, took her bag in hand and motioned for her to follow him.

She did so and as soon as they were a distance from her house, she asked him anxiously, "Are you all right?"

"I'm drunk," he said sagely as he stumbled along. "But I'm all right. In fact, I feel fine!"

She stared at him as she walked along at his side. "I never saw you like this!"

"Get used to it, kiddo," the young man told her. "I have a big thirst and lots of capacity."

Anita was glad the railroad platform was deserted but for the half-dozen members of the vaudeville troup. They were all standing huddled together and looking weary, and none of them even glanced at her. For this she was grateful.

Mr. Mooney, the station master, wasn't around and as soon as the train pulled in, Marty shoved her onto it. "Second class," he told her. "We always travel second class. Saves money."

Since she had never travelled on a train before, the big car with its battered wooden seats and smell of tobacco smoke seemed quite comfortable, warm and inviting.

The rest of the company came aboard, grumbling. She watched as they stowed their bags on the iron shelves above them and complained about the hard seats and the filthy condition of the train.

A big woman who sang ballads in a husky contralto voice sat across from them. She wore a wide-brimmed hat and a black old-fashioned dress and her stout figure, crowned by her painted and mascaraed face, looked much older and less friendly than when she was on stage.

She told Marty, "This is a rotten little railway line! Can't compare with the Lake Erie and Pennsylvania!"

"You should know," Marty said, removing his hat and bowing. "You're the queen of the second class!".

The fat woman shot him a dark look. "And I see you've fetched along a princess for yourself! I'll bet her folks will be just delighted! And wait until Sherman Kress sees her!"

"Mind your stinking business!" Marty said in a drunken, slurred voice. He sank down onto the seat next to Anita and promptly gave her a sloppy kiss.

From across the carriage, the fat woman said, "If you're smart, kid, you'll get off this train quick and run home! Don't say that Madame Irma didn't warn you!"

"That for you!" Marty told Madame Irma, fingering his nose at her. The big woman snorted indignantly and turned her back on him.

The train started with a jolt and a sleepy-eyed conductor accompanied by a shrivelled little assistant came by, punched their tickets and sent disapproving glances their way.

"What now?" Anita asked when the two railway men moved on.

"Sleep," Marty mumbled, annoyed at her making

15

him open his eyes. "Unless you want to go to the bathroom. It's down at the end of the car."

Anita felt she'd be more comfortable for making the trip, so she made her way down the railway car, holding onto the tops of the seats as it clattered unevenly along. She passed a pretty-faced young girl with her eyes closed. Seated next to her was an older man in a bowler hat and shabby black suit. He had a lined, jowled face, and his neck seemed to have shrunk inside his hard collar. He had the look of a man who might once have been fat and who was now thinner and doleful as well.

Further along sat a very suave (by Anita's standards) young man with a black mustache and long sideburns, wearing a brown homburg and an expensive-looking brown suit. He was Romero, the magician—Anita recognized him at once. Next to him sat a crabby-looking little man who had been the master of ceremonies for the troupe and who had held the stage for a few minutes on his own, telling some pretty stale jokes. Even Anita had heard them all before. As she passed, the little man glared at her.

When she returned from the washroom at the end of the car, the crabby-looking little man was standing with his hand on the back of a seat, facing Marty and glaring at him. To her surprise Marty seemed to be afraid of the sour man, and cringed before his stern gaze.

The little man introduced himself. "I'm Kress! Who are you?"

Stunned by the way he'd rasped the question at her, Anita took a few seconds before she could reply in a stricken voice, "I'm going to marry Marty!"

"So he claims!" Sherman Kress scowled. "But he's told me a few stories before! Did you run away from home or are you with us by your parents' permission?''

She gasped, ''My parents want me to marry him!''

''They must be soft in the head,'' Sherman Kress snarled with a disgusted look at Marty again. ''I don't want this company in any trouble with the law!''

''Don't worry!'' she pleaded.

''I'll worry,'' the little man declared. ''But I don't suppose it will do any good as long as you two stick to your story. But I warn you, as long as this tour goes on I'm handing out no extra money for lodgings or expenses. Just you and your Marty-boy be certain of that!''

Marty found his voice to say sullenly, ''We got money to pay our way! We don't need anything from you!''

''That's great!'' Sherman Kress said sarcastically. ''Too bad I ain't got a rich uncle like you! Well, you mind how you behave, and remember what I said!'' And he went back to sit with the magician again.

Anita was near tears as she sat next to Marty and saw that Madame Irma had been thoroughly enjoying the scene. Now the fat woman turned to the window and ignored them. She said unhappily, ''Everyone seems so hateful and angry. I though show people were kind to each other!''

''Are you nuts?'' Marty stared at her sleepily.

''It's nothing like I expected,'' she continued tearfully.

He reluctantly put an arm around her. ''You'll get used to it. Try and get some sleep.''

''Are we going to be on this train all night?'' she wanted to know.

''Yep. And most of tomorrow. We switch at the New York State border but we don't have to leave the train. Just change engines and baggage cars.''

"What about food?"

"A porter will come through selling sandwiches and drinks," he said. "You bring that money with you?"

"Yes."

"Better give it to me," he said. "Someone might slip it out of your pocketbook while you're sleeping."

Anita gave him the forty dollars and he put it in his wallet, stowed the wallet away and immediately went into a drunken sleep, snoring in her ear so that she couldn't even think of sleeping. She was afraid to move, feeling sure he'd be angry if she waked him. So she hunched there against him for hours, unhappy and uncomfortable. At last she fell into a cramped troubled sleep.

The jolting of the train moving backwards in an eerie fashion wakened her and she sat up with a start. Marty was still sound asleep.

Madame Irma glanced across at her with a sympathetic look on her broad, overly made-up face, and said, "We're just switching and hitching onto the other train, dearie. It's all right."

"Thank you," Anita said gratefully. She felt awful and there was a terrible crick in her neck.

"I saw you give him that money," the older woman said. "You sure you know what you're doing?"

"I wanted him to have it," she said, caressing her neck and hoping it would feel better shortly.

"He's no good, you know that!"

She looked at the older woman with troubled eyes. "Do you think you should say such things to me?"

"Not to hurt you, dearie," the big woman said. "Madame Irma never deliberately hurt anyone. I'm trying to put a flea in your ear, that's all!"

"A flea in my ear?"

"I'm telling you what I know about him," the big woman said. "He drinks too much, he runs after every

18

skirt he sees, and worst of all, he has a rotten singing voice and he can't even dance all that well.''

Anita gasped at the enormity of what she was hearing. She said, ''Surely there must be something good you can say about him?'' There was a brief pause as Madame Irma considered.

''He's never murdered anyone as far as I know,'' the fat woman said dourly.

''I'm going to marry him!''

''I've had three husbands,'' Madame Irma told her. ''None of them were worth sharing a double bed with. The single life, that's the best! Take it from me! I've lived and I've suffered!''

''You have a lovely singing voice,'' Anita told her.

''Thank you, dearie, I was big time once.''

''Big time?'' Anita repeated, in puzzlement.

Madame Irma shook her head. ''You don't know a *anything*, dearie. I swear I never met anyone so dumb! 'The big time' means the big houses where they pay you real money. Not a two-bit show like this where you hardly make enough to live like a galley slave!''

''Then why are you with this kind of show?''

''Misfortune, dearie,'' the big woman said. ''As you can see, I'm not all that young anymore. And I've put on a little too much weight. I relaxed the last time I married. He promised he'd take care of me for the rest of his life. The trouble was, he didn't live long! A mean Dago caught him in his wife's bed and put a knife in him! End of my third and final marriage!''

''I'm sorry,'' Anita sympathized.

''So am I,'' Madame Irma said emphatically. ''Now I'm reduced to working in a show like this, because I'm broke and I've passed my prime. But that little twerp you're thinking of marrying is never going to make it. He doesn't have much ability and he won't work hard with what he has.''

"When we're married I'll make him work," Anita said. "He'll do it for me. He says he's going to take me into the act!"

Madame Irma groaned. "You want to marry him and you want to go on the stage?"

"Yes."

The big woman rolled her eyes. "Some folks have to make all the mistakes at once!"

As the train rolled on, Anita discovered that the wooden seats were more uncomfortable than anything she had ever known. Her bottom ached. It was getting close to dawn and she was starting to feel hungry. Marty had slumped all the way down onto the seat and was snoring loudly, his clothing wrinkled and askew. She glanced down at the freckled Irish face and a soft feeling of love for him went through her. She knew he'd had a hard time getting anywhere in show business.

She remembered him as a gawky boy in Lynn with little education and no future. At least he'd managed to get himself this niche in a precarious business. And with her to comfort him and work with him, there was no reason he couldn't get to the top. "The big time!" She liked the sound of the phrase.

The train whistle blew dolefully and Marty opened his eyes and looked up at her. He stared at her for a moment, then closed his eyes and groaned again.

"Are you all right?" she asked worriedly. She sensed it was a question she'd ask often.

His answer was another groan and then he eased himself up and gazed at her. He had a sick look on his pale, freckled face and he seemed to be unable to believe what he saw.

"You're really here on the train with me!" he said in amazement.

"You made me come," she reminded him. "You brought me here!"

"I did?" he asked, showing disbelief. He groaned again. "What a hangover!"

"Don't you remember any of it?"

"Not much!"

Tears brimmed in her eyes again. "Are you sorry I'm here?"

Marty opened his eyes and smiled weakly. "No. It's wonderful to see you. You look like an angel!"

"You're not just making that up?" she worried.

He held his head in his hands. "Do you think I could make anything up in this state?"

"Are you going to be sick?"

"I *am* sick," he complained. "What I need is some coffee to get me awake! Where is that boy with the sandwiches and coffee?"

His query was answered a few minutes later when the door at the end of the car opened and a youth with a large square box suspended from his neck came along, crying out an unintelligible phrase which sounded like "cheese, chicken and coffee" slurred together into one word.

Marty beckoned the boy after he'd served Madame Irma with two chicken sandwiches and coffee. He asked Anita what she wanted. "Chicken or cheese?"

"I'll take cheese," she said nervously. "And coffee with cream and sugar!"

"I want mine black," Marty told the youth. "And I'll have a cheese as well." The boy served them and went on.

The sandwich and coffee made Anita feel better. Things didn't seem so bad after all. At least she was on this train with Marty, who wanted her to share her life with him as his wife, and that was all that really

21

mattered. Marty loved her and she was at last going to be part of the glamorous world of show business.

"Where are we going?" she asked.

"Binghampton," he said dolefully. "We play a split week there and then go on to Pumptown."

She listened blankly. "Binghampton and Pumptown? I've never heard of those places."

He sighed. "No, and neither has anyone else."

"Why are we going there?"

"Because Shermy Kress has a wicked, bad reputation for cheap shows and he can't get anything but third-rate bookings in the smallest towns."

"But you played in Lynn!"

"Which ain't exactly Broadway, New York," Marty said sourly. And then with pride, "Kress only got us in there because I was a local. I got us our only decent booking!"

"You mean Binghampton and Pumptown are smaller than Lynn?" she said with dismay.

He gave her a look. "Lynn," he told her, "has indoor toilets."

This made her think for a little. It seemed there was much she didn't know about show business. She'd realized that Marty was not at the top, but she'd felt he was in a very good, respectable troupe. It seemed he didn't share her opinion.

She turned to him and said, "What about getting married?"

"What about it?" he asked, draining down the rest of the black coffee and brushing the crumbs of cheese and bread from his wrinkled suit.

"Can we get married in Binghampton?" she asked. "I don't think we should travel around too long before we do it."

Marty eyed her bleakly. "We've already done it,"

he said, leaving her somewhat puzzled. And then he went on, "I guess we can find a JP there."

"A JP?" she asked, wide-eyed. These show people talked a different language.

"A Justice of the Peace," he said. "Don't you know anything? Lynn isn't darkest Africa. Where have you been all your life?"

"A Justice of the Peace to marry us?" Dismay was strong in her quavering voice. "We're Catholics!"

"If we keep quiet, he maybe won't notice!"

"But I want a priest to marry us!"

"Then you should have stayed in Lynn!"

Her eyes brimmed with tears. "Aren't there any priests in Binghampton?"

"Listen," he said, turning to her with a solemn look on his youthful, freckled face. "In this part of New York State they not only have outdoor toilets, but most of the people are Protestants."

"I don't believe it!" she gasped.

"Such places exist," he said. "And you better get used to the idea. You travel with me, you'll see a lot of them!"

"I'll have to travel with you as your wife," she said.

"I know," he said. "Do you still think it's a good idea?"

"Marty!" she gasped.

He bent quickly to her and took her pert little chin in his hand and carefully kissed her on the lips. "You know I love you! It's just that I'm always snappy in the morning after I drink too much!"

"I'll have to get used to that," she said, happier for the kiss. "Will a JP marrying us be legal?"

"You bet your life," Marty assured her. "Lots of people get married by JP's. I think Doug and Mary did!"

"Douglas Fairbanks and Mary Pickford were married by a Justice of the Peace?"

"I think I remember reading it in the papers," Marty said. "And I know my friend Billy Bowers was married by one. Show biz people tend to use them. Saves a lot of time and hiring a church and all."

"I guess I have a lot to learn," she sighed.

He smiled. "You're smart, kid. And you're pretty. You'll learn quick enough!"

"Are you going to put me in the act?"

He nodded. "Why not? It's the only way I'll ever be able to get Kress to pay your expenses."

"He told us he wouldn't ever!"

"He says a lot of things he changes his mind about," Marty said with a new optimism since he'd finished the coffee. "I'm going down and wash up and take a stroll through the other cars. I like to stretch my legs."

"Can I go with you?" she wanted to know.

"No," he said. "You make yourself comfortable here." And he left her.

Seeing her alone, the fat woman leaned across the aisle to her and said, "If you'll follow the advice of Madame Irma, you'll get off the train at the next stop and run home as fast as your legs will let you!"

"I couldn't do that. I'm going to marry him!"

"I heard his enthusiastic comments about that," Madame Irma said grimly. "Better go now, dearie. He'll be tired of you in a few weeks anyway. And you'll only be worse off married."

Anita protested, "I love him. And I've given him all my money!"

"The last is your biggest mistake," Madame Irma groaned. "I can see you're just like me where men are concerned. And that's not happy news, dearie."

Anita decided she would get up and stroll around

a little in the car, following Marty's example in a more limited way. She hated to go on hearing Madame Irma's doleful comments.

As she walked slowly up the aisle a pleasant young female voice said, "Hello, you!"

She halted and looked down. It was the young girl whom she'd seen sleeping the night before in the seat with the older man. She looked prettier and more animated now. She had long chestnut curls and a round, friendly face.

"Hello," Anita said. "My name is Anita O'Hara and I'm going to marry Marty Nolan."

The girl stared at her in consternation. "It would be smarter to go over Niagra Falls in a barrel."

"Why do you say that?"

"Marty doesn't marry girls, he's married to the bottle."

"May I sit down for a minute?" Anita asked.

"As long as you like," the girl said. "My name is Belle Ames and Pruneface has wandered off somewhere. Likely in search of a drink."

"I remember!" she said. "You and that older man do an act with a seal named Percy!"

"That's us," the girl said grimacing. "I'm not sure that I wouldn't rather be riding in the baggage car with Percy than here in this uncomfortable one with Pruneface. At least Percy doesn't drink!"

Anita said, "The act is called Pontiface and Percy, isn't it?"

"Right again," Belle Ames said. "I call him Pruneface. If you're going to marry Marty you must be a Catholic?"

"I am."

"So am I," Belle Ames said. "Ran away from an orphanage when I was fifteen. Been on my own ever

25

since. And Pruneface was once a brother in a seminary outside Buffalo.''

''A brother?'' Anita echoed, amazed. ''What is he doing in show business?''

''He lapsed and they decided it was better for him to leave. Too much booze! So he bought Percy and went into vaudeville. And then he added me to the act. Now get me right, he doesn't expect me to sleep with him or anything. My relations with him are pure business, just like Percy's. Only Percy gets paid in herring and I get tossed a few bills now and then.''

''It's amazing!'' Anita gasped.

''It's more than that,'' Belle Ames said with a cheerful smile. ''I not only work in the act, I have to be house mother to Percy and Pruneface.''

''Oh?''

''Percy's no problem. But every so often Pruneface gets the D.T.'s and he thinks that Percy is his father, transformed by the Devil, because he deserted the Church. He gets down by Percy's tub and begs forgiveness until I drag him away to sleep it off.''

''What a strange lot of people you are!'' Anita said.

''You haven't heard anything yet,'' the girl said. ''Where is your precious hubby-to-be?''

''He left me to take a stroll in the other cars,'' she said.

''Ah!'' Belle said knowingly. ''Do you know where he probably is at this exact moment?''

''No.''

''I'll give you two guesses,'' Belle said with wry amusement. ''I've watched him operating for weeks. Right now he is either sharing a bottle with some travelling salesman or sitting with some pretty country girl giving her a pitch about his stage career!''

Chapter Two

Anita timorously made her way from one swaying railway carriage to another. She continued on in her search for her missing fiancé until she moved from second class into first. She was at once impressed by the more elegantly furnished first class cars with their soft upholstered seats and general air of luxury. And as Belle had predicted, it was in one of the first-class cars that she found Marty hovering over a lovely blonde seated alone, and giving her the full benefit of his Irish blarney and charm.

Anita was usually a mild-tempered girl, but she was also Irish and an O'Hara. The O'Haras were noted for their fighting spirit. She bridled at the sight of Marty so clearly engaged in a flirtation with the strange girl. Fire blazing in her green eyes, she marched down the corridor to him and tapped him on the shoulder.

"Your wife is looking for you!" she said sternly. "She sent me to find you!"

Marty turned to her, his mouth gaping open. And then he managed awkwardly, "Sure! Sure! Tell her I'll be right along!"

Anita lifted her chin and said, "I think it best if I stay and see that you get back right away. She's *not* in a good mood!"

A blushing Marty now bade the blonde a hasty farewell and followed Anita back along the corridor. When they were in the next car he seized her by the arm and angrily demanded, "Why did you do a thing like that?"

She glared at him and said, "To let you know I'm not putting up with any funny business!"

Marty complained, "I just went to stretch my legs and I happened to pass this girl and she smiled at me. There was no harm in it!"

She said, "Everyone in the company is warning me against you. If you don't behave, I'm going back home!"

"That's a fine way to talk!" he grumbled.

"I mean it! No O'Hara was ever a doormat for a Nolan!"

He placed a placating arm around her and told her, "I love you! I don't want to make you a doormat!"

This interesting conversation was brought to an end by the conductor and the trainman arriving. The conductor eyed them with a scowl and said, "You're with the vaudeville company, aren't you?"

"We are," Marty said.

"Then back to second class with you," the Conductor told them. "That's what your tickets entitle you to! And don't let me catch you up here again!"

"We were just going," Marty said, attempting to show regal pride, which didn't prove convincing.

They made their way back to the miserable, hard-seated second class and Anita began to wonder if this was the usual way of life for Marty and his companions. She began to understand her father's lack of respect for theatre people. Behind much of the glamor it was apparent that many theatre folk were doomed to a second class existence which extended far beyond railway cars.

When they were back in their own seat she noted that Madame Irma had moved down in the car to conduct an earnest conversation with the shabby, sour production manager, Sherman Kress.

Encouraged by the privacy this gave them, Marty began to show some ardent interest in her. He placed an arm around her and kissed her several times.

"You're not angry with me any more, are you?" he asked in a soft voice.

She sighed. "I just won't be treated badly. Remember that!"

"I never will be cruel to you," he promised again. "You're going to be my wife!" And he kissed her with more passion and his other hand began to explore the intimate parts of her lovely young body.

She pulled away from him and thrust his probing hand away. "And I've had enough of *that*! No more funny business until we are married!"

Marty looked shocked and miserable. "What kind of a girl are you?"

"A decent one, and I'm not surprised you didn't recognize it," she replied tersely.

The gangling young man stared at her forlornly. "You're the sort drives a man to drink!"

"You don't need to be driven far, from all I hear!"

"Nita!" he pleaded. "Is this a good way for us to start?"

"As good as any," she told him. "There's no point in not being honest with you!"

"I thought you left home because you loved me!"

"I left home because I let my blind romance with the movies and theatre close my eyes to the truth. I've run away with a small time vaudeville actor who doesn't even respect me!"

He blinked at her. "You learn fast!"

"The O'Haras have always had to!"

"I'm not a small-timer," he said hotly. "And I do happen to love and respect you!"

"I'll believe it when you prove it," she told him.

"All right, I will," he said emphatically, after which he sat silent and sullen, preoccupied with what he considered her bad treatment of him.

Anita watched him covertly with an inner glow of hope. There was just a chance she might change him and help them have a decent life. If only she could instill some ambition into him and keep him from drinking and womanizing he might amount to something. Most important of all, he must really care for her since he was going to try and show her he could live up to her expectations.

The weary journey to Binghampton seemed to be endless. When they finally reached the small upstate New York village it was almost like arriving nowhere. Aside from the railway station there were two main business streets and a scattering of private houses in the surrounding area.

"We'll be staying at the Depot House," Marty told her. "The rest of the company farm out in private houses to save money. But this is to be our honeymoon."

"*After* we see the Justice of the Peace," she reminded him firmly.

"It'll be legal!" Marty said with exasperation. "You're treating me like some kind of con man!"

"I'm not certain that you aren't," she said, amazed at her newly found gift for barbed repartee.

Marty stared at her as he started carrying their bags down the railway platform. "I'm beginning to think I don't know you at all!"

"Good!" she said. "Now you're starting off right!"

The tall youth gave a great sigh and led her across

30

the street to the dingy brick building with a large black and white sign across its front announcing, "Depot House." They went inside the small, dark lobby whose only outstanding features were several potted plants and a thick aroma of strong tobacco smoke. A little bald man peered at them from behind the counter.

"You want to register?" he asked.

"Yes," Marty said importantly. "My wife and I are with the company playing the Opera House this week!" He signed "Mr. and Mrs. Marty Nolan" with a flourish.

The little clerk eyed the register dubiously and informed him, "That will be ten dollars for the week. Theatricals pay in advance."

"In advance?" Marty said with annoyance.

"Don't blame me! It's a rule of the boss!"

"Where is the boss?" Marty demanded indignantly.

"In Minnesota," the little man said. "We just run the place for him."

With some discomfiture Marty produced his wallet, extracted a ten dollar bill, and asked for a recipt. Anita was less impressed than she might have been, since she recognized the worn ten dollar bill as one of those which she had given Marty.

The little man showed them up to their room which looked out onto a trash-filled, cat-infested alleyway. Anita stared around her at the worn dresser and the chipped white paint on the iron framed bed and wondered for perhaps the twentieth time if she had been wise in running away from home.

Marty abandoned the bags and plumped down on the bed. It gave ominously under his weight. He smiled at her. "We'll be cosy as toads in this!"

"And just as cold," she told him. "No tricks until we have it all legal and right!"

"Jezebel!" he cried in an impatient tone. "Unpack

31

while I got out in search of a JP and suitable witnesses."

By the time he returned she had unpacked their scanty belongings and was stretched out on the bed resting. As soon as he burst in she could tell that he'd been drinking. And the moment he came close to her she smelled cheap liquor on his breath. She got to her feet to face him.

"You're drunk!" she accused him.

"Man going to get married deserves a drink," he said with a wave of his arm.

Her face was expressionless. "I'm not sure there's to be any marriage if you're counting on me!"

"I found him! The JP!" Marty announced. "He's also the local barber and bootlegger. So I paid him to get us a license, perform the ceremony, cut my hair and give me a couple of drinks."

"If the haircut is a sample, you got no bargain," Anita told him.

"Don't be so sour!" he pleaded, reaching out to take her in his arms. "Back in Lynn you were my little darling!"

"Little simp would be nearer to it," she said, taking a step back. "When are we going to be married?"

"Tomorrow. Right after one o'clock. And Belle Ames and Romero are going to be our witnesses."

"I'll believe it when it happens," she said.

"It'll happen, you'll see," Marty promised her. "Now let's have a bite downstairs. I have to go to the theatre early for a run-through."

About an hour later they arrived at the Opera House. Anita thought it unimpressive even by Binghampton standards. The village had more indoor plumbing than Marty had admitted and there was at least one Irishman in town, if not a Catholic, as she'd seen the windows of O'Malley's feed and grain store. They made their way inside and through the shabby lobby to the equally dismal little auditorium. It had nothing of the grandeur of the theatre in Lynn.

In these surroundings the vaudeville show had little glamor either. The music was supplied by the house pianist, an elderly, neurotic man with little interest in helping the performers do their best. He wore a green eye shade, a loud vest and a striped shirt. When Marty came on for his turn the pianist was especially unpleasant.

He waited until Marty handed down his music from the stage and then scowled at it, saying, "Okay! I can handle it!"

Marty remained center stage and told the man in the orchestra pit, "I'd like to go through a little of it."

The pianist stood up angrily. "You think I got time to waste? You're a two-bit dancer and I can handle your music any time!"

Marty folded his arms and remained where he was. "How do I know you're not a two-bit pianist? I want my act right. You'll give me some music or I'll call the manager!"

The pianist stared at him a moment, then sat down and spread the music out before him and began to play. He played well enough, and Marty went into his dance steps and measured the stage in respect to his act. The pianist didn't play long and ended with a burst of sour notes.

Marty leaned over the footlights and grinned, "That's a sample of your disposition, not my act!"

Anita, who had been seated in the dark at the back of the little theatre, heard a voice at her side say, "You must be doing Marty some good! I've never seen him stand up to anyone like that before!"

She turned to see it was Belle Ames who had come to sit beside her. The girl from the seal act was wearing a red coat with a pitiful-looking fur collar. Anita asked her, "Do you all have to battle with everyone for your rights?"

"Twenty-four hours around the clock!" Belle said with a smile.

"I didn't think show business was like this," Anita said with despair.

"We can't all be Theda Baras or Mabel Normands," Belle said. "But if you hold on there's always that one chance you may make it some day."

Anita said, "Marty says you're going to be a witness at my wedding tomorrow."

Belle nodded. "Yeah! I feel like they say in court, an accessory to the crime! You're sure you want to marry Marty?"

"Yes," she said with a rueful smile. "I love him and I feel sorry for him. I know he drinks too much and he hasn't any great prospects, but O'Hara girls have contended with things like that for ages!"

"Well, you can't say you weren't warned!" the other girl told her.

Anita attended the show that night on a special pass given reluctantly by the manager. In the end he offered it as a kind of wedding present. This time she sat in the small balcony at the manager's request, since he didn't want any of the good seats below to be occupied free. She was encouraged when the house filled almost to capacity.

Later she heard this was usually the case. If the show was awful the opening night crowd booed it and everyone else stayed away for the week. If the show was good the word went out and generally a satisfactory week's business followed. There was one drawback in this case; the manager of the Binghampton Opera House was known in the trade as one who didn't give an honest house count to the company. So, good or bad, it wasn't likely they'd leave the little town with much earned.

The main movie of the evening was a western starring William S. Hart and Anita gathered from the general conversation around her that this was the chief reason most of the audience were there. But before the western there was a two reel comedy, and of all people, it featured Billy Bowers! She was at once lost in the magic of the silver screen performance of the talented comic and found herself laughing riotously at his bashful antics. It was exciting to know that he and Marty were friends. She wished that she could tell everyone around her and impress them. Let them understand that her husband was of some importance. She enjoyed the manly Bill Hart with his two guns in the exciting western which followed. Then the canvas curtain with its advertisements of local stores dropped down, and the footlights came on. She knew that behind the canvas drop the screen was being removed and the stage being set for the vaudeville acts which followed.

The pianist had vanished for a little and now he' returned and began playing ''Avalon.'' The curtain rose on a crudely painted garden backdrop. Little Sherman Kress came from the wings in white tie and tails, trying to look warm and friendly. He didn't succeed too well, giving the appearance of an unhappy, sour, small man, which he surely was.

He sang several choruses of ''Avalon'' and then waited for an embarrassing few seconds for applause. Receiving none, he went into a series of stale jokes which drew a few boos from the audience. Undaunted, he finished with another song and introduced Romero the Great.

Anita was feeling friendly towards the mustached young magician since he was going to be one of her witnesses the next day, and his act was fairly good. He moved quickly about the stage drawing endless ribbons in gay colors from his pockets and sleeves, and from the air around him. Then he produced flowers from an empty newspaper receptacle, and he wound up by some sword swallowing. The sword bit drew applause from the audience who were clearly in a mood for adventurous happenings.

Sherman Kress bounded on again with an agonized grimace of forced geniality and introduced Madame Irma. The big woman swept onstage with an air of courage and command, looking much better than in the second class railway car. In a sequinned dress with an ostrich plume in her hair and a fan of the same feathers in her hand, she came downstage smiling. She bowed as if expecting applause and to Anita's amazement the audience gave her quite a hand.

"Thank you, dear friends," Madame Irma said in her deep contralto voice, and then began her act. It was evident that her claim to having been a headliner was justified. Whether it was due to a failing voice or some other quirk of fate, she obviously belonged in a better troupe than the present one. Her rendering of "On The Road To Mandalay" was a great success with the audience and when she sang a series of sentimental ballads, they applauded more wildly. But it was her medley of patriotic songs of the recently ended war which won her tremendous appreciation at the very end of her act. Her rousing rendition of "Over There" saw her off to tumultuous applause.

It was evident that Sherman Kress knew a good thing when he saw it. He saw that his prima donna took several curtain calls. Madame Irma came out grandly each time, bowed, waved to the little man with her ostrich fan, and then vanished.

Next to closing came the act of Pontiface and Percy,

and once again the audience were happy. The gloomy Mr. Pontiface knew how to put the seal through his paces. Percy was the favorite, but Belle Ames, in a revealing skimpy dress, added decoration to the act. Anita was sure the males in the audience paid more attention to the pretty Belle than they did to Percy balancing his rubber balls and playing his horns. But it added up to lots of applause and a satisfied audience.

Sherman Kress came back to introduce the closing act, Marty Nolan. Anita found herself holding her breath in fear that the young man with whom she was going to spend her future wouldn't be well received. After a moment of breathless anticipation the pianist began to play and Marty came dancing on from the wings. In his straw hat, dapper check suit and black and white buttoned boots he looked the perfect picture of a young man at the seaside.

When he finished his opening dance he began a patter about how badly his holiday was going, especially in the romance department. This was his cue to begin singing some semi-humorous love songs. Anita thought he did them very well but it was his dancing which was best. When he began to dance again the audience were with him. He finished to applause at least the equal of that awarded Pontiface and Percy and Company. The curtain fell after Marty took his single curtain call, and the show was over.

Anita waited until the locals had filed out and then she hurried around to the backstage door. After a difficult moment of explanation to the ancient doorman, she was allowed in. Even this modest backstage held magic for her and made her realize how much her heart was in this crazy show business. She found Marty talking to Romero and Pontiface. As soon as he saw her he left the other two men and came to her.

She said, "You were wonderful!"

He laughed happily and took her in his arms and kissed her many times. "You're a love," he said. "I knew you'd get over your sour spell!"

"Are you ready to go back to the hotel?" she asked.

"Not yet," he said warily. "As you know it is the custom on a man's wedding night to have a few drinks with his make friends."

"A stag party?"

"Yes," Marty said. "And I know you'll not deny Romero and Pontiface the pleasure of sharing a few rounds of their bootleg booze with me."

She sighed. "You won't drink too much?"

"I *never* drink too much," Marty said with righteous indignity. "Now you go back to the hotel and tuck yourself in bed and know that I'll be drinking to our future with my two chums!" He kissed her again and sent her on her way.

She was halfway down the alley to the street when she heard a voice from behind her, call out, "Wait, kid!" She turned and saw that it was Madame Irma.

She waited until the buxom woman caught up to her. Madame Irma said, "We can walk together. Company for each other."

"I'd like that," Anita said. "You were the best thing in the show."

The big woman gave her a friendly look. "Well, at least you have good taste, dearie."

'Anita said, "I can tell you were a big-timer like you said. The people really enjoyed you!"

"Even these hicks recognize talent," Madame Irma said grandly. "Oh, well, maybe some day I'll be back on Broadway."

"I hope so," Anita replied.

"Where you staying?" the big woman asked.

"The Depot House."

"High class!" Madame Irma said. "But at least

we're going in the same direction. I have a little room in a boarding house just up the street from it.''

"Marty is using my money to pay for the room because it is going to be where we spend our honeymoon.''

"Generous of him!'' Madame Irma sniffed.

"I know he's not perfect,'' Anita was quick to say.

"Not perfect? Don't start me on him,'' Madame Irma sad with wrath. "Where is he now?''

Anita smiled as they walked along the dark street side by side. "He's having some drinks with the other men to celebrate our wedding tomorrow.''

"It's nothing to celebrate,'' Madame Irma warned her. "You can still get out of it if you want.''

"I *don't* want to,'' she said. "I love Marty in spite of his faults.''

"You're in trouble, kid,'' the older woman sighed. "I know the feeling. It cost me three husbands and a lot of misery.''

They had reached the door of the hotel. Anita halted and said, "Thank you for being so kind to me. I hope we'll be friends.''

Madame Irma nodded. "I could have had a daughter your age. She died in a makeshift cradle backstage one night. I never had another baby.''

"I'm sorry,'' Anita replied with sympathy.

"Sure, but that's life. It's never easy,'' the big woman said. "You need to have some*thing* to love as well as.some*body*. I'm lucky I've got my career.''

"And you're so good!''

"I'm a damned failure,'' Madame Irma said angrily. "But you're right, I am good!'' And she walked off into the night.

Anita was a little taken back by her new friend's quick change in mood, but she knew that theatre people were famed for being temperamental and that this had

39

been a show of that quality in Madame. She could well understand that the aging woman might be lonely and discouraged, and no doubt she had reminded her of what her life might have been like if her daughter had lived and grown up.

Anita went up to the tiny room, undressed and got into bed. Then she lay awake waiting for her husband-to-be to return—the beginning of a long vigil that lasted most of the night. It was after three in the morning and she'd had only a brief nap when she heard stumbling footsteps in the hallway outside. There was much fumbling of a key in the lock until, exasperated, she got up and went in her nightie to open the door.

Marty stood swaying outside, pale and ill looking. He exuded the sour smell of vomit and had been sick all over the front of his suit. Anita groaned and helped him in, leading him to the bed. He sat down heavily in a dazed fashion and tried to say something but his words came out slurred and twisted. She struggled to remove his jacket and then he collapsed onto the bed. When Anita lifted up his feet onto the bed, he was already snoring, stretched out straight on his back.

She went to the basin in the room and used cold water, soap and one of the thin towels to try and clean his jacket. It was a sickening task but she kept at it since she knew it was his best suit and the one he'd want to be married in. At last she had it fairly decent and hung it on a chair back to dry. Then she washed herself thoroughly and, dragging a blanket from the bed, she settled down in the easy chair and promptly went to sleep.

Marty greeted the morning sun, retching and cursing. Anita went down to the coffee shop below and brought up a pot of black coffee. Only after copious amounts of the strong stuff did he begin to come around.

40

"I really tied one on," he said, seated on the side of the bed, a coffee mug in his trembling hands.

"You were disgraceful!" Anita snapped.

"What do you expect? A man has a right to celebrate the night before he gets married!"

"After seeing you last night, I'm not sure I want to marry you," she told him sternly.

"Ah, now," he said affecting a broad Irish accent, "that doesn't sound like the delight of me life!"

"I worked more than an hour cleaning your jacket," she said, waving at it where it hung on the chair back.

He got up and came to her unsteadily. "You're a darlin', that's what you are!"

She kept him at arm's length. "If we marry today, I want you to promise there'll be not more wild drinking."

"I need a little tot now and then," he protested.

"You'd be better off not to drink at all," she said. "You know that half the bootleg stuff is poison! You read about it every day in the paper! People are even blinded!"

"I'd say if you have to use a cane and black glasses, that's the ideal way to get them," he said, draining the mug of coffee.

"It's not a joking matter," Anita said earnestly. "I'm only a silly girl. But I can see you're wrecking your health and your prospects. You surely don't want to go on playing in places like Binghampton all your life?"

This seemed to reach him. He raised a hand. "Marry me and I'll do better!"

"You'll have to or you won't have a wife long," was her warning.

"Give me a kiss and let's make up," he said with some of his old charm. And he opened his arms for her.

She went to him and sighed, "What an idiot I am to be in love with you!"

"Ain't it the truth!" Marty chuckled as he kissed her and held her close, sending the usual thrills through her. There was no question that he had the gift of easily stirring her physically.

She looked up at him dreamily. "Do you know we're supposed to me at the office of the Justice of Peace in an hour?"

Marty groaned. "And I can't even think yet!"

"You'd better work on it," she told him.

He cleaned up and dressed. His jacket was presentable and he was able to wear it. Just to make sure there was no odor lingering Anita sprayed it with some cologne. Marty expressed distaste with this but she could see that he was secretly pleased.

They left for the tiny office of the JP hand in hand. The others were already there waiting for them. Romero gave her a bunch of roses and smilingly told her, "I promise I didn't pull them out of my sleeve and they won't vanish!"

"Thank you," she said, kissing him on the cheek. "You're a dear!"

Belle Ames was standing by, dressed in her best two piece woolen suit. She had a boutonniere for Marty.

"Just what I needed," Marty declared and kissed her.

The Justice of the Peace was a doleful little man with a small gray mustache and thin graying hair. He also had one turned-in eye which made him look almost a double for the cross-eyed comedian Ben Turpin. This came to Anita's mind as she and Marty stood before him and she had a hard time keeping her mind on the event.

He had a squeaky voice and conducted the brief

42

ceremony in an almost automatic fashion, no doubt because he'd married people endless times before. They all had to sign the register. Anita was proud of the wide, brass wedding ring which Marty had picked up in some local jewelery store. The little man shook hands with them and wished them well and they all left his office together.

On the street she burst into laughter and said, "I can't help it! We were just married by Ben Turpin!"

They went on to a local restaurant for a wedding luncheon, a simple affair of bacon and eggs. Toasts were drunk in water but Romero produced a flask from an inner pocket and laced the water generously with whiskey. They lingered at the table until mid-afternoon and became hilarious though not truly drunken.

Then Anita and Marty said goodbye to the others and went back to their room. Since they had several hours before having to report to the theatre Marty at once undressed her and set about enjoying his marital rights.

Making love in the afternoon seemed immoral to Anita, even though they were married. She'd always imagined that married people only made love in the dark late on Saturday night. Marty hadn't even drawn the blinds, so they romped on the bed in the bright afternoon sunshine.

The experience wasn't as painful as it had been the first time and Anita actually began to enjoy his thrustings. He seemed insatiable. He'd make love to her and then stretch out for a few minutes, only to begin again.

As the time to go to the theatre drew near she had to warn him, "You'll wear yourself out! How will you have the energy to dance tonight?"

Astride her the naked Marty leered, "Don't you worry about me, honey!"

She did worry and finally she coaxed him into get-

43

ting dressed and ready. He was in his best mood and she wondered if married life would be like this every day. If so, she knew it was going to be an exhausting experience for her.

They reached the theatre barely in time. Marty went on and did his act while she watched in the wings. When Marty took his usual curtain calls, little Sherman Kress trotted out and with one of his famous fake smiles announced that Marty had taken himself a bride that very day. And then the little man came into the wings and dragged Anita onstage, blushing and smiling. The audience were kind and gave her a fine ovation and she was very happy indeed.

So Anita's married life began. She'd been relatively innocent about sex until she'd married Marty. Now her training began and she was introduced to every variety of loving that active young lothario had picked up in brothels on the road during the several years he'd been in vaudeville.

Belle Ames and Madame Irma daily gave her stern warnings to avoid becoming pregnant, but with Marty after her every spare moment, she couldn't think that this would long be possible.

They continued to play a series of small towns first in Ohio and then in Illinois. The weather became hot and the theatres were like ovens much of the time with only weak fan systems to cool them. Percy the seal was feeling the heat badly and not his usual perky self, while Belle met the crisis by wearing no undies beneath her skimpy costumes, which brought some outraged complaints from several ladies' groups in the places they played.

When the heat was at its worst, Marty began to drink heavily again. No matter where they were playing he seemed to find a source of supply. Anita begged,

44

argued and even refused to go to bed with him, but it only kept him sober at intervals.

She was beginning to be a worldly-wise trouper's wife, but she was tired of standing during the performance and doing nothing and began to pester Marty about letting her join the act. She had written home that she was going to be his partner and she wanted to be able to send her angry folks the proof that she'd not made the mistake they'd insisted when she'd married Marty.

One hot night in their tiny hotel room she halted him as he prepared to make love to her for a third time, saying, "Only if tomorrow you begin to train me for the act!"

"Sure, honey," he said kissing her and placing his sweaty naked body over hers.

The next morning she reminded him first thing when they woke up. "Today is the day!"

Marty frowned at her and ran a hand through his touseled red hair. "What's today?"

"You start training me for the new act!"

He sat up abruptly. "Where did you get that idea?"

"You promised me last night!" she protested.

Marty grinned and reached over and caressed one of her nipples. "I'll say anything when I want it!"

Anita pushed his hand away and jumped out of bed. Pointing a finger at him, she wanred him, "You'll not be getting anything until you keep your word!"

So her dance training began. Anita picked up steps fast. Marty borrowed a small wind-up phonograph from Madame Irma for their rehearsals. He had several records especially made for tap dancing and they were played over until Anita expected they'd be worn out. She ended every session weary. But it was a new interest, and it diverted Marty from spending all his spare time with bootleg booze and sex.

Anita sweated and worked all through the summer and by the time the cooler days of autumn arrived she was good enough to make her first appearance. There was only one catch. Sherman Kress didn't mean to hire another performer, so Marty had to make a deal.

He told the little man, "Anita will work free. We'll call the act Nita and Nolan. You'll be getting two for one."

"Okay," Kress said sourly. "But don't get any ideas about holding me up. The two of you together are no better than one good talent."

Anita asked Marty in their dressing room, "Why do you let him talk to you like that?"

Marty assumed one of his jaunty poses. "Because we can wait. We'll smooth the act off with this unit and when we're ready we'll move on. Get a booking with some decent outfit!"

She saw the wisdom of the idea and went along with it. Anita's first performance was in a small Pennsylvania town with an audience of hard-working coal miners. Not an easy audience to please, she was warned.

Sherman Kress announced them with a flourish: "And direct from Broadway, New York, the flashy team of *Nita and Nolan!*" Anita and Marty danced on. Anita wore a skimpy spangled bra and a tiny skirt of the same material which displayed her long, slender legs to best advantage. She thought she would faint with stage fright but the knowledge that Madame Irma, Belle and Romero, along with Pontiface and Percy, were all cheering for her from the wings, kept her going.

Then came the comedy skit, and though Anita's voice trembled at first, she was able to make the proper saucy replies to Marty's teasing comments. This went over well.

When they went into a second dance routine, it seemed they had won the audience over completely. Th curtain fell to great applause.

Madame Irma came over and took Anita in her arms and cried, "You're a natural, dearie! You've got true talent!"

Romero kissed her, Pontiface congratulated her gravely and Percy made seal sounds of approval. Only little Sherman Kress was restrained in his comments.

He frowned at her. "You could do better than that outfit. And you should smile more, though I admit that's not easy with a partner like Marty."

Marty made a mock gesture of punching the little man. "You always say the right thing, boss!" he said as Sherman Kress marched off with dignity.

Nita (for now this became her name) felt things had to get better. And they did for a while. Letters from Billy Bowers in Hollywood continued to arrive at intervals. Billy wrote about the Fatty Arbuckle scandal and said it had calmed down Hollywood for a while, but there was lots of excitement still going on. He had been friendly with Arbuckle but thought the fat man had lost all control. And he was repulsed by his part in the death of that unfortunate girl at his party in San Francisco. Bowers again suggested that Marty try his luck on the West Coast.

Marty held the latest letter in his hand and said, "If we could only get bookings to take us out there!"

"We could make the trip and be paid along the way," she agreed. "But how do you arrange it?"

Marty's youthful face was grim. "We'll have to get away from this cheap circuit and go to New York. All the important booking is done there."

"Do you think they'd even look at our act?" she worried.

47

Marty was indignant. "I'm a name! Maybe not a big one! But I've been in the business a few years. They're bound to give me an audition. And when they see what we can do, we're on our way!"

Nita was thrilled. The drudgery of one night stands bothered her less now that she knew that they would soon be heading for New York City.

Then she visited one of the small town doctors after a few worrisome months and came away with the unwelcome information that she was pregnant.

Chapter Three

Anita had suspected for some time but she'd been afraid to face up to the truth. Now there was no question about it. She waited until she and Marty returned to their room that night and before they undressed for bed she told him in faltering fashion. Marty stared at her with shocked dismay as if she'd just informed him she'd contracted leprosy.

"Maybe it's a mistake!" he said hopefully.

"No!"

He was visibly growing more distressed. "Maybe it can be fixed! How long?"

"Almost four months," she told him.

"Four months! You ninny! Why didn't you do something about it before?"

Tears brimmed in her eyes. She had hoped he would be happy at the news of his impending fatherhood. She said, "I was afraid."

He began to pace angrily before her. "You darn well should be afraid! What have you done to us? Just when we're ready to make our big break!"

She couldn't resist saying, "I didn't do it alone!"

He whirled on her angrily. "You enjoyed yourself just as much as me! Don't deny it!"

She lashed out at him in the same vein, "And I'm not afraid to pay the price! You are!"

Marty scowled. "Smart women don't let this happen! I'm married to a dummy!" And with that he turned and left the room, slamming the door after him.

Nita knew him well enough to guess what he'd do. And he did. He returned in the small hours of the morning almost unable to walk. She helped him inside and onto the bed. Just another night of having to sleep in a chair, she thought wearily. She didn't dare allow herself to think of anything else.

In the morning she brought him the usual coffee. He drank it and sulked. After a little, he said, "I'd better start doing the act as a single again."

"I can carry on for another month or so. The doctor told me it would be safe enough."

From his seat on the side of the bed he scowled at her. "I can't let you go on with a pot belly!"

Her cheeks burning, she said, "Don't worry. I'll not embarrass you!"

He sighed. "It's all right. I just haven't gotten used to the idea."

"That's easy to see."

"I've had big plans for us. This will end everything!"

"I don't see why," she said, sitting by him. "Lots of other vaudeville people have kids and keep going."

"In the small time," he said bitterly. "Now we'll be locked in!"

"What about the Cohans? They're big time, and they built their fame on a family act."

"They were always big time," he said sullenly. "It's not the same with us."

"I'll only be out of the act a few months. We can take the baby along with us. Lots of acts do."

"Yeah, I suppose so," he said, rising. "I guess it

will be a long time before we see the West Coast and Billy Bowers.''

''You never can tell,'' she said. But she knew her optimism was lost on him. He was still down in the dumps and determined to blame her pregnancy for everything.

The rest of the company were sympathetic once the word got around. Most of them pitied her. They saw how Marty was rebelling at the prospect of the baby's arrival and thought she had made the ultimate mistake in becoming pregnant. The baby would make it harder to gain her freedom from him.

But Nita wasn't ready to give up so easily. She still loved Marty despite his weaknesses—perhaps because of them. She hoped they could see this crisis through together and he would emerge a stronger person for it. As for herself, she doubted that any woman was truly sad about becoming a mother. She was looking forward to the baby and hoping it would be a boy so she could call it Marty.

Then came a series of weeks when she felt hope ebbing away. She was ready to leave the act for the rest of her term though she still wasn't showing any outward signs of her pregnancy. Marty was drinking every night now instead of only once in a while. And worse, he was coming to the theatre drunk. She kept on in the act with him longer than she intended because she was afraid he couldn't manage on his own in his drunken state. One night he stumbled and almost fell in the last dance routine and another night he slurred his spoken lines so badly they could not be understood.

She warned him backstage one night, ''If you go on like this we won't even be able to hold this job!''

''I don't want it anyway,'' he said with drunken bravado and tipped a half-empty flask to his lips.

''What a coward you are!'' she shot at him.

"Yeah?" he eyed her blearily.

"Taking your spite out on a poor little child that hasn't even been born yet!"

He got up and faced her angrily. "Never should be born!" he said. And he brushed by her and went out to wait backstage for their second appearance of the evening.

Nita went down the iron steps to the stage level and saw Marty talking with Romero. He paid no attention to her as she took her place in the wings ready for their entrance. Only at the last minute, when she was frantic, did he finally join her and go on with her to do the act.

All went well until the final dance number. Just before the finish of the act he missed a step. He tried to cover his mistake and almost caused her to trip and fall. The dance ended in confusion instead of the usual smooth fashion, and there was only a tiny spattering of applause.

Sherman Kress came up to Marty with his fist clenched, and rasped, "You drunken bum! One more performance like that and you're out! I'm only keeping you now because of Nita!" And he turned his back on the swaying, perspiring Marty.

Marty gave her a crooked smile. "Seems you're the star now, honey!"

She didn't bother to argue with him but went back to the dressing room and changed into her street clothes, then returned alone to their boarding house room. Marty didn't come home that night or the following day when they took the train to the next town. He'd vanished for a little while at other times when they'd had quarrels but he always returned in time for the performance. She felt this would happen again.

Sherman Kress came and sat beside her in the second-class car seat. The little man was clearly concerned. "What about Marty? Do you think he'll show up?"

"I'm certain of it. He always has."

"But his drinking has been getting worse. It will be no good if he shows up again like he did last night."

"I agree," she said. "But I think he'll sober up and follow us on the next train. He could still make the first show."

Kress shook his head. "I'd have fired him long ago if it hadn't been for you. And knowing you have a baby on the way."

"That's what's upset Marty."

"He ought to be pleased!"

"He's little more than a boy himself," she said with a wistful smile. "With all a boy's dreams and lack of desire for any responsibilities. He may look like a man but I know him!"

Kress gave her a disgusted look. "So why marry a silly kid? Especially one on the booze!"

"I think he needs me," she said. "And I guess in a strange way I need him. He first represented all my illusions about the stage. And if I lose him I'll lose all my dreams of the theatre."

"Show business" the sour little man said with disgust. "I'd like to get out of it! Look, I've got a brother who's a tailor, pressing, repairing and cleaning. He owns two apartment houses already. Not bad! I can hardly pay for my room and have any money left!"

She smiled at him. "I've seen you on stage. You're as proud as a peacock. You love it and you know it!"

He looked slightly guilty. "You're a smart girl! I wish I was as smart. Why don't you go back to your folks and have the baby like any young woman should?"

"I couldn't," she said. "My father told me never to come back because I ran off with Marty."

"Go back anyway!"

"I couldn't," she said, though she knew he was right. Her father and mother would take her in and look after her without a murmur. And then she asked him, "Do you honestly think I have any talent?"

He blinked at her. "You want I should tell you?"

"Tell me the truth. I promise it won't cost you any money."

"All right," he said. "You got looks and you got a certain quality. You show up on stage and people like you. That's important. All my life, people hate me when I step on stage. So what does it matter if I have talent?"

"You really think I have a chance in the business?"

He nodded. "I tell you what I've been thinking. But I didn't tell *him*. And don't you tell him either. I think with your face and figure you'd do great in the movies."

She was surprised. "You really think that?"

"Don't tell Marty-smarty!"

"I won't," she said.

The little man got up dolefully. "All I know is, he better show up tonight." And he moved back to the rear of the car to sit alone.

Nita considered all that he'd said. She was secretly more concerned about Marty than she'd let on. He'd been angry at himself for spoiling the act the previous night and he'd surely gone off to finish the job of drinking himself into unconsciousness. She hoped he would come around in time and that he would stop drinking so crazily.

Kress had told her she had talent and that she might do well on the silver screen. Nita had confidence in the sour little man's opinions. He was not her favorite

54

person but he did know show business. Perhaps if she could somehow keep Marty from destroying himself they might get to Hollywood and have their chance . . .

Belle Ames came to sit with her and said, "Was Kress giving you a bad time?"

"No. He wasn't bad at all. But he's worried about Marty."

"Do you think he'll show up?" her friend asked.

"I can only pray that he does. We can't afford to lose a job now."

"Marty doesn't care," Belle warned her.

"He must have some character," Nita said. "How can he let me and the baby down?"

Belle's big eyes were sympathetic. "You oughtn't to be still dancing. You're at least five months, aren't you?"

"Just."

"It's time you quit," her friend warned.

"I will at the end of the week."

"You said that last week," Belle reminded her.

Nita smiled wryly. "I intended to. But then Marty got worse."

"He's no good. We warned you!"

"I know," she said.

Belle sighed. "If Marty doesn't show I suppose we can fill in for a night or two. The Madame can go on for a second session of songs."

"She's good enough," Nita agreed. "But it would hardly be fair to her."

"Kress won't worry about that."

Nita gave her friend a glance. "Maybe I could fill in as a single."

"A single?"

"Marty did the act as a single before I joined it."

"That's different!"

"Not so much," Nita protested. "I can do the first

55

dance solo, and go into a monologue using some of our patter. And I can surely do the last number.''

''You'd be dancing onstage for almost twenty minutes,'' Belle warned her.

''I could do that,'' she said, though she knew she'd be taxing herself to the limit if she tried.

Belle shook her head. ''I don't know what's wrong with Marty. He has talent and a nice wife like you. What is it?''

''A wild Irish taste for drink which he inherited, for one thing,'' she said. ''And he's proud! Far too proud! It killed him the other night when Kress said he was only keeping him on because of me.''

''He should know Kress talks ragtime!''

''Even so, Marty can't take things like that. He knows he's good and he's afraid he may never get his chance. It's different with Madame Irma, she's also good but she's past her prime. And she knows what it means to be a big headliner. She was there.''

Belle smiled ruefully. ''And she never lets you forget it.''

''I don't blame her,'' Nita said. ''She has a right to be proud.''

The Opera House in Milton was no more enticing than any of the others they had played in. But it was a novelty in one respect—after playing a long series of one-nighters they were going to play in the old house for a week. The manager had encountered some booking troubles and was willing to give them a better deal than usual so Sherman Kress accepted it.

But as curtain time of opening night drew near all the little company were on edge. There was still no sign of Marty. Nita had privately discussed with Kress the possibility of her filling in as a single for the act and he had agreed after a good deal of argument. As the time approached she lined up a new cue sheet for the piano player in the pit and improvised a new routine.

She maintained hope that Marty would appear all during the screen section of the program. The main feature was a society drama starring Neil Hamilton and Lois Wilson. The comedy which preceeded it was another Billy Bowers two-reeler. It seemed that Marty's old friend was gaining in popularity.

Sherman Kress came to her tiny dressing room as Madame Irma took over the stage. He was in a tense state. "No question now, he won't be here," he said. "Are you ready to go on alone?"

"Yes," she promised.

"And the piano player?"

"I've given him a new cue sheet."

"I'll introduce you as a single," Kress said grimly. "I've got to get back on stage now." And he hurried off.

Nita sat staring at herself in the murky dressing room mirror. So this was to be her big night! It was the sort of break many girls only dreamed about. But under the circumstances it meant nothing to her. She saw the sad-faced young girl in the mirror and knew that she wanted Marty back more than any stage fame.

Yet once she went on alone and proved herself, she would have a new independence which had never been hers before. It did not matter that this was a small time troupe in a minor theatre, it would make the start of her appearing alone as a professional. If she won the audience it could open an entire new future for her. But she wanted to share the future with Marty and their child, and it didn't seem to matter to him at all.

They called her. She dabbed a last bit of powder on her nose and hurried out to the backstage area. Pontiface and Percy were just finishing their act. Percy was playing "The Star Spangled Banner" on his horns

57

with the help of Belle. The act ended in the usual burst of applause. Then the curtain came down and it was her turn.

Belle hurried off stage and paused to pat her on the arm. "Best of luck, honey!"

"Thanks," Nita said weakly, the pit of her stomach heaving.

Sherman Kress gave her a look of utter despair and then with a smile frozen on his mean little face bounced out and with great zest announced, "A new act tonight, ladies and gents! A fine singing and dancing star from Broadway's bright lights, I give you that charming comedienne, Nita Nolan!"

The announcement brought scattered applause, cheers and a few boos from the gallery. The curtain rose and the piano player began the opening music. Nita took a deep breath and then, smiling, danced out on stage. What happened afterwards she was never quite sure. After her dance she launched into her improvised comic routine, then sang some romantic melodies and ended with a long, strenuous session of dancing, all in a sort of excited daze. When she finally danced offstage to a good round of applause the whole episode was jumbled in her mind.

Madame Irma was waiting in the wings to give her a kiss and hug. The older woman said, "You're a real trouper, dearie! And they loved you!"

It was true. As a single she had drawn as much, if not more applause, than she and Marty had together. Sherman Kress came and dragged her on again. She thanked the audience in a thin voice and then did an encore of her closing number. It went well and the show finished on a happy note.

Kress came to her saying, "You were great! If Marty doesn't come back we can do without him!"

She gave the little man a wry look. "Don't forget,

I've an act of my own to break in a few months from now.''

He frowned. "I'd forgotten."

"At least I can carry on now," she went on quickly. "That's the main thing."

"You're not too tired?" he wanted to know.

"No," she said. "I feel fine." Which wasn't exactly the truth. She felt extremely weary and she was conscious of carrying the baby for the first time. It seemed like a weight bearing her down, which in fact it was.

Yet she had no choice. She must continue through the week at least, and decided to tell Sherman Kress at the end of the week that he had better wire for a replacement act. She would carry on until one arrived and then she'd have to take a room somewhere and hope her small savings would carry her over until the baby was born. It was also possible she might get some easier job like being a cashier or a clerk in some store. This thought, however unappealing, gave her hope.

By Thursday it was a torment to go on. Each time she came to the last dance she had pains in her abdomen which were more than fleeting. But she spoke of these to no one.

On Saturday night she was feeling truly ill. The pains were striking at intervals all around the clock. She knew that she must stop dancing as soon as possible. She sat alone before the dressing room mirror praying that Marty might return. How could he desert her and their unborn child?

She was asking herself this for the hundredth time when the door of her dressing room slowly opened as if in a perverse answer to her prayers, and a thoroughly washed-out and dejected Marty appeared. His face was

59

covered with a stubble of beard, his eyes were sunken and feverish, and his clothes were a wrinkled mess. He came inside the door and closing it, leaned against it and stared at her.

She jumped up and went to him. "Marty!"

He kept her at arm's length with a sour smile, saying, "I ain't very sanitary!"

"I don't care," she sobbed. "Oh, Marty, you did come back!"

"What made you doubt it?"

"I didn't really! But we've all been so worried!"

Marty said sarcastically, "That's not the way I heard it. Kress tells me you're doing so well alone he never wants to bother with me again."

"He's only saying that!"

"You look great," Marty said. "Maybe he's right! I offered to go on tonight and he refused. So I guess its no longer Nita and Nolan. Just Nita Nolan!"

"That's nonsense!" she protested. "I don't want to go on. I'd much rather you did the act!"

"I'll be watching from the rear," Marty drawled. "And in between I've got some important drinking to do."

Then he was gone. She could scarcely believe that he had been there, or that he had said the things he had. It was like some crazy nightmare. How could she reach this stubborn man and let him know she loved him? That all she had gone through was for him? She had a throbbing headache now as well as the shooting pains in her abdomen. She was ill and heartbroken. Sinking into the hard chair she bowed her head and sobbed quietly.

There was a brisk knock on the door and Sherman Kress let himself in. He peered at her with concern. "Did he come in here and upset you?"

She looked up. "He was here. He said you refused to let him go on."

"Did you take a good look at him?" Kress demanded. "Do you think he's fit to go on tonight?"

"No."

"I told him to go out and sober up before he came to me again," Kress said sourly.

She gave the little man a pleading look. "You will give him another chance? Take him on again! You know I filled in only to keep our place in the show. But I can't go on after tonight. I wanted to hold the job for him. We need it so badly!"

Kress nodded impatiently. "I ain't the Salvation Army! If he turns up clean and sober on Monday, he can take over the act again. But no more drinking!"

She felt better. "I'll tell him," she said. "And I promise he'll be all right."

"You ready to go on??" Kress asked.

"Yes."

"Well, better move, it's near time!" Kress said and went on his way.

Nita fixed her mascara in the mirror and then followed him. She knew the time onstage would be an ordeal. Together with her headache she had to contend with those occasional pains in her mid-region, which invariably seemed to get worse when she danced. On top of everything else there was the knowledge that a drunken Marty would be somewhere in the theatre watching her. And she had no idea what kind of behavior might be expected from him.

Onstage she waited while Percy finished his patriotic horn playing. Kress stood by her nervously. There was an added tension among them all because of Marty's return.

She whispered to the little man, "Be sure Marty

61

doesn't get away. Send someone down to tell him I want to speak with him.''

Kress shrugged. ''I won't guarantee it'll do any good.''

''We can't let him vanish again!''

''I'll do my best,'' he said.

Then the curtain fell and Kress rushed out with his usual zest to introduce her. Belle came running over to her, concern in her face. ''I hear Marty is back, causing trouble,'' her friend said.

Nita nodded. ''I think it'll be all right.''

Belle stared at her worriedly. ''You look sick!''

''I'll make it,'' she told the girl. And as the piano player began her music she danced onto the stage.

Because it was a Saturday night the theatre was filled to capacity, and the audience was in a gala mood. They took to Nita at once. She went through her act in a dazed state. By the time she had reached her final tap dance to the tune of ''Gimme A Little Kiss, Will You, Huh?'' the pains became unbelieveably acute. She wanted to cry out each time she whirled about on the stage, but she gritted her teeth and hoped she would manage to finish.

She ended her routine and almost staggered off. There was a roar of applause and Sherman pressed her on again, ''Give them a little more!'' he urged her.

''I can't!'' she wailed. But he had already pushed her out onto the stage.

The pianist automatically picked up the lilting tune once more and Nita forced a mechanical smile and began to tap dance once again. She managed to continue for about a minute longer; then the pain in her abdomen blacked everything else out and she collapsed right there onstage.

She opened her eyes to darkness and a strange noise. Belle was leaning over her, an arm around her. ''It's all right,'' her friend said, ''we're driving you to a hospital!''

Nita heard the words in a daze and then the terrible sharp pain came back and she became unconscious once more. She had no recollection of anything after that until she opened her eyes to dull daylight in a small room with a window and another bed in it. The other bed was screened from her. She tried to call out but no sound escaped her lips. All her body seemed on fire.

Ages seemed to pass. She lay there unable to collect her thoughts. It was just enough to endure the pain. Then she heard a sound and looked up to see a white-capped nurse staring down at her.

''You've come to,'' the nurse said with a slight smile. ''Your friends will be glad to know that.''

Nita made a great effort to speak and only managed a whisper, ''Hospital?''

''Yes,'' the nurse said. ''You're safe in a hospital and you are going to get better soon.''

Nita stared up at her and then fainted again. She was aware of being given a sweet, thick liquid to drink and then she fell into a blissful, painless sleep. When she awakened again the sun was shining in the window. The screen had vanished from around her bed and the bed across from her was empty.

A nurse came and asked, ''Are you feeling better?''

''Yes,'' she said, the miracle being that she had a voice, even though it was small and weak.

''The doctor will be in to see you shortly,'' the nurse said briskly. ''You've had quite a time!''

''How long?'' she asked.

''You've been here three days,'' the nurse said. ''Your friends have been constantly calling about you. The show has moved on to a town about fifteen miles from here.''

"I see," she said, remembrance coming back. She had fallen on the stage. The pain had been beyond bearing.

The doctor and another nurse came in to examine her. He nodded and went through his professional duties and made several comments to the nurse, who wrote down his instructions. Then he gazed at her sharply. He was middle-aged and stern.

"You're finally coming around," he said.

"Yes."

"You know you might have died?"

"No."

He frowned. "You did a very stupid thing, dancing like that in your condition. You were aware of your condition?"

"Yes."

"Did you not have medical advice? Did no one tell you that dancing so late in your term was a stupid and dangerous thing to do?"

"I had no choice," she said meekly.

"We all have a choice," the doctor told her. "You must have been in great pain. Why did you go on?"

"There were—reasons."

"I hope they were good," the doctor said brusquely. "Not only did you put your own life in danger, you lost the child."

Tears choked Nita and she was unable to say anything.

He stared at her. "You are married?"

"Yes."

"You have had serious internal damage. You must not dance again for a long while. Months. And I cannot guarantee you will ever again be able to conceive a child."

She listened in abject silence. She knew it did not matter that he had broken her heart in a matter of seconds. She was of no real interest to him, merely a creature who had caused him a good deal of what he considered needless bother.

She managed, "When can I leave?"

"It will be a week at least. Maybe longer. And then you'll be very much of an invalid for awhile," the doctor said. "I don't know what's wrong with you young women today. You want to be mothers yet you carry on as if it made no difference at all. You have paid quite a price for your bad judgment, Mrs. Nolan."

He left her then and she was able to let the tears flow freely. She had been too proud to cry when he was there to see. Now she gave way to her despair.

The elderly nurse came and patted her hand. "There, there, Mrs. Nolan, it may not be as bad as he said. Dr. Cronin is a stern man with little consideration for anyone, including himself."

Days passed and Nita received flowers from Madame Irma, and letters from Belle and Sherman Kress. They both wished her well and told her they were sure she would soon be well and out again. There was no word at all from Marty.

What had happened to him after her collapse? There was not a word concerning him in the letters. And they did not tell her how they were managing without the act. They simply let her know they cared for her and wished her well.

As her strength returned, her curiosity grew. Before the end of the week she was able to walk about a little. The doctor saw her again and informed her that it would be two months before she could dance again.

The week passed and she knew she would soon be released. Her problem was where to go and how to support herself. There would be hardly any money left after she had paid her hospital bills. She began to try and work out some plans and decided the first thing she must do was attempt to get in touch with Sherman Kress. She could not resume the act again but at least he might have some word about Marty.

She was deeply hurt that there had been no word from her errant husband. Before she allowed herself to condemn him too greatly she forced herself to realize that he also might be ill and unable to get in touch with her because of that. He had looked completely down and out when she'd seen him the night she'd collapsed. He had surely abused himself badly with drink and could well be in the hospital also.

Sunday afternoon came and the hospital was filled with weekend visitors. She strolled in the hall for a little in a worn robe which Belle had donated when she'd been admitted to the hospital. After a while the press of people bothered her and she went back to her room and sat on the side of her bed.

She was sitting there thinking bleakly of her future when she heard someone enter the room. She turned and saw Marty, clean and dressed in his best suit, with a bouquet of roses in his hand.

She jumped up and cried, "Marty!"

"Darlin'!" he said brokenly and came to her. He threw the roses on the bed and took her gently in his arms and kissed her.

She stared at him, smiling, her eyes filled with tears. "You didn't write me or anything!"

He held her. "I was too ashamed."

"You look so well!"

"I'm sober at least," he said contritely.

"Where have you been?"

"With the company."

"You've been doing the act?"

He smiled. "Sure. You didn't think I'd let them

down? Not after what you went through to keep them on the road.''

She pressed herself against him happily. "Oh, Marty!''

"You're almost well again," he said.

"I must look a sight," she worried. "I've lost weight and I'm so pale."

"Makes you look all the more the angel you are!"

She smiled up at him. "You and your Irish blarney."

"They've all missed you, Nita. They asked me to tell you so," her husband said. "They love you, which is more than they do me."

"They were so good to me, saw that I got here," she said.

"I know," he sighed. "While I was too drunk to do anything but stand by and weep."

Touched, she said, "That was enough."

He released her and retrieved the roses. "I've brought you some flowers."

She smelled them. "They're lovely! You oughtn't to have wasted the money."

"Not anything to what I've thrown away on booze," he said grimly. "Can you forgive me?"

Her answer was a joyous kiss. "I've wanted to see you so badly," she said.

"And I wanted to be here," he told her. "But I didn't have any way. The show kept moving on. And I didn't know what to write, or whether you'd bother reading any letter I sent."

"It's all right," she said gently.

"I've put you through hell," he said contritely. "And you lost the child."

"My own doing," she sighed. "I should have known better. I ought to have told Kress about the pains. He would have sent on Madame Irma."

"You did it for us," he said. "For me! To try and make sure I'd have a job to come back to."

Nita said, "I did what I thought was best. I was wrong, but I suppose I'd do the same thing again in the same circumstances."

He said, "When can you leave?"

"In a day or two. But I won't be able to dance again for months."

Marty smiled. "There's no need for you to do anything but play the lady and rest. You're married to Marty Nolan, one of the best single acts in the business!"

"That's true!" she said.

"I'll ask at the desk when I can come for you."

"What about the show?"

"I left last night. We're not going back. Kress wired and another act is coming to join them on Monday."

Nita felt a great sadness. The troupe had become a haven for her. It was where all her new friends were. She'd be lost without them. She said, "I wish I could have seen them again just once!"

"You will," he assured her. "In show business you're always running into people again. It's a small world, really. And a warm one."

"I've come to know that," she agreed. "But what are we to do?"

"I have a job," he said proudly. "And an advance of salary to pay our bills and get us to it!"

"Glory be!" she cried happily. "Tell me about it."

"Billy Bowers!"

"From Hollywood?"

"Yes," Marty said. "He's been after me to go out there. He thinks I might be the new Wallace Reid. And there'll be work for you as well."

"When do we leave?"

"As soon as you're out of here," her husband said.

"A friend of Billy's is opening a circuit of vaudeville theatres in and around San Francisco. He's hired me, on Billy's word, to head the bill. He sent me the money. And when we play the circuit of eight weeks there I'll buy me a little car and we'll drive on down to Hollywood. How does that sound?"

"Grand!" she cried. "Just grand!"

He took her in his arms again and said tenderly, "I'll make it up to you, I swear I will. And we'll have another kid."

She knew it was not the time to tell him the chances of that were slim. It could wait until later. With a small smile, she said, "Time for that after we've made our way to Hollywood!"

"I've treated you badly," he said. "I know it. And I promise from now on it will be different."

"Just so long as you keep away from the booze," she said. "It's the booze that changes you."

"I know," he said sadly. "It's held me back. But I'm making a fresh start and nothing will stop me this time."

Nita left the hospital three days later and they stayed in a lodging house for another few days until she was stronger. Marty proved a loving and considerate husband in every way. Then the morning came for them to board the train on their first lap of the journey to San Francisco.

It was second-class cars again becuaause they had to make their money go as far as possible. Nita had brought along pillows to sit on and spare her mending body from the worst of the jolting. She slept a lot as the days and miles went by. She could see that Marty was restless but he remained close to her and was on his best behavior.

San Francisco was all that she'd hoped for. The

weather was good and they had pleasant lodgings in a vine-covered brick house. Marty's report on the vaudeville circuit was excellent but they agreed that she should remain at the house while he played the eight weeks. Then they would drive down to Hollywood together.

She did not even give him a last warning about his drinking. He seemed a completely different person. She rested and explored the fascinating city and the time passed quickly.

One morning Marty appeared in front of the old house with a car. It was a beauty and she couldn't imagine how he could have afforded it.

"It's grand," she said, staring at the tan touring car with its handsome lines, "but how did you pay for it?"

"Won it in a poker game," said the irrepressible Marty. "The owner of one of the theatres bought it and ruined the engine in a month. It has a broken head and it heats up when you don't expect it. But it'll get us to Hollywood in style, and maybe when we get there I can somehow buy a new motor for her!"

"A Cole Aero-Eight!" she said in wonder, not knowing what the journey ahead would bring.

Chapter Four

The Cole Aero-Eight proved their undoing. The deceptively attractive car was in even worse shape than Marty had admitted. It broke down continually and their journey from San Francisco to Los Angeles took twice as long as it otherwise would have. Still Marty enjoyed being at the wheel of the luxurious car (when it was moving) and refused to consider parting with it.

As they drove on down along the coast road, he promised her, "When we get to Hollywood I'll have Billy find me a garage and get this baby in good shape!"

Nita gave him a distressed glance. "I think it's hopeless!"

"This car is almost new!" he protested. "It can't be that bad!"

Nita didn't want to argue with him. It was enough that they were together again and he was easing up on his drinking. She hoped that when they reached Hollywood they would both be able to find work. She'd not forgotten that Sherman Kress, not given to empty compliments, had vowed she was an excellent type for the movies. If Billy Bowers could get Marty work in some of his comedies it would be a beginning for them.

Despite their faltering car Nita was enjoying the drive south. The lovely blue skies, the sweet flower-scented air and the multitude of gardens in perpetual bloom made it seem an enchanted place. As they came to a smart suburb adjoining Hollywood she had a glimpse of a succession of great mansions behind iron gates and fences, many with shaggy royal palms decorating their grounds.

The traffic grew heavy as they came into Hollywood and Nita was at once excited by the sight of buildings she had read about but never seen before; Grauman's Chinese Theatre, the Brown Derby Restaurant and the famed bungalow court, The Garden of Allah, owned by the famous actress, Nazimova. She was so caught up in the sights and the people strolling along the sidewalks of this gaudy, almost tacky place that she paid no attention to Marty at the wheel.

All at once her attention was riveted by a groan from him as he cried, "The brakes have failed!"

She turned to him in dismay and saw his frightened, pale face as he reached for the emergency brake. She realized they were going ahead at much too fast a rate for a city street and coming to an intersection where traffic was streaming in from every direction.

"Stop it somehow!" she exclaimed.

"I can't!" he cried as he swerved quickly around a slow-moving car ahead.

But in avoiding that collision he placed them in new danger. Nita saw it almost too late to warn him as they reached the intersection.

"The truck!" she cried. "On your side!"

She saw his dismay at the approach of the heavy truck and his frantic effort to avoid being hit side-on by spurting ahead, since he couldn't brake the car to a halt. What he hadn't noticed was another truck coming out of another street at an equally fast pace. Nita screamed as she realized they were directly in the path of this second monster! She was aware of a jarring impact and a sensation of being hurled up out of the car. Then all was silence and darkness.

Much later on, it was the pain which wakened her, pain in her right arm and in her head. Nita opened her eyes slowly and saw that she was back in a hospital room again. It took her a moment or two to remember the events which had preceded her being there. And when the frightening replay of the accident came to memory she sobbed aloud.

A young nurse came hurrying into the room and over to her bedside. The girl peered down at her sympathetically. "You must not be afraid. You're quite safe here. You're going to recover fully!"

She stared up at the nurse. "How long have I been here?"

"Four days," the young woman said. "We've been waiting for you to come around."

Nita rolled her head on the pillow and gazed about the nondescript little room. Her eyes sought the nurse's face again as she put her second question. "What about my husband?"

"Your husband?" the girl said vaguely.

"Yes," he was driving our car at the time of the accident."

The young nurse looked uneasy. "You mustn't talk too much," she warned her. "I'll send Dr. Watters in to see you. He is in charge of your case."

"What about my husband?" Nita asked again, frightened now.

The nurse was already on the way to the hall doorway. She looked back over her shoulder, calling, "I'll get the doctor!"

Nita moved a little in the bed and felt a surge of pain in her left forearm and the surging throb in her head once more. In addition to this it was as if she'd been pounded over every inch of her body so that she was a mass of tortured flesh.

Then figures appeared in the doorway again and she concentrated her attention on them. The nice young nurse had returned with a tall man in a white coat, a stethoscope slung about his neck. Nita knew he must be her doctor.

He came close and bent down to smile at her. "Well, Mrs. Nolan!"

"You know my name?" she said in wonder.

"We've had you here the better part of a week," he told her. He was brown-haired and had a tanned, rather broad face, a snub nose and a friendly smile.

She gazed up at him, still not completely clear-thinking. She said slowly, "The truck! I saw it coming—too late!"

"Most unfortunate," he agreed. "Happily you have nothing more than a concussion and a simple fracture of the lower arm. It was the concussion which was worrying us. And now you've come around."

"My husband," she said, returning to that most urgent theme.

The doctor's smile faded. He said, "Of course, you do not know."

"Know what?"

He hesitated. "I think you should rest now and I'll tell you all about the accident and your husband later. You're taxing yourself too greatly."

Nita's eyes filled with tears. She said in a taut whisper, "He was badly hurt?"

The young doctor nodded. "I'm afraid so."

"How badly?"

There was a second of silence and Watters took her

74

good hand in his and said in a sad tone, "You must be brave, Mrs. Nolan. Your husband was killed."

"No!" she moaned.

"It was instantaneous, he didn't know what happened," the doctor assured her, still holding her hand. "You must try to bear it." He turned to the nurse and gave her some instructions.

Nita continued to sob. "He can't be dead!"

"You have a good friend who has been here every day and is looking after everything for you," the doctor went on. "Billy Bowers, the well known comedy star."

Nita had closed her eyes and was crying silently now. She felt her head lifted slightly and a tiny glass applied to her lips. She swallowed some sweet-tasting liquid and then was gently settled back on her pillow. The action of the liquid was almost immediate. First the pain lessened, and she had a sensation of being a distance from it, outside her injured body, floating in a kind of cloudlike atmosphere. Her mental anguish also succumbed to the magic of the liquid. She was only conscious of a faint sensation of sorrow. Then she knew nothing at all for another long while.

When she came out of her drugged state the first thing she saw was a familiar face gazing down at her. She thought for a moment she was seeing the boyish face of Billy Bowers on a movie screen. Then she realized it was real, that he was here in her hospital room studying her with deep compassion.

He said, "I'm Billy Bowers."

"I know," she replied in a small voice. "I recognized you."

The comedian looked like a sober business man in his dark blue suit and sedate tie. He said, "I'm terribly sorry for what happened. I feel partly responsible since I encouraged Marty to come out here.''

"You couldn't have guessed there'd be an accident," Nita reminded him.

Billy said. "You're just as lovely as Marty described you. I'll try to make up to you for what happened.''

"Where—is he?''

"He was buried yesterday," said Billy. "I've bought a plot for him in Hollywood Memorial Cemetery. All the important motion picture people are buried there.''

Nita managed a rueful smile. "Marty would like that. He always wanted to make the big time!''

"And he would have.''

"He admired you," she said. "Your letters gave him the courage to go on.''

"Marty was my friend," Billy said quietly. "We played the vaudeville circuit together before I came to Hollywood.''

An anxious look crossed Nita's face. "Did he have a priest to bury him?''

"He did," said Billy. "Rest assured, everything was done as you would have wished it. Now we must look to the future. As soon as you are well enough to leave the hospital I'm going to have you come to stay with me.''

"I couldn't," Nita protested.

"You must," he said. "I have a big house with a swimming pool and more than enough servants to look after it. You can have the entire guest wing to yourself.

"I want to find a job in pictures," she said. "Marty intended us to make something of ourselves out here.''

Billy nodded. "And you will! I'll give you work in my comedies as soon as you're ready. This is a crazy town, let me warn you, but I can help you over the hard spots.''

She gazed up at him in wonder. ''You're not a bit like you are in pictures. You're so solemn.''

The boyish-looking actor managed a small smile. ''People are inclined to confuse the screen image with the real person. You'll have a lot of surprises here in Hollywood as you meet your favorite stars.''

''Marty said you and Fatty Arbuckle were good friends. Or you were before he got into all that trouble.''

''Roscoe and I are still friends,'' Billy sighed. ''He's a sad case and I don't know what will become of him. No one will touch his films and he ought to leave Hollywood. But he can't seem to bring himself to do it.''

''You're so famous!'' she said wonderingly.

He shook his head. ''Limited fame, I promise you. I'm a star of two-reelers. And today that's the small end of the business. The features are everything. Chaplin, Keaton and all the big names are making long comedies.''

''Why don't you?''

''No one wants to back me in a feature. They think I'm best in two-reelers. Until I can convince them differently I'll stay in the short stuff.''

''The two-reelers are important,'' she said loyally. ''I think they are the part of the program everyone enjoys most.''

''I hope it stays that way,'' Billy Bowers said. ''But it's getting late and you're not supposed to overdo. I'll go now.''

''Thank you for everything,'' she said, stretching her good hand out to him.

The star took it and held it for a moment. His eyes

met hers with great earnestness and he said, "Don't worry about anything! Get better for Marty's sake!"

Then he was gone. Nita watched after him, thinking what an odd meeting it had been. Marty had always planned a boisterous reunion with his friend with plenty of drinks for them all. How different it had turned out! From what she could tell by observing him, Billy Bowers was a much more steady type than Marty. Yet she knew the two had once been very close and the friendship apparently continued to mean much to the comedy star. She was surprised by his modest appraisal of his talents and the fact that two-reeler stars were not particularly well thought of in Hollywood.

Slowly Nita came back to health until finally the afternoon came when Billy Bowers was to pick her up and take her to his home. She was able to look after her own packing and the sight of her battered suitcase on her bed brought back sad memories of the accident. As she straightened things out in the suitcase she came upon her precious doll. It had come through the crash without harm. She smiled at it wistfully and moved it so that it opened and closed its eyes.

A voice behind her with an amused edge suggested, "I would expect you to be somewhat beyond the age of dolls."

She turned to see that it was young Dr. Phillip Watters who had seen her through her ordeal. She smiled wryly, still holding the doll in her hands. "It has a special meaning for me," she said. "We've travelled a long way together. I used to believe it brought me luck."

"Don't let me come between friends," the young doctor said. "I'm sure you're both glad to be leaving us."

78

Nita put the doll back in the suitcase and turned to him to tell him, "I shall never forget your kindness."

"No more than my regular duties," he said, clearly embarrassed. "By the way, we're both leaving the hospital at almost the same time."

"I don't understand."

He smiled. "I'm taking another job. Master Films have made me an excellent offer to be their studio physician. I'm leaving tomorrow to take over there."

She said, "Do you think you can do as important work there as you're doing here?"

"I have given that a good deal of thought," he admitted. "And I think the position will be worthwhile. The studios are faced with all sorts of medical problems."

"I wish you luck, then," she said, holding out her hand.

He took her hand. "And I wish the same to you. Mr. Bowers tells me he has plans for you in films, so perhaps our paths will cross."

"I hope so," she said sincerely.

After he left, Nita completed the task of packing. The young doctor had made all the difference in her speedy recovery. She was amazed at how well he seemed to understand her and how easily they got along together. She was still thinking about him when Billy Bowers came for her in his Cadillac.

The star carried her suitcase and took her out a side door of the hospital to the waiting car. A husky, middle-aged man with a puglilist's battered face was waiting for them. Billy at once handed her suitcase to the big man.

"This is Murphy," he said. "He's my man of all work. He combines chauffeur, secretary and bodyguard in one, as well as being my physical fitness instructor. This is Nita Nolan, Murph."

Murphy gave her a warm, Irish smile. "Pleased to meet you, Mrs. Nolan."

"And I to meet you," she said, liking him at once. "I need some Irish around me to feel at home."

"There are plenty of us here in Hollywood," Murphy told her with good humor as he stowed her suitcase away and saw them safely in the back seat of the car. Then he took the wheel to drive them to Billy's home in an affluent section of the film city.

Nita thought that Billy Bowers looked taut and haggard as she sat next to him in the glaring sunshine. In films he definitely looked more boyish. She could see now that he was a good many years older than Marty.

The comedian gave her an uneasy smile and said, "I'm going to start you working right away."

"Fine," she said. "I need to have my mind occupied."

"We're working on a comedy now," he went on. "And day after tomorrow we're shooting a scene in which I try to elope with a girl against her father's wishes. I've arranged for you to play the girl."

"Knowing I have no film experience?"

"You can do it," he said. "I'm part owner of the company that turns the two reelers out. Hammons only owns forty per cent. The rest is mine."

"I see," she said. "So you control it."

"In almost everything," he agreed.

"Could you make a long film if you wished? You said you wanted to."

Billy Bowers shook his head. "I'd never get Hammons to agree to it. If I insisted I'm sure he'd sell the company shares he owns to someone else. And he's too good a production manager to lose."

She accepted this explanation and turned her attention to the wide boulevards lined with rich, green bushes and occasional palm trees. Behind the trees were the homes of the more successful Hollywood stars and executives.

They finally reached Billy's home, a brown stucco building in Mexican hacienda style. It had a kidney shaped pool at the rear surrounded by a large stone patio and a cabana also of Mexican design. A maid came out and Murphy gave the elderly woman Nita's bag, which she took inside.

Billy smiled at Nita as he accompanied her to the entrance door, saying, "I want you to feel at home here."

"I'm afraid I'm intruding," she protested.

"Not so. This is the least I can do for Marty. And for you."

"I'll try to repay your kindness," she promised.

He took her inside where it was shadowed and very quiet. As time progressed, she was to be further amazed at the silence of the sprawling big house. It was a distance back from the street and surrounded with a heavy, exotic growth of trees and shrubbery. Inside there was hardly ever a sound. It reminded Nita of the reading room of the Public Library back in Lynn. She'd thought a lot about Lynn during her recovery. There had been warm letters of sympathy from Marty's parents but only a rather cool note from her own mother. She was not yet forgiven for running away.

Billy led her to the open doorway of a room in the right wing of his mansion. It was a huge bedroom furnished tastefully in the Spanish style. The furniture was dark and elegantly carved. He said, "This will be your room while you are here. In fact, the entire wing will be yours."

"It's much more than I need!"

"I'm glad to have someone in the house," the comedian told her.

She said, "I'll promise not to bother you."

"That would be impossible," Billy said. "I have my own section of the house. The servants have the wing at the other end. We have space to spare." He halted and then added, "There is just one thing."

"Oh?"

He frowned. "I have frquent migraine headaches. They strike when I least expect them. When they come I lock myself in my part of the house and must have absolute quiet."

She was concerned. "Do they bother you often?"

"Enough to be a nuisance."

"Has no one been able to help you?"

"I'm afraid not," he said. "But I've learned to deal with them."

"I'm glad."

He gave her a wary look. "The thing is that you mustn't be upset when I have an attack. Don't try to reach me or cause any noise in the house."

"Be sure that I'll be considerate," she promised.

He lost his gloomy look and seemed pleased. "So that settles that," he said. "I'll give you a chance to move in and then we can have lunch by the poolside."

Nita changed into a blue linen dress and went out to join Billy. Murphy in shirt-sleeves waited on them. They had salad, melon and coffee under the shelter of the table umbrellas.

Billy studied her across the table. "How do you like it?"

"It's a palace! I only wish Marty had lived to see it!"

"And I," he agreed.

Nita gave him an anxious glance. "You must keep a strict account of all you spend. I intend to pay you back."

"No need."

"Marty would want it that way," she said firmly.

"As you like," Billy said without further argument. He wore slacks and a white shirt with short sleeves, open at the throat. "Tomorrow night I'm taking you to Charles Ray's house for a party."

"Charles Ray who starred in 'The Coward'?" she exclaimed with awe.

Billy smiled his crooked smile. "He's the only Charles Ray I know of in Hollywood."

"I won't know how to act!"

"Just be yourself and they'll like you," he said. "A lot of the people who'll be there were once in vaudeville or on the stage. And there'll be some of the business people as well. A lot of them were running nickleodeons back East a few years ago. There is plenty of money here but not a lot of real class!"

"What about people like De Mille and D.W. Griffith?" Nita wanted to know.

"They keep to themselves," he said. "Have their own small circle socially. But they don't even rank with the true Los Angeles society out here. Not one of them can belong to the exclusive country clubs."

He talked on and she began to understand that except in their own circle, movie people in Hollywood were no more accepted than were show people anywhere else. The stigma of grease paint and footlights continued on the West Coast under the klieg lights and before the cameras. But it was still a magical world that she aspired to, just as Marty had, and she wanted to make her way in it. Become a star if she could.

Billy seemed to have read her thoughts, as he told her, "I think you have the looks and personality for movies. But a word of warning. Don't think it will be easy."

"I'm sure it won't," she agreed.

"The hours are long and the work is hard," he told

her. "There will be men along the way who'll offer you short cuts. In every case they'll ask a price. And often when you'd kept your part of the bargain, they'll conveniently forget all about you."

Her cheeks crimsoned. "Marty spoke of that. He said the studios were known to have a lot of casting couch experts."

"Marty knew," Billy said grimly. "A few stars have made it that way. But you'll do better to avoid those couches."

"I have you to help me get started," she said.

"I can only help you so far. After that you'll be on your own," he said. "That's why I'm being frank with you about the hazards."

She said suddenly, "You were married once."

"Yes."

"What happened?"

He sighed and sat back in his lounge chair. "Mary had big ambitions. She met a director who made her a lot of promises. She left me to live with him."

"And it didn't work out?"

He stared at her. "Don't tell me you haven't read about it in the papers or the fan magazines?"

"No," she said, regretting now that she had brought the matter up.

"I forget you're just a kid," he said, staring at her. "It happened three years ago."

"I was still in parochial shool. I didn't read the papers much."

"Mary killed herself," he said without emotion. "They found her in a rundown hotel in Los Angeles with her wrists slashed. Her director friend had not only not kept his promises but had deserted her."

"I'm sorry," she said, distressed.

"It's an old story," he told her. "I thought everyone knew."

"I didn't hear of it before. Marty didn't tell me."

Billy smiled wryly. "He was probably afraid it might make you think twice about coming to Hollywood. By the way, you can sleep late in the morning. Murphy or Mrs. Case will bring your breakfast. And I must ask you to excuse me for tonight. I think one of my bad headaches is coming on and I will have to rest."

"Don't let me upset your regular routine," Nita said.

"I won't," he promised quietly. He came over to her as she also rose from the table and taking her by the arms he gave her a gentle kiss. Then he nodded and walked back into the house, leaving her alone by the swimming pool.

His gesture had been entirely unexpected. During her time in the hospital he had been a model of reserve. He had often kissed her on the cheek or temple but never on the lips, and never before with such warmth such as he had shown now. She had never though of the shy, rather haggard man as a romantic type, especially not in relation to herself.

She could only assume he was trying to be kind to her because he was Marty's good friend. But his kiss now made her wonder if he might be interested in her on his own. Could it be that he was falling in love with her? If so, she was entirely unprepared for it. Following the shock of losing Marty she had concentrated on surviving, made stronger by her plans for a career of her own, and encouraged by the young doctor in charge of her case.

Staring at the azure surface of the swimming pool with its shining tile steps and its high diving board Nita realized that she had indulged in more speculations about Dr. Phillip Watters than she ever had about Billy Bowers. She had looked on the star as merely a family friend. Now it seemed his interest in her might go deeper.

She knew she would have to watch and wait and be careful not to encourage him until she knew her own feelings. Once again, as she had many times before, she wished that Marty was at her side, holding her hand, cracking jokes and yet making plain his love for her. Drunk or sober, she believed he'd really cared. Now that part of her life was at an end. She must continue alone.

But Marty had taught her how to sing and dance and had given her the chance to learn about the trying profession in which she meant to make her name. Also through Marty she had the friendship and help of Billy Bowers. Things surely were looking better for her. Her arm had healed rapidly and she had recovered completely from her head injuries. She had much to be thankful for.

Nita sat and wrote letters that afternoon. And when time came for the evening meal Mrs. Case brought her a tray of delicious food. She did not mind eating alone in her room, finding it a pleasant change from the cheap atmosphere and bad food of the small town restaurants which she'd become used to on the road. When dinner was over, the housekeeper came for the empty tray.

"You shouldn't shut yourself in your room," Mrs. Case told her as she prepared to leave with the tray. "You have the run of the house."

"I know," Nita replied. "But I understand Mr. Bowers isn't well and I wouldn't want to disturb him."

"Don't worry about disturbing him," Mrs. Case said. "He's shut up in his own rooms at the back of the house where he can't hear anything."

Later Nita decided to stroll out by the pool to enjoy the balmy evening. It was near twilight when she ventured out and Murphy in white slacks and a green sweater was standing by the pool smoking a pipe and gazing at the water. He turned on hearing her footsteps on the patio tiles.

Removing his pipe from his mouth, he said, "Good evening, Mrs. Nolan."

"It is a lovely evening," she agreed. And then she added, "I can't get over this house. It's so quiet!"

"Yes," Murphy said thoughtfully. "It is."

"Is it like this all the time?"

The big man nodded. "A good deal of it."

"I'm sorry about Mr. Bowers' headache," she said. "It's too bad."

"Yes," Murphy said, gazing at the pool again.

"Isn't there anything can be done to help him?" she asked.

The Irishman gave her another of his solemn looks. "I'm afraid not."

"It seems such a tragedy. He has everything and yet it's spoiled for him."

Murphy said, "Hollywood is full of men like him."

Feeling let down, she ventured, "I guess Hollywood isn't all glamor and parties as the screen magazines tell us."

"Not at all," he said.

Nita felt uncomfortable. She sensed that Murphy didn't want to engage in small talk with her. Rather awkwardly, she said, "I'll be going back to my room. I'll see you tomorrow."

He nodded. "Yes."

Nita went back to her room in a puzzled frame of mind. There was something strange about Murphy and in the cautious way in which he had talked with her. He seemed part of the austere quiet of the elegant Mexican style house and heightened the odd atmosphere of mystery which she felt shadowed it. She fell asleep wondering if the house held some dark secret.

Nita wakened in the middle of the night with a start. She had been dreaming wildly and suddenly her nightmare had been pierced by a loud, sobbing cry. She sat up in bed staring into the darkness of the big room, not certain whether the cry had been part of her dream or whether the sound of it had made her awake.

It was hard to be certain. Yet without question the house was silent now, just as grotesquely quiet as it had been for most of the day. She listened for other sounds and heard none. At last she lay back and after a time passed into an uneasy sleep which lasted until morning.

Mrs. Case dutifully came with her breakfast tray and the morning paper. The woman placed it on a table by a window and then lifted the window sash to allow the balmy air to come in.

The woman smiled at her and said, "I think I've brought you everything you mentioned."

Nita put on her dressing gown and went to the table to study the savory contents of the tray. The sight of coffee, toast and marmalade stimulated her appetite. "It looks delicious," she said.

"The boiled eggs are in the covered dish," Mrs. Case indicated a silver dome.

"Thank you," Nita said, sitting down and picking up a glass of orange juice. "Another lovely day."

Mrs. Case glanced out the window. "We've had little rain lately," she agreed.

Nita paused with her orange juice to ask, "Did you hear any strange sounds last night?"

Mrs. Case showed concern. "Strange sounds, madam?"

"Yes," she said. "I wakened in the middle of the

88

night and I'm almost sure it was a loud, sobbing cry which broke into my sleep.''

''Indeed, madam?'' Mrs. Case stared at her with incredulity.

''You heard nothing?''

''No,'' the woman said. ''But then I'm a deep sleeper and my hearing is not the best.''

Nita smiled at her. ''I'm sure you would have heard this cry. It was most eerie. Perhaps I dreamed it after all. I could have.''

''Yes, madam,'' Mrs. Case said and lost no time in taking her leave.

In the early afternoon Nita put on her only black dress for the memorial service. She fashioned a veil to wear with her black cloche. Billy was waiting for her in the living room, also dressed in black. She noticed at once that he appeared even more tense and haggard than on the previous day and it worried her.

She asked him, ''Do you feel well enough to attend the service?''

''Of course,'' he said, seeming irritated that she should ask him such a question.

''It was only your headache I was worried about,'' she went on to explain.

The comedian at once looked apologetic. ''I'm sorry,'' he said. ''I'm afraid I'm still a little edgy. I didn't mean to speak sharply.''

''It's all right,'' she said, drawing on her black gloves.

''You look amazingly well in black,'' he said in admiration. ''Most women find it unflattering.''

Nita shrugged. ''I hadn't thought about it. I have little choice.''

Billy looked sympathetic. ''Are you sure you feel

up to it? You don't have to come if it will be too much of an emotional strain.''

"No," she said. "I've braced myself. Best to get it over with. It's the least I can do for Marty.''

"Brave girl," he said warmly. "I'll have Murphy bring the car.''

The drive to the famous Hollywood Cemetery took a half hour. Billy tried to distract her from her melancholy by pointing out famous places along the way, but Nita barely heard anything he said. Her mind was with Marty, back in those early days when she was learning about show business and what it was to be a show-business wife. It was Marty who had encouraged her ambitions and had brought her here to Hollywood. Now she was about to say her final farewell to him.

But suddenly Nita realized that this was not true. She would never truly say goodbye to the boisterous young Irishman she'd married. He would always be a part of her and, in a subtle way, would influence her. The experience, good and bad, which she had gained as Marty's wife was the foundation on which she would have to build her future.

She broke her reverie to glance at Billy Bowers, and said, "Billy, do you honestly think Marty would have made it in films if he'd lived?''

The comedian nodded. "I do. I really do.''

She sighed. "Perhaps its just as well. I'm sure he'd never have been able to handle success. His drinking would have ruined him.''

"Marty had a big thirst," the man at her side said. "But it's a part of the Irish character.''

"I know," she said ruefully. "I've heard it all said before. I come from a large Irish family myself. I've seen my share of Irish drunks.''

Billy said no more. Shortly they arrived at the

chapel, a brick building in English style. An usher in full morning dress greeted them and escorted them to their seats. A thin, sad-faced priest of late middle age waited inside the small chapel.

Nita swayed a little and her eyes filled with tears as the service began. She was unable to concentrate on the priest's words. All she could think of was that her Marty had dreamed all his short life about making the "big time," but for him the "big time" was burial in a renowned Hollywood cemetery.

The service ended and the priest came to her with words of comfort. Billy explained to Nita that he had made arrangements for a fine memorial stone which they would come and see it when it was erected. They turned then and walked slowly out of the chapel, Nita clinging to his arm.

It was only then that she noticed they had not been the only ones present at the service for Marty. Standing together towards the rear were a large, fat man and a smaller, very thin one. They were about the same age and made a strangely contrasting pair.

As she and Billy made their way outside the two followed them and the small, hollow-cheeked man with an aquiline nose and a head of unruly hair came forward to her awkwardly and said, "I knew Marty, Mrs. Nolan. We once were on a vaudeville bill together for two weeks."

She warmly took his hand and said, "Thank you for coming!"

"I wanted to pay my respects," the thin little man said soberly. "I'm also a friend of Billy's. I'm in movies myself. My name is Buster Keaton."

Nita's eyes widened. "Of course! I've seen your films!"

"I'd like you to meet a friend of mine," Keaton

continued, turning to the baby-faced fat man who had been standing quietly with his cap in his hand.

Nita turned to the fat man and shook his hand, "How do you do? May I ask your name?"

The fat man hesitated, then quietly said, "Arbuckle. Roscoe Arbuckle."

Nita was taken back. Then she said, "Of course! I've seen you many times as well."

"Not lately," the fat man said soberly.

Buster Keaton spoke up quickly, "We have to be going. I have to report on the back lot before the end of the afternoon. Good luck in Hollywood, Mrs. Nolan."

"Thank you," she said. "Thank you both for coming."

Arbuckle started away, his cap now on his head, followed by Keaton. As they walked out of the cemetery to the distant street they were indeed a unique couple.

At her side Billy Bowers said, "Buster has been a staunch friend of Arbuckle's through all his troubles. That's not the usual Hollywood story." They followed the two famous actors as they went back to Billy's car and the waiting Murphy.

Chapter Five

It proved to be a twenty-four hours of strange contrasts for Nita. After the sadness of Marty's memorial service, she was catapulted into the midst of a roaring Hollywood party that very night. As he had promised, Billy took her along to the gala event being held at Charles Ray's house. Murphy drove them and on the way over the comedian seemed to regain a lot of his jovial good humor. Nita assumed that he was feeling much better.

During the drive to the Ray mansion, he warned her, "You may find Charles and his wife a little unusual."

"In what way?" she asked.

Billy Bowers smiled, "Charlie is one of the new rich. For years he played the juvenile lead in dozens of stock companies. Then Thomas H. Ince picked him up and began starring him in movies. Now he's making at least a half-million a year."

"It sounds as if he came from the same background as most of the show business people out here," she said.

"He does," Billy agreed. "But Charlie has strange tastes. He and his wife Honey always dress formally for dinner, even if they are alone and even if they're giving an informal party!"

She smiled. "That must become tiresome for them."

"Charlie thinks he should, that he's acting like high society," Billy went on. "And if you look carefully you'll see the gold plumbing fixtures in the bathroom and the gold doorknobs in the living room."

"Who will be there tonight?" she asked.

"You never know," Billy said. "But Charlie Chaplin usually comes. He thinks Ray is amusing. He pokes fun at him but they get along well."

Nita could not help being excited at the prospect of a party where she would meet many famous people of the screen. Whatever poor taste Charles Ray might display, it seemed he had a lot of friends. She remembered him from the movies and had always thought of him as a wistful young man. She had worn her most elegant dress, a green crepe de chine with beaded trim. She hoped it wouldn't look dowdy.

Billy pointed out the house as they drove into the circular drive before it. The house was large, white and rambling with several wings, all having peaked roofs. Before the house were a number of cars.

Billy said, "There are at least five Rolls Royces here. I see Chaplin's."

"I'm frightened!" she told him.

"You don't need to be," the comedian said, smiling at her. "You are prettier than most of the women. Don't judge by what you see on the screen. They're all glamorized with make-up."

Still, Nita was trembling as he led her from the car to the front entrance of the house. The door was open and they went straight in. Most of the guests were in a huge drawing room whose walls were covered with fine paintings and tapestries. The room was crowded with men and women, all with glasses in their hands. From the midst of the chattering group there emerged a tall moon-faced man in evening dress whom she recognized at once as Charles Ray.

"Greetings!" He shook Billy's hand warmly and bowed when he was introduced to Nita. "My place is yours!" was his sweeping invitation.

There was a bar with three busy uniformed bartenders. Seeing so much liquor in one place in these Prohibition times was a shock for Nita. But there were greater shocks in store for her. Billy pushed his way through the clusters of chattering people until he was within reaching distance of the bar. Nita had asked for rye and he came back holding her drink high so as not to have someone bump into him and spill it. He smiled at her as he handed her her glass and began sipping from his own.

"Are Hollywood parties always this large?" she asked in awe.

"Charlie's are," he said with a smile. And he nodded towards a sleek-looking man with slicked-back hair and a small mustache who was giving all his attention to a rather bored looking lady.

"That's Lowell Sherman," the comedian told her. "He was at Fatty Arbuckle's the night that girl was killed. But it hasn't seemed to hurt his career."

As they were talking a sexy blonde girl came over with a drink in her hand and smiled at Billy. She exclaimed, "Darling! How nice to see you here!" And she stood on tiptoes to bestow a kiss on his cheek. "I'm Thelma Stone," she told Nita.

Billy, looking slightly embarrassed, introduced Nita, adding, "She's going to begin working in one of my comedies tomorrow."

The shapely Thelma gave her a wink. "I warn you he's a slave-driver. I started in pictures with Billy."

"I'm not all that bad," he protested.

Thelma laughed. "He's all right." Staring at Nita she said, "You're new here, aren't you?"

"Yes," she agreed.

"Where are you living?" the blonde girl asked.

Embarrassed, Nita said, "I'm at Billy's place now."

"Wonderful," Thelma replied blithely. "I'm living in a fairly reasonable cottage court, called Gardenia Court. If you ever need a place, there's always a vacancy or two."

"I'll remember," she promised.

"Introduce her to Chaplin," Thelma suggested. "He's over in the corner holding court!"

Billy Bowers asked Nita, "Do you want to meet him?"

She shrugged. "Why not?"

He led her across the room to where a small man was standing talking quietly to an interested group, none of whom Nita recognized. As the small man saw them approach he turned away from the group and came to them with a smile on his pleasant face.

"Good evening, Billy," he said in a soft British voice. "May I enquire who the lovely lady is?"

"I brought her over to meet you," Billy said. "This is Nita Nolan. She's the widow of an old friend of mine from vaudeville days and she's going to start work with me in the morning."

Chaplin took Nita's hand and kissed it with great gallantry. His eyes met hers and he said, "I salute the arrival of a new beauty in Hollywood."

She smiled. "So you're the little tramp! I would never have recognized you!"

"For you I'll put on my mustache and walk funny," Chaplin promised.

She shook her head. "That won't be necessary!"

Chaplin smiled at her. "So you've been in vaudeville? Where?"

She told him, ending with, "I'm on my own now. My husband was killed in an auto accident."

"You'll do well," Chaplin replied. "Billy Bowers can get you started. But you must aim for higher things."

"So I've been told," she said.

"I began in vaudeville in England," Chaplin told her. "Came over here with Fred Karno. Stan Laurel was in the company also. He's making two-reelers like Billy."

"I think they are important to the movie house programs," she replied. "I always enjoyed them."

"I began with two reelers," Chaplin agreed. "I think you are right." He glanced around and then told her, "Let's get away from here. I see Ford Sterling coming our way and I want to avoid him. We're having an argument about a contract."

As he said this the immaculately dressed little man led her out the french doors by which they were standing. She found herself standing on a small balcony outside. It was dark now and the only light was what glimmered through the curtained windows from inside.

"Where are you living?" Chaplin asked.

She wondered if everyone in Hollywood were going to ask her this question. She said, "Billy has kindly allowed me to stay with him for a while."

Chaplin laughed softly. "I gave Billy credit for good taste. And for taking care of you. I can hardly call you there."

"Why not?" she asked.

"I wouldn't want to annoy Billy," he said.

She felt her cheeks burn as she understood the comedian's words. She said quickly, "I'm not living with Billy. I'm merely staying in his house!"

97

Chaplin was at once abject. "I didn't mean to suggest anything unseemly. But if you tire of staying there I wish you'd phone me."

"I'm not likely to do that," she said sharply, ready to go back inside.

Before she could manage this the famous comedian had taken her in his arms and kissed her. At the same time one of his hands was carressing her in a most intimate fashion. She tried to free herself from his embrace just as the french doors opened and Thelma Stone came out.

She said, "You've always had my admiration for being a fast worker, Charlie."

Chaplin was at once all self-righteous. He straightened his tie and looked indignant. "I have no idea what you're talking about. If this young lady and I wish to enjoy a kiss I doubt if there's any state law to prohibit us." And with that he marched back into the room, highly annoyed.

Nita exclaimed indignantly, "I didn't encourage him!"

"I'm sure of that," Thelma replied. "But you'd have a hard time proving it, even in court."

"I can't believe what happened!" she said.

Thelma rolled her eyes. "Better get used to it. It's going on all the time here. One of the first rules is don't let yourself be alone with any man you don't know well. Coming out here was dumb!"

"I realize that now," Nita said unhappily. "I think what started him was my saying I was living with Billy Bowers. He at once assumed I was Billy's mistress."

Thelma smiled good-naturedly. "So did I, to be truthful. But then I saw that I was mistaken. So I mentioned Gardenia Court to you. It's not too bad a place."

"I'll remember it," she promised.

"Billy hasn't tried to play any funny games with you, has he?" the blonde girl asked.

"No," she said. "Has he a bad reputation?"

"Not with women. You know his wife left him and later killed herself."

She nodded. "He told me."

"At least he's being honest with you. A lot of people feel sorry for him. His wife's suicide seemed to do something to him. His work on the screen hasn't been as good since."

"He's a sensitive man. It was bound to affect him."

Thelma closed the door so they could talk on the balcony and not be heard from inside. Earnestly, she said, "You're a nice kid, so I want to try and level with you. Billy and I spent a little time together. It didn't work."

"Oh?"

"You've met Murphy?"

"Yes."

"You know what he is?"

Nita's eyebrows raised. "Billy said he employs him as a chauffeur and man of all work."

Thelma shook her head. "Billy doesn't employ Murphy. The studio employs him."

"Really? But then Billy owns part of the studio."

"The big share is owned by Hammons no matter what Billy's told you," the other girl told her. "And Hammons hires Murphy to police Billy."

"To police him?"

"Yes," Thelma said grimly. "Hammons has a lot of money tied up in Billy's career and he's not about to lose it."

"But I thought Murphy was employed to help Billy," Nita said, bewildered.

"Don't be a child," the other girl remonstrated with

99

her. "You don't know much about Hollywood yet, I can tell that. Murphy is hired by Hammons to keep an eye on Billy and make sure he doesn't drink too much."

Nita said, "I haven't seen him drink much of anything."

"I know," Thelma said. "I lived with him. He's a solitary drinker. What do you think happens when he locks himself up in his house away from everyone?"

"He does that because of his headaches!"

"No," Thelma shook her head again. "I'm sorry, kid, but that's when Billy dips into the booze. He drinks himself unconscious and it's Murphy's job to look after him and have him ready to work in the morning."

Nita listened, realizing that it was all very likely true. She had noticed an oddness about the house and the way Murphy and Billy related to each other. So Billy was an alcoholic, as Marty had been.

She sighed, "I guess I'm naive. I should have guessed it."

"Well, you know now. Murphy runs the place. And he answers to Hammons, not Billy Bowers."

"It's a shame. I mean that he drinks as he does."

Thelma said, "He's always been a heavy drinker. That's why he'll not get beyond the two-reelers. He'll die from his drinking one of these days."

"I wish I could do something to help him, he's so nice," she worried.

"I tried to help him," the other girl said. "So have a lot of others. It didn't work. He wants to drown himself in drink. It's hard to stop someone from trying to kill himself if he's made up his mind to do it. And I'd say he did that the morning he learned that his wife had taken her life."

100

"That probably has a lot to do with it," she agreed.

"So let me be your friend," the blonde said. "You need some new clothes, I can see that."

"Not until after I get my first paycheck."

"You should do it right away."

"I can't," she protested. "I haven't the money."

"I can let you have some," Thelma said. "You can pay me back."

"Sorry. I make it a rule not to borrow."

"Whatever you like," the other girl said. "Billy will likely want to fit you out with a wardrobe. He'll need to so you'll look good in his comedies."

"We'll see," Nita said. "I suppose we'd better go back in."

They returned to the party which was going on at an even livelier rate than before. A girl was on top of a table dancing, her short skirt was flying in the breeze showing that she wore little or nothing under it. The males were crowded around the table laughing and applauding.

"Clara Bow!" Thelma said with annoyance. "Crazy-headed! I don't know what they see in her!"

"She's very popular with movie audiences," Nita pointed out.

"Not with me, she isn't," Thelma snapped.

It was then that Billy came towards them. He looked pale and weary and he halted before them with a look of curiosity. "What are you two conspiring about?"

"Not a thing," Thelma told him with an arch smile. "I've been handing the little girl some good advice."

"Coming from you, I'm sure it was the best," Billy said with a wry look.

Thelma laughed. "You know me, kid!" And with that she moved on and left them.

Billy gave Nita a tired glance. "I don't know about

you, but I've had enough. We're starting work early tomorrow. And it will be a long day.''

"And all new to me," she agreed. "I'd like to go home!"

He looked pleased. "Good! I'll find Murphy!" And he left her in search of their driver.

Nita moved away from the excitement in the living room and went out to the reception hall to stand by the front door. She had only been there a moment when the front door opened and a distraught-looking Charles Ray entered dragging and half-supporting a slim, good-looking dark man with his hair parted in the middle. Nita thought he looked vaguely familiar.

Charles Ray halted for a moment with his drunken friend leaning on him, and said, "Are you leaving so soon?"

"I have to," she said. "I'm working early in the morning."

"So am I," the big moon-faced man said with a frown. "And it looks as if it'll be morning before this breaks up!"

"I wish you luck," she smiled. "I enjoyed it!"

"So did I," the drunken man leaning on the host said, coming alert suddenly and smiling at her in drunken fashion. "Who are you? I'm Jack Pickford!"

"I knew I'd seen you on the screen," she said. "I'm Nita Nolan."

Pickford eyed her with drunken amusement, then turned to Charles Ray laughing and said, "This is little Nita Nobody! Nita Nobody!"

"Excuse him, please," their host pleaded and then angrily to Jack Pickford, he said, "Come along!" And he dragged him off down the hall.

Nita watched in dismay and was glad when Billy appeared with Murphy waiting in the car outside.

When she was in the car she told of her meeting with Jack Pickford.

Billy sighed. "Mary has spoiled him. No matter what he does it's funny. And the sad part of it is he has plenty of talent. But he's throwing it away!"

They were driving through the cool night air and darkness with Murphy sitting silently behind the wheel as he headed the open car homeward. She glanced at Billy and said, "May I make a comment?"

"Why not?" The comedian asked.

"I've never seen so many tense and unhappy people in one place," she told him. "I thought vaudeville was filled with strange people, but Hollywood is worse!"

"You think so?"

"Yes. Everyone was drunk and there was so much hostility! And no one really respected Charles Ray and his wife as their hosts."

"That's Hollywood!"

"I don't think I'm going to like it," she said. "All these people who've seemed like gods and goddesses to me are less than pleasant!"

"The party did you some good then," Billy said with a grim look her way. "Took the stardust out of your eyes."

"I'm not sure I'll want to stay here," Nita declared.

"There are a good many decent, happy people in the town," Billy assured her. "You won't find them on every corner. But they are here. And some great talents as well. Thomas Meighan, Billie Dove, Lila Lee and Milton Sills. They're all good people whom you'd enjoy knowing."

"I think your friend Thelma is nice," she said.

"Go easy with her."

"Why? I thought you and she were close."

"We were once. Not anymore."

"She seems independent and getting ahead."

Billy nodded. "She's had several good parts in Wallace Reid features lately."

"Well, what's wrong with her?"

The comedian was silent for a moment. Then he said, "I may be wrong. But I've heard some strange stories lately. Someone who knows Thelma well told me that both she and Wally have been taking drugs."

She gasped. "I can't believe it! Wallace Reid is a fine looking man! He'd never take drugs!"

"The way I heard it he's been addicted a long while," Billy said in a tired voice. "And he's been trying to start Thelma on them. But it may all be gossip. It can be venomous in this town!"

"I'm sure that it has to be," she said defiantly. "I like Thelma and I can't see Wallace Reid as a drug addict."

Billy didn't argue with her. By this time they were only a short distance from his house. When he later saw her inside he said goodnight and gave her a chaste kiss on the forehead. She went on to her own room much confused by the unusual evening. If all she had heard was true, Hollywood was worse than the most narrow-minded bigot might imagine.

Mrs. Case came with her breakfast at dawn the next morning. And by seven o'clock Murphy was driving Nita and Billy to the small studio where the two reelers were put together. In addition to the back lot Billy explained they often went out into the Hollywood streets for location backgrounds.

Murphy drove up to gates with a small guard house and an attendant inside, who let them pass inside. Within a few minutes they parked opposite an area where camera men and prop men were already at work. It was a mock street scene with a bake shop and a police station featured in the backdrops. Some actors in comedy police costumes were standing about in groups talking gravely.

Billy stood with her a moment. "Well, here it is," he said. "Here is where the miracles come to pass!"

She laughed. "The street scene looks familiar."

"It should. We use it over and over. Sometimes we change the shop names. A bakery becomes a clothing store or the police station becomes city hall or a fire station."

A nervous looking man with a tanned face and his cap on backwards came towards them. In his hand was a megaphone.

He said, "Hello, Billy! Who's the new doll?"

"This is Nita Nolan," Billy said. "She's going to play the baker's daughter." And then to her, "This is Johnny Dale, our director. He can really help you!"

"I'm happy to meet you, Mr. Dale," she told him.

His black eyes snapped and his thin face showed disdain. "Unless you've got more than a nice face and figure you'll hate me! This comedy stuff requires talent."

"I think I can catch on," she said. "I've watched a lot of movies and I've worked in vaudeville."

Johnny Dale looked slightly less disgusted. "At least you have some experience. Most of the dames they bring me are straight out of Woolworth's!"

"I've never done that to you," Billy chided him.

Johnny was studying her. "You got strong legs and lots of wind?"

"I've done a lot of dancing," she ventured.

"Good," he said. "In this comedy you do a lot of running in and out of the bakery when the fellows from the police station try to steal samples of your father's cooking. You run in and out after them, slap them in the face with pies and such."

Billy smiled at her. "A real art form!"

"If it makes people laugh, I'm satisfied," she said.

"That's the idea," the director told her. "Keep that in your mind all the time! All of us here are supposed to be funny! And you have to make faces and not worry about not looking pretty!"

"I understand," she said.

"Okay," the brusque little man in the turned-around cap said. "After you're made up, come out and be ready to work. When you're on just do what I tell you! I'll be shouting directions all the time. If you do anything wrong just keep on until you get it right."

The director went on his way and Billy took her to a row of makeshift bungalows. He pointed to one, "That's the women's make-up room. I'll see you on the set."

She entered the room and found a harried looking man of middle age making up a stout, character woman. There were also two younger women waiting for his talents.

The little bald man frowned at her and groaned, "Another one!"

She sat and smiled politely though she felt very discouraged. Last night she'd been disillusioned at a Hollywood party, and now she was seeing the drab, factory-like operation the making of pictures was. She felt a great longing to be back with Sherman Kress, Madame Irma, Percy the seal and the others.

What would Marty have made of it all? If Billy were right, and he probably was, Marty would have conquered the town with his Irish charm and talent. Then no doubt he would have joined the suicide brigade to drink himself to death. Marty had wanted her to share his Hollywood chance. Now she was facing the big opportunity alone. For his sake she couldn't give up easily.

The make-up man roused her from her reverie with a curt, "All right, you're next!"

She went and sat on the stool which the others had vacated. He glared at her and said, "What role are you playing?"

"The baker's daughter."

He looked impressed. "That's the lead, next to Billy." He went about completing her make-up. When he'd finished and she saw herself in the mirror she thought she looked like a witch, daubed with pasty yellow. But he seemed satisfied. He sent her on to another bungalow marked "Wardrobe."

A woman with a foreign accent was in charge there. She asked Nita her role and when she learned it was the baker's daughter, the wardrobe mistress gave Nita a dark brown dress. She warned her, "I haff only three of these. If you get them all dirty you'll haff to vait until they're vashed and dried. So be careful!"

"I'll do my best," Nita said wanly, taking the dresses with her into the tiny cubicle of a dressing room. She removed her own dress and put on the brown one. Then she went out to sit on a canvas chair behind the cameras.

The director was already at work with Billy and the policeman. Billy was having an argument with a fat policeman and when the fat one stuck his finger in his face, Billy bit it. This sent the fat man into a dancing rage as Billy ran off. The cameraman was busy filming the scene and the lighting man was adjusting his reflectors to get the best effect.

The director had Billy and the fat man repeat the scene two or three times. Then he ran another scene where the fat policeman and a thin one conferred in front of the bakery shop. It was clearly their plan to steal some dainties from it. The thin man stood guard while the fat policeman furtively made his way into the bakery.

There was much shouting by the director and changing of pace before he was satisfied with the results. Then he shouted into the megaphone, "The baker's daughter!"

Nita came forward and stood by him. "Ready!"

The director scowled at her. "Your eye make-up is too heavy, but we can't wait now. It will have to do. Now I'll tell you what your action is!"

And he did. He took her behind the store front and explained that when the fat policeman came in and stole two pies she was to follow him out shouting. He was to stop and argue with her. She was to continue accusing him. The fat man would give the pies to his doleful thin accomplice to hold and then turn to shake her like a puppy. At that moment Billy would appear, see her plight, and taking the pies from the thin policeman, slap one of them into his face and then the other one into the fat policeman's face. After which he would take Nita by the hand and rush her to safety inside the shop.

"Okay," The director shouted. "Let's do it!" He came forward and gave her further instructions about her timing and facial expressions. She listened carefully and tried to follow his instructions. Her first dress was stained with pie and she had to rush to the dressing room and don another. Then the filming resumed.

It seemed an age until the noon break. Nita had been told film acting was hard work. Now she really knew it. She joined Billy Bowers with a wry smile.

"What a morning!" she said.

"A good morning," he told her. "You were great!"

"You honestly mean that?"

"I do," he said. "And to prove it I'll reward you.

108

Go change and I'll take you to lunch at the Master Films Commissary. It's just across the street.''

"Have we time?''

"Plenty,'' he said. "And the alternative is eating sandwiches her from a truck which comes in to provide food and drink for the company. We aren't rich enough to afford to dine in style.''

She smiled. "I won't be long!''

He called after her, "Don't take off your make-up. Just change your dress.''

So a few minutes later she found herself strolling across the street with Billy. She felt odd in her heavy make-up but she soon discovered all the other players took their lunch breaks with make-up on. The guard on duty at the Master Films gate recognized Billy and greeted him warmly. Nita walked into the wondrous world of major film making and saw that this was a truly busy lot.

They passed a set of ancient England with castle, moat and green fields surrounding it, then moved on to where a unit was still working. She was entranced to hear a trio of musicians playing romantic background music for the scene. It was an outdoor café and a tall, handsome man and a blonde girl sat across from each other at a sidewalk table conversing in an intimate fashion.

Billy told her, "That's Rod La Roque and Vilma Banky. They're very big at the box office these days.''

She was awed. "I never expected to see them in person!''

"You'll see a lot of people here,'' he said, amused.

They walked on to the commissary and found most of the tables occupied. Billy led her to the rear of the room and she recognized Dustin Farnum sitting talking to an elderly man as went by. She didn't dare look around. It seemed there were familiar faces from the screen everywhere.

"I feel I don't belong," she said as she sat with Billy at the empty table he'd found.

"You will," he promised her. "After you finish the film we're working on today people will be seeing you on the screen. You'll be one of us."

She laughed. "It will be a long time before people point me out on the street."

"It can happen quickly," Billy said. "Look at Mabel Normand. She became famous almost overnight."

The food was served buffet style from a long counter. Nita was too shy to want to stand in line, so she told Billy what she would like and he went off to bring back lunch for her and for himself.

She sat transfixed by the chatter of the glamorous group around her. One woman dominated a nearby table with her exotic looks, pale white skin and coal black hair drawn straight back from her forehead. She was surrounded by two men and two other women, none of whom were as stunning as she.

"Star gazing?" The question was put to her in a pleasant male voice.

She glanced up in surprise to see a familiar face smiling down at her. It was Dr. Phillip Watters. He looked even more handsome in a brown jacket and fawn slacks. Belatedly she remembered that he had told her he was going to become physician to one of the studios.

She said, "Hello! So this is where you've ended up!"

His brown eyes twinkled. "Let's say it is where I'm working at the moment."

"Whatever you like," she said. "It's good to see you again."

"And to see you," the young doctor said. "Judging by the fact you're in make-up I would suppose you are working here."

"I am working," she told him. "But across the street at Hammons Pictures. Billy Bowers brought me here as his guest."

"Of course, Billy Bowers," the doctor said. "He came to see you often when you were in hospital."

"And now I'm working in his new two-reeler," she said.

"Good," Phillip Watters replied. "I wish you luck."

"How do you like it here?"

He shrugged. "Fair. I'll stay a while. It's been a quiet day so far. An extra fainted on one of the sets. I sent her home with a fever and told her not to report for work until she had recovered. And Barbara La Marr had one of her weak spells but she came out of it with a little medication."

"Different from the hospital," she said.

"Very much so," he agreed. "But it pays well and I'm getting a different kind of experience."

"This is a different world!"

He nodded. "You're right. I hope we meet soon again."

"I hope so," she said, and he left her.

When Billy came back with their plates of food she told him about seeing the young doctor again. She said, "He has an office right here on the lot."

The comedian nodded as he attacked his salad with vigor. "Most of the companies have doctors on the lots and always a nurse or two. It pays. There are many accidents and with a lot of people around, there is bound to be some illness."

They finished lunch and went back across the street to work again. New action was introduced and Nita

did much running around and tripping of the police-
men. Sometimes they would halt for a little while new
ideas were evolved. She was amazed to discover that
much of the story was made up on the set as they went
along.

This marked the beginning of a long period in which
Nita worked almost constantly on the Hammons lot.
She made a dozen or more of the two-reel comedies
in which Billy starred. Soon she was accepted as a
veteran of the troupe. She quickly caught on to the
tricks of the trade how to work before the cameras.

Nita went on living at Billy Bowers' chiefly because
she didn't wish to hurt the comedian's feelings, but
she would have preferred more freedom than the mon-
astic life at his mansion offered. Murphy continued
to be polite but distant, and there were many days and
nights when Billy vanished into his own quarters on
what she now knew to be extended drinking bouts.
When he emerged he was invariably shaky and haggard.

It hurt her to see him slowly destroying himself
because she felt he had great talent. But it was precisely
his feeling that his talents were not being properly
recognized that seemed to make him drink all the more.
It angered him that Chaplin, Lloyd and Keaton were
all making successful feature films while the best he
could manage were the two-reelers.

Nita also discovered that he was a creature of
moods. At times he would be in the depths of depres-
sion and then he would swing again to an excitement
which was more than normal. It was on one of his
high days that he happily revealed to her it was his
thirty-fifth birthday.

"I'll have a party for you," she exclaimed. "Invite
everyone you'd like to have!"

The tall, shy man gazed at her fondly. "I'd like to celebrate with just one person. You!"

Surprised, she quickly recovered and said, "Very well! Just the two of us! Where will we go? Musso & Frank's? The Victor Hugo? The Biltmore? You name it."

"Why not a quiet dinner here at home?"

Again she was surprised. But she said, "If that is what you wish."

"I'd like that," he said. "And let us have it in the living room of your wing."

"At least that will be a change of scene," she said, smiling. "I'll tell Mrs. Case to have the cook fix all your favorite dishes."

That evening Nita wore a yellow dress which was one of Billy's favorites. Rather than have thirty-five candles on the cake, she had only one. She used candelabra on the table and made the setting as attractive as she could.

When Billy arrived to join her he was wearing a dressing gown. He said, "You don't mind my being comfortable?"

She kissed him lightly and said, "I approve of it. How do you like the table?"

"Lovely. As I knew it would be."

Mrs. Case served dinner and then there was a special ceremony over the cake. Nita explained she'd used only a single candle because it stood for the year she'd known him.

"Proper," he said. "I began a new life when you came here." He blew out the candle and there was a slice of cake for each of the staff including Murphy, and for herself and Billy. Then they sat together in the candlelight sipping after-dinner wine.

He told her, "This is the most perfect birthday of my life."

113

She laughed. "Does it make you want to see thirty-six?"

They were seated side by side on a chaise lounge. He put an arm around her. "If I can spend it with you, yes."

She smiled. "I'm sure that can be arranged."

He put his glass on the coffee table before them and turning to her soberly, said, "Nita I have a confession to make."

"What?"

"Something has happened which I never expected. Something which I never hoped for. I have found feeling again. I have fallen in love with you."

His impassioned words brought her fear and unhappiness rather than joy. She had come to understand and like him as a friend but he simply did not appeal to her in a romantic way. She knew she had made a mistake in remaining in his house so long. How could she correct it now without badly hurting him?

She said, "It's your birthday, and the wine. We're good friends. That's wonderful. I've never had a better friend than you!"

His eyes showed anguish. "I need more than your friendship, Nita. You can save me! I want you for my wife!"

"Billy!" she protested quietly, not knowing what to say.

"I can stop drinking if I know I have you. My career won't be that important to me," he went on. "I have come to be dependent on you. To resent the minutes and hours when I'm not with you."

"Billy, it won't work!" she protested. "You don't really know me at all."

"I do," he said, and he prevented her making any further protest by putting his arms around her and covering her lips with his.

Nita realized what was happening and that it was going to be impossible to prevent it. She hated herself for having been so stupid as to remain in his house and fervently prayed that when it was all sorted out he would not be hurt. As he lifted her in his arms and carried her into her bedroom she knew he expected her to surrender herself to him. To save him from further pain she knew that she would.

Chapter Six

When Nita awoke the next morning Billy was no longer in her bed. He had left sometime towards dawn. It was raining. There would be no work at the studio today. She lay there naked beneath a single sheet and in a sleepy reverie reviewed the events of the previous night. Billy had carried her into her bedroom and after undressing her had removed his dressing gown and got into bed with her.

Nita had not remonstrated with him since she partly blamed herself for the situation. He had been a considerate and most gentle lover, but there had been little thrill or satisfaction for her. And she had a secret suspicion that their love making had not excited him much either. It had ended soon and then he had remained next to her in the bed, stroking her hair and whispering endearments. Shortly after that he'd fallen asleep, but Nita had remained awake for a long while, worrying. Then she also slept. He had left without waking her and she tried to decide what she must do now. The main thing which came out of her thoughts was that she must no longer remain as his house guest. It was not fair to either of them, and surely no longer necessary for her.

She hoped that he would be in an amenable humor

so she could try to reason this all out with him. Nita remembered Thelma Stone's offer to help find her a cottage apartment at Gardenia Court. This appealed to her and she felt that she must discuss it with Billy and hoped he would agree. She also worried that because of the previous night and the rainy day he might decide to hide himself in his room for another extended bout of drinking.

One thing she had discovered about show business people, and especially the Hollywood stars, was their extreme vulnerability. It was not strange when one considered how exposed they were to the public. Small fears and insecurities became magnified in the spotlight of the press. The results were often temperamental and insane behavior from people of whom it would not ordinarily be expected.

Nita was sure that the comedian was right. Not all the stars were continually living on the edge of disaster, taking drugs or drinking too much. But it seemed to her the majority of them were and she did not wish to join their ranks.

There was a knock on her door and she quickly rose and put on her dressing gown. Then she went and opened the door. To her surprise it was Murphy who was outside with her breakfast tray in hand.

"Mrs. Case has a few days off," he explained with a smile on his broad, tanned face. "Her daughter is sick."

"I'm sorry," Nita said, standing aside to let him enter with the tray. "You didn't need to bring me my breakfast. I could have made it for myself."

Murphy put the tray on the usual table and then turned to her. "Begging your pardon, Mrs. Nolan. But Mr. Bowers would never approve of that."

"Well, thank you," she said. "It's raining so there'll be no studio call."

"No," the big man agreed. "Mr. Bowers is taking an easy morning. He'd like you to join him in the dining room for luncheon at twelve."

Nita sat at the table with the tray and unfolded her napkin. She smiled at Murphy and said, "You can tell him I'll be delighted to accept his invitation."

"Good!" Murphy said moving to the door to leave. "He'll be pleased."

"And what about you, Murphy?" she asked.

He looked surprised. "Me, madam?"

"Yes. I understand you are living here to keep an eye on Mr. Bowers. That you're doing this for the studio. Do you think I'm a good influence on him?"

Murphy looked startled. After a moment he said, "I think you've made this house a much more pleasant place."

"Thank you," she said.

"Why did you ask that?" Murphy wanted to know.

She raised her eyes to meet his. "Because I plan to leave soon."

"I see."

"I hope Mr. Bowers will approve."

Murphy shrugged. "It's hard to tell about him. But for the most part he's a reasonable man."

"But a sad one."

Murphy nodded. "He's that, all right."

"The trouble is, I'm not sure I can do anything about his sadness."

Murphy stared at his shoe tips. "There's not too much any of us can do," he said.

"You're really fond of him, aren't you, Murphy?" she said quietly.

"Yes, I am," the big man said. And with a final glance at her he added, "I'll tell him you'll come to the dining room at twelve."

The rain continued in a heavy downpour. Nita felt

her nervousness increase as the time drew near for her luncheon with Billy. She hoped that she could carry it off as she'd planned, but she was by no means sure. She needed to make him understand that the time had come for her to strike out on her own without hurting him. And she worried that this would not be easy.

Nita donned a simple blue dress and went to the dining room a few minutes before twelve. She found the table set and Billy waiting for her. He was staring out the french windows at the rain, a half-emptied martini glass in his hand. He turned as she came in and greeted her with a smile on his shy, boyish face.

"I had Murphy make up a pitcher of martinis," he said. "I know you like his mix."

Nita smiled. "I'll have one."

He came and poured her out one from the pitcher on the table. "Just one?"

"You know I hardly ever drink during the day."

"This is special, it's a rainy day," he said.

"I know," she smiled, taking the drink from him. "What a grand excuse for not having to work!"

"I couldn't have arranged it better," he agreed.

She stood beside him, watching the garden being drenched with heavy rain. "Is it supposed to last long?"

"Clearing tonight," he said. "So we'll be working tomorrow morning now matter how many puddles on the set or how deep they may be."

"Johnny Dale will likely find a way to include the puddles in the story line," she laughed and sipped her drink.

It was apparent that Billy had been drinking for some time, yet he was by no means drunk. His mood was subdued as it often was when he was drinking.

Without looking at her directly, he said, "I'm sorry about last night."

119

"Nothing to worry about," she said.

"It was a mistake, I know that now," he said. "It wasn't good for either of us."

"We all make mistakes."

He glanced at her anxiously. "We've had a good friendship. And I need friends. I was a fool to risk destroying it by adding sex to our relationship."

She grimaced. "Most men would do the same thing."

"I don't want to imitate most men," he objected. "I want to act according to my own lights. And I know last night was a disaster for us both."

"Even so," she said, "we can forget it and begin over. Our friendship need not suffer."

He gave her a hopeful look. "You mean that?"

"I do," she said.

"Thank you," he said with great warmth. He kissed her gently on the forehead.

"There's just one other thing," Nita went on, aware that this was the moment when she must try to reason with him.

He frowned at his empty martini glass, then went to the bar and refilled it. He took a sip of the crystal clear liquid and asked, "What is it?"

"My living here is no longer practical."

"Why not?"

"It was all right at the start," she said. "But now that I've been here a long time I'm sure it must be a strain on you. And I could frankly do with more freedom."

The comedian looked surprised. "I have never tried to interfere with what you do!"

"I know that," Nita said. "But merely living in someone else's house imposes certain restraints, and creates certain tensions!"

"You're talking about last night," he said. "I promise it will never happen again."

"I'm not thinking only of last night," she protested. "I'm thinking of things generally. But you are right in one sense, the only way I could remain here would be if we became lovers."

"And you don't want that?"

She shook her head. "No. And if you'll be strictly truthful about it, you'll admit that neiher do you."

He sipped his drink again and stared down at it. "Lately, I'm not sure what I want."

"You need a placid existence," she said. "I can't give you that as a mistress. But I can offer something as your freind."

He eyed her unhappily. "So you propose to leave here?"

"Yes."

"Where do you want to go?"

"I haven't decided," she said. "Thelma Stone suggested I take a cottage where she lives. It's called Gardenia Court."

"I warned you she's working with Wallace Reid and that several of the company are taking drugs," Billy said.

"I know that," she said. "But I doubt that Thelma is taking anything. She's too level-headed and ambitious. And I certainly have no intentions of taking drugs."

The comedian sighed. "I hope you are right in all you've said. If you leave the house that doesn't mean you intend to stop working with me?"

"Of course not! I want to go on with you and Hammons."

"You're not ambitious to escape two-reelers like Thelma?"

"That's another place where Thelma and I differ.

I'm happy to continue as an actress in short comedies.''

"Good!'' Billy Bowers said. "The first films in which you worked are in release now. The word on you is good.''

She brightened. "I'm glad! I'd like to see one of them,'' she said, excited.

"We'll do it just as soon as one of them comes to play in a Los Angeles movie theatre.''

Nita's eyes were wide with excitement at the prospect. "I've seen the day's rushes, of course. And some of the complete films before they were properly cut. Seeing the finished product in a theatre with other people around is something else.''

Billy's smile was wistful. "I remember I felt exactly like that once, long ago.''

"You make it seem ages ago. You're not that old!''

"Old enough,'' he said. He put down his glass. "Murphy has promised us a wonderful lunch. Let's see if he lives up to it, and while we eat we can discuss when you're to move.''

So it was settled as easily as that. Nita had expected Billy to offer other objections. But aside from warning her not to count too much on Thelma, he said nothing. They returned to work on the latest two-reeler the next morning as if nothing had happened. But she quietly started to make preparations for establishing her own place.

It began with a phone call to Thelma and an appointment to visit the blonde girl at her cottage and be shown one of the cottages which were vacant. It was a pleasant evening as Nita drove to the plain but well kept cottage court. Thelma's cottage was in the rear, some distance from the street. She parked her small Chevrolet roadster outside the cottage, went to its front door and rang the bell.

122

Thelma answered and at once threw her arms around Nita as she welcomed her. "Do come in," she said, ushering her into the plainly furnished living room distinguished only by some posters of Billy Bowers comedies with the star's face featured large and a similar one of Wallace Reid in "Across The Continent." Wally as a racing driver looked healthy and handsome.

Nita thought that Thelma had accquired a new kind of beauty. She was thinner and her radiance had a kind of sparkle. She glowed with loveliness. Nita told her, "I think you're looking marvelous!"

Thelma laughed. "I'm out of Billy's two-reelers and doing different kinds of parts now. It's hard for a girl to grow in grace in those crazy comedies!"

"Surely it's a good place to begin," Nita said.

"To *begin*," Thelma repeated. "But if you remain in two-reelers too long you're typed. It's even happened to Billy himself, and he could have been a great star."

"I'm only leaving his house," Nita said. "I mean to go on working with him."

"Until you get a better chance," Thelma said. "You must look out for yourself in this business."

"I'm not sure Hollywood is right for me," Nita said. "It was Marty who wanted to come here. He was more dedicated to show business than I've ever been."

"You're in it now," the blonde told her. "You'll stay on. Why did you decide to move out on Billy?"

Nita blushed. "It was getting awkward. I felt I should be on my own."

"You were right. But something must have decided you. Did he make love to you?"

Her cheeks burning, Nita glanced down at her folded hands. "Yes. But that was only part of it."

"I know the scenario, kid," Thelma said with sympathy. "I played it myself. I lived with him for a while and we were lovers but it didn't work."

"And you left?"

"Just about like you," Thelma said. "I knew he wasn't in love with me and so did he. He's in love with his dead wife who killed herself for another man. He's hopeless."

"I'm terribly sorry for him," Nita said.

"He has his booze," Thelma said. "That's the big thing in his life now."

"But he's slowly drinking himself to death. He says the doctors have warned him."

"Murphy tries to keep him from doing that," Thelma said. "As long as he has Murphy he should be all right. Murphy sees he's sober enough to work and keeps the booze away from him whenever he can."

"I know," Nita agreed. "I like Murphy. Now what about yourself?"

Thelma smiled happily and pointed to the Wallace Reid poster. "I just finished that feature with Wally," she said. "And he wants me in his next one."

Remembering, Nita said, "There are some strange stories going around about him."

Thelma's lovely face shadowed. "I know. I've heard them. Don't believe any of it."

"How did they get started?" she asked. "The drug rumors?"

"Wally hurt his back finishing one of the stunts in a picture," she said. "Since then, whenever it bothers him while he's working they give him morphine. It's purely medicinal and prescribed by the studio doctor."

Nita was relieved to hear the innocent explanation of the gossip. "So that's what started it all!"

"You know how vicious they are here!" Thelma

124

said. "I'm going to work in an Alma Rubens picture next. She's wonderful and a friend of mine also."

"What about romance?" Nita asked.

"I'm seeing Monte Blue," Thelma said. "But it's nothing serious. He's handsome and talented—and part Indian. Did you know that?"

"No," Nita admitted. "I've always liked him on the screen."

"I must get Mrs. Denny to show you the cottage. I'm sure you'll like it," Thelma said. "Then I have to run. I'm meeting Monte at the Biltmore."

Nita was delighted with the cottage. They were all much alike except that hers was closer to the street than Thelma's and a few of the others in the rear of the courtyard. Mrs. Denny was a mannish lady with a handyman husband who attended to repairs. She demanded a month's rent in advance.

"You're a movie person," the big woman said firmly. "I have to get my rent in advance from all my movie tenants."

Nita gave no argument. She could hardly blame the woman, knowing what a frantic place Hollywood was. Within a week she moved in but she saw little of Thelma in spite of their friendship. The blonde girl had her own circle of friends and her hours were different from Nita's.

One day on the movie set of a cowboy and Indian satire with Billy starring as a pioneer, the comedian told her, "Reserve tonight. I have something planned."

She and Billy had continued to be friends and to go out together. They mostly went to modest restaurants away from the main strip and not the popular places where the stars congregated. One day he took her to the cemetery where Marty was buried and she saw the handsome memorial stone Billy had had erected over his grave. She would never doubt that Billy had been sincere in his friendship with Marty and now was perhaps her best friend.

That night he picked her up in his new Packard and took her to Musso-Frank's for dinner. On the way to their table they passed a table where Douglas Fairbanks was chatting with his wife Mary Pickford, and with them were Gloria Swanson and the dapper Charles Chaplin. As she hurried by Nita was glad that none of the quartet had noticed her entrance. She would have been embarrassed to have faced Chaplin after their last meeting.

At the table Billy ordered lavishly and told her, "This is a special evening for two reasons."

"What are they?"

"One, I'm taking you to see a comedy in which you have the co-starring role with me. Remember 'The Baker's Daughter'?"

"I'm not liable to forget it," she laughed.

"You'll see it in a theatre tonight and tomorrow night I'm taking you to a party at Pickfair."

"At *Pickfair*?" she echoed. "I saw Douglas Fairbanks and Mary Pickford just as we came in!"

"I saw them too," he said. "They'll be on hand to greet everyone tomorrow night. The place is large. Too large, I think. But it's Hollywood magnificence and you'll have a chance to meet the right people there. People who can help you get ahead in this town."

She smiled at him. "Are you trying to be rid of me altogether?"

"You have talent," he said seriously. "You deserve something better than my two-reelers."

When they left the restaurant they drove to the neighborhood theatre where the comedy was showing, and for the first time she was able to sit in a theatre and hear the audience around her enjoy her efforts. They laughed at her funny antics and she heard one

126

say aloud to a friend, "I think that new girl is adorable!" It was a heady experience.

But it was nothing compared to attending the party at Pickfair. Marty wore a tuxedo and Nita donned an evening gown. The stars' famous house was reached by a winding roadway which led high up in the hills. The stucco house was in a setting which included magnificent grounds, and at the rear of the rambling mansion there was a vast swimming pool.

On this pleasant evening the roadway was lined with parked cars. At the door Billy turned his Packard over to a servant who drove it away. Music emanated from the house and they went inside to the reception hall to be greeted by a smiling, sun-tanned Doug and sweet-faced Mary in a ruffled pink gown.

"We don't see you often enough, Billy," Doug said shaking the comedian's hand. "What's the news on Arbuckle?"

"Just the same," Billy said. "I wish he'd leave Hollywood altogether."

"I heard he was writing some scripts," Fairbanks said.

"Yes. But that doesn't pay much," Billy told him. He introduced Nita to both Doug and Mary.

Doug was clearly more interested in having a few words more with Billy before other guests arrived, but Mary took a special interest in her.

"You have good bone structure," Mary told her. "That's important for the camera."

"I've been told that," Nita said with a smile.

"I want you to meet Lew Meyers," Mary said, "Don't be misled by his size. He's a big man when it comes to Hollywood, even though he is only five feet tall."

"He owns Master Films, doesn't he?"

"Yes," Mary said. "And he hires far too many of

his relatives for the studio's sake. But in spite of them all, he's so smart he is making money and moving up in the film world every day."

Mary led her to a group of three people talking together away from the main room where the dancing was going on. She recognized one of them at once, the dark, sultry Barbara Lamont. With her was her husband, suave Eric Gray. He had starred in his own films as well as appearing with his wife. The third member of the trio she did not recognize but knew it had to be Lew Meyers, the studio head of Master. He was, as Mary had told her, short and bald, with a fringe of gray hair around his bald pate, and sharp eyes peered nervously from his wrinkled, sour face through thick horn-rimmed glasses.

Mary offered one of her famous smiles and introduced Nita to the trio. Then she said, "I must desert you. I can't leave Doug alone to receive." And she hurried off.

Barbara Lamont, pale skinned, her black hair drawn back tightly and wearing a black evening gown with a double strand of pearls at her swan-like neck was regarding Nita with such warm interest that she felt embarrassed.

She said, "What a lovely face you have! And this in a town of lovely faces. Don't you agree, Lew?"

The elderly Lew Meyer shrugged. "I don't go by faces, but by what's behind them. I like actors with brains!"

Barbara Lamont raised her chin loftily. "This girl has brains as well. You can see that!"

Elegant and poised, Eric Gray beamed at Nita and said, "My opinion was not asked but I'll offer it in any case. I think you are quite lovely but that you shouldn't be subjected to this kind of comment! Let us have praise with subtlety!"

128

Barbara drew on her cigarette in its long holder and said wearily, "My husband pretends to be a gentleman. I assure you he's no more genteel than the rest of us."

Little Lew Meyers had been staring at Nita in a hard, interested fashion for several minutes. Now he turned to his two stars and barked a command. "Why don't you two go and dance? Mix around with people! They like to see you!"

"Lew wants to be rid of us," Barnara Lamont said. "And I'd hardly call him subtle, either."

"When the master commands," Eric Gray said, offering his arm to his wife. And to Nita, he smiled and said, "I shall expect a dance when you've finished with Lew."

As the two went off to join the others, Lew Meyers glared at her and said, "I can't ask you to dance. I don't dance!"

"That's all right," she said.

"A few years ago I was running a string of nickleodeons in New Jersey," the small man went on. "I decided I'd never make any money unless I made my own films. So I came out here and started a new career."

Nita said, "There's a lot more to your story than that, I know. I read about you in *Photoplay*. You gambled all your life's savings and you worked hard. You still do!"

The bald man eyed her sourly. "You know all about me."

"At least what I've read in newspapers and magazines."

"I don't know anything about you," he said. "Do you want a drink?"

"Not just now. I don't drink much."

"I don't drink at all," Lew Meyer snapped. "Boot

leg booze rots your stomach and ruins your brain. I smoke Havana cigars.''

"I've never tried them," she confessed.

"Sarah Bernhardt smokes cigars," the little man said. "You know who she is?"

"A famous French actress."

"What have *you* done?"

"I've only been in Hollwood some months. Before that I did an act in vaudeville, singing and dancing."

"Your voice doesn't matter here. It's what you can do with pantomime and how you project."

"I've been playing in the new Billy Bowers comedies."

The little man showed new interest. "Are you the one who played in something about a baker's daughter?"

"Yes," she said.

"Ha!" Lew Meyers glared at her. "One of my scouts mentioned you to me."

"Did he, really?"

"He said you were pretty and had talent but you made too many faces. You can't make faces at the camera. You have to play into it."

She said, "In the comedies, everything is overdone."

"I know," the little man snapped. "Slapstick! All right in its place! I want no part of it!"

And no part of me, Nita decided. But she said aloud, "I think I can do other things."

The shrewd eyes fixed on her again. "You do?"

"Yes."

"Barbara seems to like you. She has pretty good taste in girls," Lew Meyers said. "I'll tell you what I'll do. If you can begin work the first of the week I'll give you a supporting part in her next picture. And we'll talk about a contract with options."

She was surprised and ecstatic. "Mr. Meyer! You can't mean it!"

"What can't he mean?" Billy Bowers, who had joined them, asked the question.

The little man gave the comedian a sour look. "I'm trying to steal your girl from you."

Billy laughed. "That's the reason I brought her here!"

For the first time Meyers chuckled and said, "Honest sonofabitch!"

Billy looked at Nita fondly, "I don't want her playing in two-reelers for the rest of her life, like me," he said.

Nita reproached him, "You know I'm satisfied."

"That's not enough," the comedian replied. "When do you want to see her, Lew?"

The little man shrugged. "Tomorrow morning. Around eleven."

"I can't be there," she protested. "I'll be working on the lot in the new comedy."

"I fire you as of now," Billy told her. "She'll be there, Lew!"

The next morning Nita presented herself at Lew Meyers' office and was introduced to his Austrian director, Conrad Mirnoff.

Mirnoff studied her from several angles and then told the studio head, "She vill do!" then walked out of the room disdainfully tapping his puttees with his riding crop.

Lew Meyers gave her a sour look across the desk. "He must like you," he said. "He usually complains."

"He's very awesome," she said.

"He knows camera angles and not much else," Meyers said grimly. "I've had to keep a producer on his back all the time or the costs would go sky high. He wants real Persian carpets on the floor, knowing they're going to be stained with fake blood."

She said, "Then I will be in Miss Lamont's film?"

"She wants you," Lew Meyers said irritably. "Mirnoff accepts you. I think you're a good risk. I'll give you a six month contract at hundred a week with options and raises to seven years."

Nita had dinner with Billy that night and told him all that had gone on. She said, "I hope if it doesn't work out I can come back to Hammons."

"Any time," he assured her. "But you won't be back. You'll never make another two-reeler. I've lost you."

She pretended it wasn't so but secretly she hoped it would turn out that way. The following week saw her in costume and make-up on the set of Barbara Lamont's latest torrid romance called simply "Desire." Nita played a cousin of the star, a minor role. The story told of the numerous love affairs of an actress, who broke many hearts until her own was broken.

Barbara's handsome husband Eric Gray played the man who finally broke the heart of the cruel beauty. Both stars seemed to enjoy their roles. Conrad Mirnoff did countless retakes while a string orchestra in the corner played romantic waltzes and such tunes as "Lonesome and Sorry" and "Wonderful One" to keep the actors in the right mood.

The two stars were experts in this type of film and they were also kind to Nita. She could hardly credit the interest which the exotic Barbara showed in her. The star halted everything one morning because she felt that Nita's make-up was faulty.

"The girl is beautiful," Barbara ranted. "What two-bit make-up man smudged her eyes like this?"

The errant make-up man was found and the damage repaired. Nita enjoyed her scenes in the movie and found the pace of work much slower and more pleasant than on the two-reel lot.

Eric Gray told her, "Hammons Pictures is a poverty row outfit, my dear. You must *never* think of returning there!"

They were standing on the sidelines as Mirnoff was slaving over some important close-ups of Barbara Lamont. Nita felt that Eric Gray worked almost as hard as his wife to make her feel wanted on the set.

She said, "You really think so? Billy Bowers is a star and he works only for Hammons."

"He's part owner," Eric said with a weary gesture of his slim hand. "We all know it's his drinking problem that keeps him out of features. You must be aware of that. I understand you lived with him."

She blushed fiercely. "I stayed in his house. I saw little of his drinking. When he goes on those bouts he locks himself in his room."

"Sorry," the leading man said contritely. "I didn't mean to upset you. So much of this sort of thing goes on in Hollywood. I really didn't consider what I was saying."

"It's all right," she said.

"Barbara and I are interested in you, my dear," the elegant man went on. "And I think she's going to invite you to spend a few days with us in our beach home when we finish this dreadful film."

She was surprised, "Don't you like it?"

"Utter trash," he said. "But it's what Barbara's fans want."

Nita was shocked by his attitude. "Doesn't your wife have the privilege of choosing her own starring vehicles?"

He shook his head. "Lew Meyers makes all the

decisions here. He's a business wizard but he has no taste at all!''

Nita was to hear this over and over again at the studio. Yet everyone gave in to Meyers because he had the touch of gold and none of them wanted to risk offending him. Occasionally he came onto the set and sourly watched the shooting. He generally left after a short stay, having given Mirnoff some suggestions.

Once again Nita met Dr. Phillip Watters, this time in the café reserved for stars and executives at Master Films. He sat with her and congratulated her on her move up in the world.

She asked, ''What about you?''

''It's an interesting experience,'' he said. ''But I wouldn't want to spend the rest of my life on the lot.''

''What would you like to do?''

''Specialize.''

''In what?''

''Treatment of diabetics,'' he said. ''If I can manage it I'm going to New York City and open my own clinic there. I have a number of theories about the disease. My mother had a bad case.''

''It sounds worthwhile,'' she agreed. ''Quite a change from playing nursemaid to movie stars.''

He grimaced. ''Too many of them are only interested in prescriptions for drugs.''

Nita thought it was a good time to ask, ''Is there as much drug abuse in Hollywood as gossip has it?''

''It could be even worse,'' he frowned. ''Wallace Reid collapsed midway through the production of 'Mr. Nillings Spends His Dime' and had to be replaced by Walter Hiers. He's in a sanitarium right now being treated for drug addiction.''

''I was told there was nothing to the story of his being addicted,'' she said, remembering Thelma's indignation.

"I'll stake my medical reputation, such as it is, on the truth of it," Phillip said. "And he's not the only one. There'll be more casualties before long."

Nita and Phillip saw each other nearly every lunch time after this, which led to evening engagements. Phillip had become popular in the community and was invited to many private parties. On one particular night they had drinks with Richard Dix and his wife, went on to dinner with Lew Meyers and some of the great man's relatives, and ended the eveing at a dancing party at the Trocadero with Richard Barthelmess and a host of his friends.

Nita rarely saw Thelma. But one afternoon as she drove up from work she saw the blonde girl enter her bungalow. She went over and pressed the bell and Thelma answered. Nita was at once surprised to see that she had been crying and that she looked thinner and more fragile than when they'd met last time.

"I haven't seen you in so long," Nita said.

Thelma dabbed a hanky to her eyes. "Sorry. You caught me at a bad moment. Do come in." She was wearing a blue cloche hat and matching suit.

"I've been busy," Nita told Thelma as she seated herself in an easy chair. "We're just finishing the new Barbara Lamont film."

"I heard you were over at Master," Thelma said, standing and staring at her. "You look well. How do you like it?"

"I feel I'm getting somewhere at last."

"Master Films is a fairly good outfit," Thelma said rather grudgingly.

"What are you doing?" Nita asked.

Thelma sighed and sat down. "I'm going to New York. I've an offer to do a part in a new play there. I've had enough of Hollywood for awhile."

"When are you going?" Nita asked in surprise.

"Tomorrow," the blonde said. "I'm settling with Mrs. Denny and taking the train in the morning."

"But why?"

"I'm tired of this town," Thelma said and took out a pack of cigarettes and lit one.

"You look weary," Nita said, alarmed by her loss of weight. "Have you had problems?"

"I've had plenty," the other girl said, puffing on the cigarette.

Nita ventured, "I've heard that Wallace Reid had to give up his latest film and he's in hospital."

Thelma froze. "They're saying that now, are they?"

"Isn't it true? They say he's badly addicted to drugs."

"Wally's ill," Thelma said. "Very ill. He many not live."

"Have you seen him?"

The girl shook her head grimly. "They won't let me near him. None of his old friends can see him."

"That's too bad," Nita said.

"What about you?" Thelma asked. "How's your love life?"

She smiled. "I have none. I go out with Dr. Watters occasionally. He's the studio doctor at Master."

"I know him," Thelma said. "My friends don't like him. He's very bigoted and arrogant. Thinks a lot of himself."

"I've never noticed that in him," said Nita.

Thelma smiled wryly. "You're fond of him. Makes a difference how you see him. What about Billy Bowers?"

"I see him now and then."

"Not too often?"

"No. Not all that often."

"He'll be the next one in hospital," was Thelma's warning. "They say his drinking is worse than ever."

"He seems to want to destroy himself," Nita said sadly.

"Don't we all?" was Thelma's enigmatic reply.

That was the last Nita saw of the blonde girl. The cottage was rented to a middle-aged couple who'd deserted a tend show in the Middle West to try and find a niche in Hollywood. They were both older than Nita and so she did not make friends with them. She was too busy preparing for a new film at Master and having an exciting social life.

At a party given by the Francis X. Bushmans she told Phillip she was going to spend the weekend with Barbara and her husband.

Phillip and she were standing alone on the patio. The young doctor said, "You're going to spend the weekend with Barbara and Eric? How did you get to be so friendly with those two?"

"I worked with them in 'Desire'," she said. "And they were both very kind to me."

"I'll bet," he said quietly.

She stared at him. "Why do you say that?"

"Nothing," he said. Then hesitating a moment, he went on, "I think you should know that he and Barbara are not the ideal happily married couple they seem."

Puzzled, Nita said, "They seem happy enough."

"They may be genuine in their liking for you," he said. "But be on your guard. Don't be surprised at anything."

She said, "Are you suggesting that her husband might make a play for me?"

"That would be surprising, indeed," Phillip told her dryly. "Let us see what happens."

"I've been looking forward to it," she said. "I'm told their beach home is lovely. You can walk from the bedrooms out onto the sand, and into the ocean if you like. In addition there's a huge pool.''

"It has also been the scene of some wild parties,'' he warned her. "Did anyone tell you that before?''

"No.''

"Well, it's true.''

"I don't think they expect any company this weekend,'' she said. "Just me.''

"Perhaps I'm doing them an injustice,'' Phillip said. "This might be a pleasant experience.''

"I certainly hope so,'' she said. "Though you haven't helped any.''

He laughed and said, "Maybe it's because I'd rather you spent the weekend with me. I'm becoming terribly possessive of you.''

"Phillip!''

"I mean it,'' he said, taking her in his arms. "I don't like seeing an innocent like you running about loose in this jungle.''

She smiled up at him. "You can't be serious!''

"When it comes to you, I'm most serious,'' he said. "The trouble is, you have your eyes fixed on stardom.''

"And you want your diabetic clinic in the East.''

"Guilty,'' he agreed. "But what would you say if I asked you to marry me?''

"Would that change anything?''

"I'd leave Hollywood tomorrow and take you with me. Far away from this crazy place!''

She laughed. "That's why I won't marry you. In spite of everything, I intend to make it here. I've gone through too much to give up now.''

His arms still around her, he said, "May I warn you that you might have to go through much more before you get what you want?''

"Then I will,'' she said.

"Why have I let myself fall in love with you?" he wanted to know.

"I'm just a stand-in until the right girl comes along," she teased.

His answer was to silence her with kisses. She was still in his arms when someone came out onto the patio to join them. The young doctor released her and they both turned to see their smiling host, the romantic leading man, Francis X. Bushman.

The big, blond man's eyes held a twinkle as he said, "I never indulge in moments like that unless it's before a camera and I'm being paid!"

Chapter Seven

Barbara and Eric's beach house of exceeded Nita's expectations. Its ideal location on white sands with the ocean only steps away was awe-inspiring. The various bedrooms including Nita's were located on the side of the house facing the beach. Each bedroom had its own bath and balcony. Steps led from the balconies to the perfect beach. All that was required for an ideal weekend was good weather and it also was just right. Warm air and azure blue skies with plenty of sunshine blessed this special holiday excursion.

When Nita arrived on Friday evening Barbara and Eric hosted her to a candlelit dinner. She was amazed at their interest in her and decided they were two of Hollywood's nicest people.

At the talble, she said, "How can I thank you for being so kind to me?"

The exotic Barbara, at her best in a low-cut yellow gown, reached over and patter her hand. "By merely being your sweet self," she said.

Eric Gray, handsome in white dinner jacket and black tie, smiled at her and said, "It's not easy for people like us to make new friends. We have to be wary of being wooed for our position. And too often people try to use us in one way or another."

Barbara daintily touched her napkin to her full lips and agreed, "Eric is so right. We must be extremely discreet."

After dinner they sat in the living room with its fine view of the ocean and its array of fine paintings on beige walls. Only after an hour or so did Nita notice that the elegant Eric was drinking a good deal. Occasionally his voice would slur and he would sit for long periods saying nothing and smiling vacantly.

Around nine o'clock a visitor arrived, a young leading man who Nita had seen in several Eric Gray pictures. He was English, and had a rather feminine manner and a girlish style of good looks. The most masculine thing about him was his small moustache, which Nita felt had been grown in an attempt to minimize his female qualities.

Eric Gray seemed delighted to see the young man and greeted him warmly. With an arm around his shoulder, he brought him over to her and said, "Nita Nolan, I want you to meet Richard Wright, my closest friend!"

Wright smiled at her and said, "Delighted to meet you, Nita. Eric has spoken to me about you."

Barbara Lamont did not seem to be particularly pleased with the arrival of her husband's friend. She puffed on her cigarette in its long holder and asked him, "Aren't you supposed to be working on location in Mexico?"

Richard Wright smirked over his martini. "Murnau gave us the weekend off. He's having a big party at his place."

Eric explained, "F.W.Murnau is the director of Richard's film."

Barbara gave her husband a cold look and said, "Everyone in Hollywood knows about Murnau."

141

Eric took it in good nature. "I'm sure Nita doesn't. Do you Nita?"

She smiled. "I'm fresh from the two-reel lot. I know little about the big names."

"You see!" Eric declared triumphantly. And to her he explained, "Murnau is a very talented foreign director."

Richard Wright waved a slim hand gracefully declaring, "He's a complete and utter genius."

Barbara showed increasing annoyance. "I do not intend to spend the evening listening to the virtues of Murnau."

"Sorry," Eric apologized. He turned to his friend and said, "It's a lovely night. What do you say we take a walk on the beach, Richard?"

"Fascinating idea," his friend said to Nita and Barbara, he added, "Do excuse us. We'll join you later."

When the two men left the room Barbara made herself another drink and told Nita, "I'm sorry, but I can't bear Richard or any of his crowd."

"Oh?"

Barbara frowned. "He's a bad influence on my husband."

"They seem so friendly. And he's in all Eric's films," Nita said.

"Eric sees to that," the exotic black-haired beauty said with disgust. "I'm certain he does it to annoy me!"

"But you have such a happy marriage!"

Barbara lifted her eyebrows. "You think so?"

"The fan magazines are always extolling you as the ideal married couple."

"You surely don't read that rot!"

Nita blushed. "I used to when I was younger. I think most young girls read some of that sort of thing."

Barbara sipped her drink. "There are some truths

142

you must soon learn about Hollywood, my dear. You must be friendly with the people who can help you. I plan to have you in every film I make from now on. The rushes show you are excellent in 'Desire'."

"I'm so glad to hear you say so," Nita said. "I've been really worried."

"Don't worry any more. As long as I have any say you'll have work at Master Films."

"You're too kind."

"If Eric can have his favorites in his films so can I," Barbara said.

"I must find out more about the director they were discussing, F.W.Murnau," said Nita.

Barbara grimaced. "I wouldn't give him a second thought. I consider him an undesirable person."

"Why?" Nita asked innocently.

Barbara turned away from her. "I'd rather not discuss it."

They talked for a little longer. Then Barbara went over to the big windows overlooking the beach and pulled back one of the drapes which had been drawn closed when darkness came. The beach was floodlit to keep burlars from approaching the house by that way.

Staring out the window into the darkness broken only by the beams of the floodlights, Barbara said, "Jesse Lasky has the place next door."

"He's the producer, isn't he?" Nita said.

"The best of the group here in Hollywood," Barbara answered. Then all at once she froze and gasped as she went on staring outside.

Nita saw her stunned reaction to whatever was happening and went to her. "What is it?"

"Look!" Barbara said in a taut voice.

It took Nita a moment to see what had so disturbed her hostess. Just to one side of the floodlight's glow two figures stood in the bushes. Two male figures, embracing and kissing.

"Why, it's—" she turned to Barbara in dismay and didn't finish.

"It's my husband and Richard making love," Barbara said bitterly. "We won't see them again tonight!"

Nita stared at her incredulously "What . . . ?"

"They'll go off to one of their private places. Perhaps to Richard's apartment. He has one near here. Or maybe to the orgy at Murnau's. He's having another one of them tonight, so Richard said."

The shocking truth was now dawning on Nita. She said, "Richard Wright is a homosexual—and your husband?"

"Is 'double-gaited,' if you want to be especially kind to him. The truth is, his homosexual nature takes over every time he has an opportunity."

"How awful for you!" Nita gasped.

Barbara put out her cigarette in a nearby tray. "I've grown used to it. I go my way and he goes his."

"He'll spend the night with that man?"

"Yes."

"And when he returns?"

"He'll tell some preposterous story for your benefit, make it seem an innocent case of drinking too much and falling asleep on a friend's couch. Eric is an old hand at explaining his pecadillos."

"I'm so sorry," Nita said.

Barbara smiled at her sadly and took Nita's hands in hers. Her soulful eyes studied her closely and she said, "Now you know why I sought you out. I'm desperately lonely and in need of companionship."

"It's a hateful position for you," Nita said. "Why don't you divorce him?"

"It would ruin both our careers," the lovely, pale woman said. "Neither of us can afford that just now.

144

Later, when it is more convenient, we'll surely separate."

"In the meantime you're living a sham existence! How unhappy you must be!"

Barbara bent close to her so that her perfume filled Nita's nostrils and kissed her gently on the cheek. "It helps me having you here, dear Nita. I need feminine friendship."

Nita said, "There are many fine men. You should pay Eric back by seeking out some good man to keep you company!"

Barbara sighed and moved away. She said, "I have suffered too much at the hands of men. Eric is only the latest sad example of the misery I've known."

"Really?" Nita said. "I was married, you know."

"And?" her hostess said.

Nita sighed. "He was killed in an accident. I was deeply in love with him at first. But he drank a lot. I almost left him but towards the end he seemed to be straightening out. I think he did truly love me."

"There's always some flaw," Barbara said despondently. "Men are invariably inconsiderate of women in one way or another."

"I think it's just that they don't understand," Nita suggested.

Barbara touched a hand to her temple. "I think I'll go to bed if you don't mind. And you should also. You're here for a rest. The camera seeks out every wrinkle. Rest is all important."

Nita nodded. "I'll be glad to get to bed early, unless you'd like me to remain up to talk with you."

The dark beauty smiled languidly. "Not tonight. I'll come by and say goodnight before I go to bed. Just to be sure you are comfortable."

"I'm sure I will be," Nita said.

Nita went to her room, still stunned. She now had

145

evidence that there were other things beside drink which could destroy a marriage. Here in Hollywood there were drugs, the race for power, and homosexuality. As she recalled Eric Gray's performances in his films she realized that he had a carefully masked feminine side to him. In Richard Wright this peculiarity was more noticeable. But according to Barbara they were two of a kind. Nita knew little about homosexuals and was not anxious to know more. The incident had sickened her and even though she had much sympathy for Barbara she made up her mind not to accept any invitations to their beach house in future. This must have been what Phillip Watters was alluding to but had not wanted to say straight out.

Nita undressed and filled the tub with perfumed bath salts. She lingered in it for a good half-hour. Then she rose and dried herself before the mirror in the large bathroom. She could not help being grateful for her youth and the shapely, long legs, and firm, not-too-large breasts with which she had been kindly endowed.

Still nude, she was crossing into the bedroom to get some body lotion when the door to her room suddenly opened and her hostess, wearing a long golden dressing robe, came in. Nita felt herself blushing at being caught naked in this manner and stood awkwardly for a moment between the bathroom door and her bed.

"Don't be embarrassed!" Barbara said with a smile. "You have a beautiful body. You should be proud of it."

Nita managed a small smile. "New England Puritanism, the Irish variety." she said. "One is only nude in the bathtub on Saturday nights!"

Barbara's laugh was a musical tinkle. She said, "How dear you are! You should have been with me in the South of France. I spent some time with a group of women who walked about naked most of the day and night! Such wonderful freedom!''

Nita moved towards her bed where her nightgown was lying. She said, ''I doubt if I would make a good nudist.''

''Nonsense! You have the body for it!'' Barbara said. And she came close and with an outstretched hand restrained Nita from slipping on the nightgown.

''Thank you,'' Nita said, a tremor in her voice, aware that there was something disturbing in the manner of her hostess. ''I'll put on my nightgown now.''

''Wait!'' Barbara said, and with a quick gesture she opened her golden robe and let it drop to the floor. The lovely body of the exotic star was perfectly revealed—the curve of her luscious breasts, the firm stomach, the perfectly proportioned limbs.

''Please!'' Nita's cheeks continued to burn and she tried to move away.

''You mustn't be so shy,'' the other woman said, keeping that steel grip on her arm. ''Sit down beside me,'' she said softly and Nita found herself doing as she was bid, hoping that at any moment she might escape.

''We must get to know each other better,'' Barbara said softly, and horrified Nita by leaning forward and greedily kissing her breasts. Then the lovely woman's hand began to carress Nita's most intimate parts.

Nita was frozen with horror for a moment. Then she lifted her free hand and slapped Barbara across her beautiful face so hard that it left a patch of red. Barbara released her grip and fell back a little. Nita jumped to her feet and held her nightgown in front of her.

''Leave my room!'' she demanded.

Barbara's hand covered the spot whcih Nita had slapped. She stood before her, cringing and pleading. ''Please!''

"I only want you to leave!" Nita cried.

Barbara's manner changed abruptly and the cringing look became one of hatred. She nonchalantly reached down and picked up her golden robe and put it on.

As she tied the cord, she sneered. "You little fool!"

"Go!"

The lovely star's face was distorted with anger. She moved to the door and turned to tell her, "I'll see you finished at the studio! Remember that!" She slammed the door behind her as she stalked out.

Nita hurried across the room and turned the key in the lock. Then she leaned weakly against it. Her experiences since coming to the beach house had been as shattering as anything she had ever known. She was sick and frightened. Most of all she wanted to get back to her own place in Gardenia Court, back to her little cottage and away from these depraved people!

She hastily dressed, then packed her bag and quietly made her way out to her roadster in the parking area. She got into it and was backing it up when she saw Barbara come to the window. Nita paid no attention as she wheeled the car around and started out to the road. All she wanted was to get away from the horrible house and its occupants.

As she drove towards Hollywood she began to feel desolate and alone. It was natural that she should think of Billy Bowers. She momentarily considered trying to reach Phillip Watters but remembered he'd spoken of going to San Francisco for the weekend. With Thelma gone to New York she had no one to turn to but Billy.

Nita changed the direction of the car and drove to Billy's house. She was glad to see some lights in the windows indicating someone might be home. Murphy opened the front door to her.

He looked surprised. "Mrs. Nolan! What are you doing here?"

"I want to speak with Billy," she said urgently.

The big man gave her a knowing glance. "He's in his room. He's been there most of the evening."

Desperately, she forced herself to ask, "Is he—very drunk?"

"He's been drinking."

"Can I just see him for a few minutes? I need to talk to him," she begged.

Murphy gave a sigh. "I'll see how he is and try and arrange it. Come inside."

Nita waited in the shadowed reception hall while Murphy went to the rear of the house to check on Billy. She realized with dismay that she was trembling violently. After a brief time Murphy returned.

He said, "He'll see you but you'll have to go to him in his room."

"All right," she said.

"I'll show you the way," Murphy told her.

"Thank you," Nita said, following him. Along the way, he asked her, "How's the career shaping up?"

"I've been working hard. I'm not sure," she faltered.

"No one in Hollywood ever is," Murphy said dryly. He halted before an oaken door. "In there."

She knocked on the door and a Billy's weary voice invited her in. When Nita entered the room she was shocked by his appearance. He was slouched in a big leather chair, wearing a bathrobe and pajamas. He had a two-day stubble of beard, and there were dark circles under his eyes.

He managed a smile for her. "Don't be afraid. Come in and sit down."

The smell of bottleg whiskey filled the room. He poured her a drink from a bottle on the table beside him and held out the half-filled glass. Looking at her closely, he said, "You look as if you need this!"

"Thanks," she said, and, taking the glass, sipped from it and gingerly perched on the chair facing him.

"To what do I owe this late and unexpected visit?" he asked.

"I'm so sorry to bother you," she said.

In spite of his appearance Billy seemed relatively sober. "No apologies needed. Unless they be mine. I'm not quite—presentable, as you can see."

"I need a friend tonight, Billy."

"You look as if you'd witnessed a murder," he said.

"I've seen enough," she replied grimly. She swallowed some more of the burning liquid in the glass and as it trickled down her throat, it gradually warmed her. She said, "I decided to spend the weekend at Barbara and Eric's beach house."

Billy shook his head in disbelief. "Didn't anyone warn you?"

"Several people gave me guarded warnings," she admitted. "But no one came right out and said what was wrong."

"I thought I told you about them," Billy said. "They're one of the 'twilight tandem' couples. Several of Hollywood's most vaunted marriages are in the same category."

"Everyone knows this?"

"And no one talks about it, or at least not in public," the comedian said. "Barbara was a well-known lesbian before she married Eric, and he is know to have been involved with both women and men, with a preference for men."

"He went off with one of his friends for the night and left me alone with her. Then she came to my room and tried to seduce me!"

Billy smiled grimly. "I assume you fought her off!"

"I made her get out of the room and then I packed and left as swiftly as I could!"

Billy poured himself another drink. "I'm glad you passed the test. You were bound to face something like that sooner or later. Some girls have tried to play along with the likes of Barbara to further their careers. It's a sad way to stay in show business."

"As she left she told me she'd finish me at the studio," Nita said.

"She'll do what she can to hurt you," Billy agreed. "But you have a legal contract with Lew Meyers, and I think he believes in your talent. So he'll not likely let you go."

"I don't care," she said unhappily. "I'd rather go back to vaudeville than get caught up in anything like that."

Billy smiled. "You can always come back to two-reelers. I'll see there's a job for you."

"What about you?" she worried. "I heard you'd been ill."

He sighed. "I drank a little too much one night and they took me to the hospital."

"They say you've been warned that you're drinking yourself to death."

"Let it be my road, then," he said.

She went to his chair and knelt by him. "You mustn't! It's such a waste of talent! Of a fine human being!"

He smiled down at her. "Other talents will come along."

"I need you!" Nita cried.

He raised an eyebrow. "Now there's an excellent argument for sobriety."

"I do need you, Billy!" she said tearfully, her head on his knees.

151

"But not enough to marry me."

She looked up at him. "You don't really want that. I know you'd be tired of married life in a few weeks."

He stroked her hair. "You're lovely and you're smart! You're right, I don't want to marry, but if I did, it would be you."

"Take care of yourself for me," she begged him.

"I'll try," he said. "What about that doctor you've been out with so often?"

"He's in San Francisco for a few days."

"So I'm a surrogate doctor?"

"No!" she protested. "I would have come to you first anyway. I couldn't have talked to him about that awful business."

"I'm sure he knows more about it than you guess. Or than he's told you."

"Probably," she agreed.

"Now go home and try to get a good night's rest. I'll come by tomorrow afternoon and we'll drive somewhere and have a nice dinner. Somehow we must save your weekend."

She reached up and touched her lips to his, ignoring the whiskey fumes and his stubble of beard. "You really are a darling," she said.

It was late when she reached her cottage. Nita unpacked, took a sleeping tablet and went to bed. Since she rarely used sleeping aids the tablet did its work and she slept soundly. She felt better when she got up the next morning, so she decided to try to put the entire incident out of her mind.

She fixed breakfast and then read the Sunday paper for a while. Billy would not come by for her until later in the afternoon so she would have plenty of time to bath and dress later. She was still in her dressing gown she she heard a knock at her door. Thinking it might

152

be one of the neighbors, she went to the door and opened it.

A contrite Eric Gray in white sweater and flannels stood in the doorway. He said, "Can I speak with you for a few minutes, Nita?"

She said icily, "I don't think we have anything to discuss."

"Please!" he said. "I know what happened with Barbara last night and I've come to say I'm sorry!"

"Don't tell me your leaving with your boy friend wasn't planned," she said sharply.

He looked guilty. "Don't judge me too hastily or too harshly. I beg you to listen to my side of it."

There was something in his manner that forced her against her will to feel sorry for him. He gave all the evidence of being sincere.

With a sigh, she said, "Very well. Come in."

Eric smiled his gratitude. He said, "It's nice and cosy here."

"Hardly an item for a Hollywood sightseeing tour," she said grimly. "But I could skip some of the mansions that are."

"I know what you mean," he said, standing before her awkwardly.

"Would you like coffee?"

He nodded. "Yes. I would."

"Sit down," she said. "I'll make some."

He was glancing at the paper when she came back in. He said, "Wallace Reid is very ill in a sanitarium."

She put the coffee tray down, shocked. "I didn't hear anything about it."

"It's a front page story," he said, showing her. "Pneumonia, they say. Actually, it was complicated by drug withdrawal."

Nita was trembling again. "So he really is deep in drugs?"

"Has been for a long while. And there are others," he said with a deep sigh. "He's been treated before, so he may pull through."

She poured their coffee and let him help himself to cream and sugar. Then she sat down near him. She was thinking of Thelma in New York and how the news would effect her. And she was worrying about the change in Thelma's appearance and wondered if her new frailty might also be due to drugs.

She said, "What do you want to tell me?"

"I'm sorry your weekend was ruined."

"It doesn't matter. I have a friend coming to take me out later."

"I'm glad," Eric said. A frown crossed his handsome face. "I'm unhappy about what happened. That Barbara so forgot herself."

"Didn't you expect it?" she said. "I had the idea I was being set up."

"Never!" he said vehemently. "I'd not be a party to that."

"You went off with Richard Wright swiftly enough," she said.

His cheeks crimsoned. "Yes."

"It seems to me you and your wife are two of a kind. I don't mind that as long as you don't menace others. There must be many innocents like me."

Eric sipped his coffee. "It's very complicated, Nita. Let me say first that I really like you. I was attracted to you when we first met on the set."

"Really?"

"Yes," he said earnestly. "And I have known and loved many women in my time."

"I understand that men are your preference."

"Not so," he retorted. "I have tried to fight that side of me, I really have. But it's not easy. It's worse than being a drunk like Billy Bowers. It's something

154

deep within me and often I let down my guard as I did last night.''

"What has this to do with me?"

"I want you to understand," he said. "I married Barbara knowing she was a lesbian. I thought we could help each other. But she soon let me know she had no intention of changing her ways. And her shocking behavior drove me into seeking satisfaction with my men companions.''

"You're telling me you're an unwilling homosexual?"

"Believe it," he insisted. "Had Barbara been the right sort of wife, I might have put that other life behind me.''

"I find that hard to accept," she said.

"You have never been in my place," he told her soberly. "You can ask Lew Meyers if you like. He knows! I really wanted to lead a normal life. I still want to!''

"But you keep returning to friends like Richard Wright," she pointed out.

"These things are not easy to break off.''

"If what you say is true, I'm sorry for you," Nita said. "But I have problems enough of my own without yours.''

He put aside his empty coffee cup and leaned forward to her. "I think if I had married you instead, you might have helped me. I'm sure of it.''

She smiled thinly. "Your wife tried to seduce me last night, and now it's your turn.''

"Nothing like that!" he argued. "I want a chance to prove myself to you. You could help me more than you realize. My liking for you had nothing to do with Barbara.''

"All right," she said. "I'll take your word for that.''

He offered her his hand. "Can we still remain friends?"

"Yes," she said, shaking hands with him.

A shadow crossed his face. "You must be on guard against Barbara. She does not forgive easily. She's going to be looking for a chance to harm you."

"She made that clear."

"I'll do what I can to prevent it," Eric said. "But she's truly wicked and she acts on her own. So you must be wary."

"I understand," she said.

"Lew Meyers knows what she is and all about her tricks," he went on. "He doesn't approve of her, but sometimes she forces him to accede to her will because she is his single biggest box office draw. And she never hesitates to use that power."

"I expect my option at Master won't be picked up," she said.

"I hope it will. You have talent. The studio can use you."

"Thanks," she said. "And thank you for coming to apologize."

"I had to do that," Eric said. Then he asked, "Are you still seeing Dr. Watters?"

"We're friends," she said.

"Nice fellow," Eric said with a sign. "But not for anyone who loves our business. I think he's only marking time until he can get away from show people and Hollywood."

"That's probably true. I'm not sure I don't agree with him."

"Eric smiled sadly. "Don't say that! You're too near the top to give up now."

"I wonder," she said.

His reply was to suddenly take a step forward and embrace her. His kiss was ardent and, taken by surprise, she found being in his arms a not unpleasant experience. As he let her go, he smiled and said, "Just to convince you I do care!" The next second he had gone.

She watched from her cottage window as he stepped into his long cream sports car and drove away. His kiss was still tingling on her lips, as she thought ironically that surely he was the ideal image of a stalwart Hollywood hero. So much for Hollywood heroes!

When Billy came by later she told him over the dinner table of the strange aftermath to the weekend. She said, "It was the last thing I expected. There he was in my doorway!"

Billy, shaven and pale, looked more like himself than he had the previous night. He said, "I think he was being truthful with you."

Nita stared at him. "You're saying he may truly be interested in me?"

"Yes."

"How could he be?"

"He had at least one bona-fide affair with Clara Bow," Billy said. "And any girl who cheerfully takes on a football team plus the coach isn't going to be satisfied with a pale imitation. I'd say he proved his virility with her."

"But since then he's turned to men again," she pointed out.

"Would you say being married to a creature like Barbara was apt to help him?"

"No."

"Then there's your answer. People like Eric live a difficult and dangerous existence. If the truth about him or Barbara comes out it would ruin them in films."

"I pity the people taken in by their facade."

"It happens in many areas of life," Billy said. "But

157

I think the important point Eric made is that he wants to straighten out his life and Barbara doesn't.''

"You think so?"

"What other reason would he have for coming to you as he did? He made no plea for Barbara but only for himself. And he's important enough in this town not to be worried about your opinion of him unless he really cares for you. So I think he does.''

She smiled. "You make a very persuasive argument.''

"I think I'm right.''

"I don't want to try and reform another actor. I had little success with Marty.''

Billy reminded her, "You said he had improved in his last months.''

"After we lost the baby," she said. "I didn't tell him I couldn've have another. But I think he may have guessed.''

"Still, you wanted to be in this business. So you have to be prepared to deal with the people in it. We're all rather complicated, I fear.''

"I've recently learned that," she agreed with a small smile. "You're surely no exception.''

Billy gave her a teasing look. "I think I know where your heart lies. With the good Dr. Phillip Watters.''

"That could very well be," she said thoughtfully.

Chapter Eight

Within a few days two events happened which were to make an unexpected chance in Nita's plans for the future. She was home on a short holiday from the studio when she picked up the morning paper to the confronted by huge headlines: "LATEST FILM ROMANCE, Film Star Sally Stark and Dashing Dr. Phillip Watters!" She could hardly believe her eyes when she saw the smiling photos of the two standing with their arms around each other.

The story went on to tell of their secretly dating for some time and that they had recently spent two weeks together in a hideaway on the outskirts of San Francisco. Sally and the handsome doctor insisted her mother had been along as chaperone, but did not deny there was a possibility of marriage in the offing. The story gave other details about the two, indicating that the vivacious Sally felt this new man in her life was the one she'd been waiting for. Her two previous marriages had ended in divorce.

Nita threw the paper down with a feeling of despair. She knew now that she cared for Phillip a great deal more than she'd been willing to admit, but had been so intent on her career she'd let them drift apart. He had been away several times and she had not thought anything about it. Now it became clear. He and Sally Stark had been having an affair.

No doubt the newspapers had managed to get onto the story and the studio had made Sally indicate that marriage was in the offing, whether it was or not. Sally Stark was still one of Master Films' biggest grossing stars but she was known to everyone as a woman of flagrantly loose morals. Her affair with a handsome prop man had been mentioned in the gossip columns, as had numerous other affairs.

There had been times when Nita had speculated about agreeing to marry the young doctor. Now it would clearly be impossible. The studio would likely put pressure on the Phillip to marry Sally, thus avoiding further scandal. Nita felt that the handsome Phillip had degraded himself in getting involved with a person like Sally Stark.

She was moping about the cottage when the phone rang. Phillip was on the line. He sounded worried. "I've been trying to reach you," he said. "I thought you'd be at the studio."

"I'm waiting for a new assignment," she said. "And I see you've found one."

"That newspaper story!" he groaned. "You mustn't believe any of it!"

"I thought you both looked charming. So adoring!" she said.

"I want to talk to you," he insisted. "Let's go out to dinner tonight."

"I don't think that would be wise," Nita snapped. "You'd better not be seen with anyone but Sally Stark."

"I must explain to you," he insisted. "Where can we meet?"

"Do you think it necessary? I'd expect Sally to be taking up most of your time!"

"Can I come over to your cottage?" he pleaded.

"All right," she said without enthusiasm. "But I don't think we have anything to discuss."

"Wait until I see you," was his reply.

Nita worried that she shouldn't have consented to see Phillip at all, and tried to prepare herself mentally for the confrontation with him. Her great weakness was that she'd really cared for him and she hadn't expected him to act in such a scandalous fashion. On the other hand, she had kept him at a distance and not given him the encouragement she might have.

Phillip arrived less than an hour later, looking pale and weary, as well he might after finding himself in the headlines with so notorious a figure as Sally Stark.

After Nita had shown him in and given him a martini they sat down in her living room. He said, "Surely you know better than to believe everything you read in the newspapers."

"Does it matter what I believe?"

"It does to me," he said. "I'm in love with you. I always have been."

"What about Sally Stark?" she wanted to know.

Phillips shook his head in despair. "I turned to her out of sheer boredom. First, she was my patient. She kept calling me to her bungalow on the lot and complaining about headaches. It wasn't until later I discovered she was interest in me."

"And?"

He sighed. "Call it a case of male vanity! I saw her a few times. We went to Santa Barbara for a few days."

"So you were lovers?"

"I don't deny that," he said. "I can only tell you that all that while I was unhappy and wondering how I was going to get myself free of her."

161

Nita said, "Judging by the headlines today you didn't make much headway."

He raised a hand in protest. "Give me a chance to explain. Sally was far too devious for me. I know that now. She was always one step ahead of me. And I made her angry by foolishly admitting that I really cared for you."

"That was obviously a mistake," Nita agreed with a bitter smile. "Especially as you were still carrying on with her!"

"I intended to break it," Phillip insisted. He got up and with a hand to his forehead began to pace back and forth. "Then all hell broke loose! Sally went to Lew Meyers and told him she was two months pregnant and I was to blame!"

Nita was shocked by this, even though she knew many dirty games were played and studio politics entered into everything. She covered her repulsion, saying, "By your own admission you could have been responsible!"

Phillip turned to face her unahppily. "I could have been, but I'm sure I wasn't. The timing was all wrong. But you know what Lew Meyers is like. He demanded that she go to San Francisco and be attended to by a doctor there who specializes in abortions."

"That sounds like Lew," she said dryly. "Save the studio no matter what."

"And worse, Sally pretended to panic and insisted she wouldn't go unless I went along to take care of her and make sure everything was all right."

"So that's how you came to be in San Francisco together," she said. "Did she had the abortion?"

"Yes," he said wearily. "I thought I would finally be rid of her. Then the press caught on to the fact we were staying in a seaside house together and came hounding us."

"So you decided to say you were engaged?"

"That's not the worst of it," the young doctor said. "We had a call from Lew Meyers. It seems someone tipped off Louella Parsons about Sally's abortion. Maybe some doctor friend of her husband, who is also a doctor, got wind of it. Louella told Lew she was going to print the story."

Nita listened to the growing complexity of it all with amazement. "So what then?"

"Lew Meyers swore that Sally and I were genuinely in love, that she'd only had the abortion because her health was not good. He also said that Sally wanted a child later on, she and I were going to be married soon and Louella would have the scoop!"

"Hence the headlines."

"Yes," he said. "Louella has promised to say nothing about the abortion and Meyers has vowed that Sally and I will marry."

"Are you?"

He spread his hands. "What can I do? Sally still says I'm to blame. She's agreed to divorce me in a year if I marry her now and save her career from collapsing in scandal."

"I don't believe it," Nita gasped. "Even in Hollywood!"

He took a step towards her. "I don't give a damn about Sally but I don't see how I can avoid marrying her now."

Nita leaped up, facing him. "And you were the one who refused to consider becoming part of the Hollywood mire! You said you were leaving to practice in New York."

"I still intend to!"

"I wonder," she said grimly. "Hollywood is filled with people who meant to leave long ago. But they're still here, holding on to what they think are careers."

163

The young doctor said, "What about you and Billy Bowers? Or you and Eric Gray? There's been plenty of talk."

"Whatever you've heard, Phillip, I'm still my own person. And I intend to continue being so. Would you kindly leave? I think I've heard enough."

His arms were outstretched towards her. "Nita, I do love you!" he pleaded.

"We've lost our chance," she said. "Just leave me alone!"

"I won't give up," he promised. He took her in his arms and kissed her with great passion. She pushed him away and he stood staring at her a long moment, hurt and indignation on his handsome face. Then he turned and rushed out of the cottage. A moment later she heard him driving away.

Only then did Nita throw herself on her bed and sob aloud until she was exhausted. There seemed little hope for Phillip now. He would be caught up in studio politics on the one hand and tied to Sally on the other.

Nita had barely recovered from this shock when she was brusquely summoned to the studio by Lew Meyers. The little Napoleon of the Master Film company received her in his huge, sumptuous office. His small, bald figure perched in a throne-like chair behind a massive desk was ludicrous in contrast to his impressive surroundings.

Nita timorously approached him across the wide expanse of maroon carpet from the entrance to his desk. It was rumored the little man used this long open stretch to intimidate his underlings. Now he sat apparently absorbed in some papers as she approached him.

"Mr. Meyers?" she said in a small voice.

The wizened, crab-apple face lifted and she was subjected to a stern glance. "Ah, it's you, Nita!" he

164

said as if her coming was a surprise and not one arranged solely at his request.

"Yes."

"We have a problem here," Lew Meyers said. "It seems there is no suitable part for you in our present productions. I'm lending you to Classic Films."

Nita had heard of these loans of contract players. Generally the studio made a handsome profit on the deal and paid the actor only his regular salary. Also it was a favorite way of punishing some recalcitrant actor or attempting to get rid of him if his being on the lot was an embarrassment. Nita felt it was a little of each in her case.

She said, "Barbara Lamont seemed to think I had promise and that I did well in my last film with her and Eric Gray."

Lew Meyer scowled. "Miss Lamont has changed her mind. She doesn't want you in her new picture. And she has the final word."

"I see," Nita said quietly, understanding all too clearly.

"You'll get some good experience and you'll be working," the little man said. "It is good neither for the studio nor for you to have your idle."

"Who will I be working with?"

"A famous director," Lew Meyers said. "Rudolph Von Eltz. You must be familiar with his work."

The name at once conjured up an image of the erratic German director who had won fame in Hollywood during the war playing vicious German officers. Now he was exhibiting his real talent as a director, and had become notorious for his realistic orgy scenes in nearly all his films. She had glimpsed him once in the studio cafe, a stocky, bald man with a marked Teutonic accent. His shaven head and the monocle he wore in one eye made him a formidable looking figure.

She said, "I have heard he is rather difficult to get along with."

"Good discipline for you," Lew Meyer said. "I'll expect you to report at Classic Films on Monday and that you'll do well in the new Von Eltz movie. That is all!"

So Nita was summarily dismissed. She drove back to her cottage feeling extremely low in spirits. A letter from her mother did not cheer her up, but only made her more homesick. Her father was suffering from arthritis and one of Marty's sisters had died in child-birth. It seemed that, like many Irish matrons, her mother took some macabre pleasure in lamenting the woes of the world.

After a series of phone calls to Murphy she finally was able to reach Billy Bowers. For once the comedian seemed in a good humor and immediately suggested that they go to the Cocoanut Grove for dinner and ancing. She was a little surprised by his genial mood and his willingness to go out but she accepted. Her own spirits were at a low ebb and she needed to talk to someone.

Billy picked her up in his own car. Nita noticed that he was at the wheel rather than Murphy. He also looked better than he had for some time. She sat beside him and as they drove to the popular night spot, he told her the reason.

"I had a call from Louis B. Mayer," he said. "It seems they are interested in grooming a new star for a series of comedies. My name was suggested. He interviewed me and told me if I could keep off the booze three months he'd give me a contract."

Nita was delighted. "What did you say?"

"That was a month ago," he said, glancing from

166

the wheel with a smile. "I've had nothing but an occasional glass of wine since."

"You look so well," she said.

He nodded. "I think I'm going to make it this time. It's my last chance to escape from two-reelers."

"I know you can do it!"

He laughed. "Just don't expect me to join you in martinis tonight."

"I'll do better than that," she said. "I'll drink wine with you."

All kinds of ruses were devised for the serving of liquor in public places during prohibition. The simplest one was to secretly carry flasks and spike the mixers which the various eating places served. Another was to make a club a membership affair with a private stock of liquor for the use of various members. Often liquor was poured from bottles with a mineral bottle label. There were frequent raids, whereupon fines were paid and the various practices cheerfully continued.

On this particular night the Cocoanut Grove was crowded but Billy had reserved his favorite table under a palm tree near the entrance. No sooner had they been seated when Phillip Watters arrived with Sally Stark on his arm. The entire room suddenly turned all their attention to the headline couple. Sally, famous for her platinum blonde hair, waved to some favorites and smiled as she clung to the young doctor. Phillip merely looked embarrassed. They were taken to a table some distance away.

Billy smiled, at with ironic amusement. He said, "Your doctor has been getting a lot of publicity lately."

"I know."

"He made a mistake in even looking Sal's way. She's a man-eater."

"I'm sure he's found that out," she said.

"The story is they're going to be married."

"So I hear."

Billy stared at her. "Doesn't that mean anything to you? I thought you were in love."

"I thought so, too," she said.

"What happened?"

"Call it Hollywood," she said. "Lew Meyers ordered them to marry."

"The mighty midget!" Billy said with a wry smile.

"And I'm not to be in the new Barbara Lamont and Eric Gray starring vehicle. I'm being sent off the lot on loan."

"You know why!" Billy said at once.

"Of course," she said. "Barbara."

"You turned her down and now she's doing the same to you in a different way."

"I don't think Eric had any part in it."

Billy shrugged. "He does what she says. They protect each other."

"It isn't fair to strike back at me in my work," she said with indignation.

"What is fair in this town?"

"Not much," she said. "I'm to report to Classic for the new Rudolph Von Eltz film on Monday."

"Aha!" Billy said. "Now I'm sure it's Barbara's doing. She's turned you over to the 'Dirty Hun.' "

She said, "Is he called that because of the orgy scenes in his pictures?"

"Partly," the comedian said. "And because much of the filming of his orgies is so realistic. Do you know that filming of them sometimes goes on for twenty-four hours behind locked studio doors and he treats both principals and extras to squab, caviar and champagne? His extras are hand picked for their loose morals. Some of the women he uses have been imported here from bordellos.''

Nita was shocked. "I can't believe it!"

"Ah, but it's true," he replied. "And there's also drugs. I've heard stories of girls coming out of these sets bleary-eyed and staggering. Some of them covered with bites and whip marks!''

"Don't tell me any more!" Nita protested, appalled.

"I'm simply warning you about the kind of cesspool they're sending you into," he said.

"But Von Eltz is praised by many of the critics. He must have talent!''

"He's a mad genius," Billy said. "Personally, I can do without him.''

"If I don't take the job I'll be suspended, and probably end with my contract broken.''

Billy frowned. "You'll have to take the job. But be on your guard all the time. You're smart enough to take care of yourself.''

"I'm glad you think so," she worried. "I'm not all that sure.''

Billy ordered rack of lamb and they drank red wine. After dinner the orchestra played and Billy and Nita danced to "California, Here I Come," "Sweet Georgia Brown" and "Toot, Toot, Tootsie Goodbye." She had never seen the normally shy man in such an outgoing mood. It was apparent that sobriety agreed with him.

"I feel wonderful," he told her as they returned to their table.

"You must stay as you are until Louis B. Mayer sees you again," she said. "You're bound to get a contract.''

He nodded. "I hope so."

Then Nita saw Phillip and Sally on the floor. The young doctor noticed her and nodded. She saw Sally

169

speak to him angrily and they moved to another area of the floor. Shortly afterwards he and Sally left. As Sally passed Nita's table on the way out she held her shapely chin high in the air. Phillip slowed a little and offered her a small smile, then hurried on to join Sally.

Billy looked amused. "They're not even married and she already has him on a leash!"

"He's a fool," she said bitterly. "Why doesn't he get out of Hollywood? He's not tied to movies like the rest of us."

"A scandal about an abortion wouldn't be an ideal way for him to open a medical practice," Billy said. "And Sally would ruin him without even worrying about it."

"I know," she sighed.

They went back to dance again. While they were moving about the floor she saw the smiling face of Eric Gray moving towards them. He came to Billy and touching him on the shoulder, asked, "May I cut in?"

Billy raised an eyebrow at Nita and said, "Why not?" The comedian let Eric take his place and went back to the table to wait for her.

Eric smiled at her. "I didn't expect to have this pleasure tonight."

"Are you here with Barbara?" she asked.

"No," he said. "Richard and I decided to stop by for some food. I saw you and wanted to talk to you."

"What about?"

"I know you're being lent to Classic."

"You ought to," she said. "Since you and Barbara are responsible."

Eric shook his head. "Not me! Just Barbara! But you need not worry. Rudolph Von Eltz is a friend of mine and I promise you will be given good treatment."

"Not drugged, whipped or raped?"

"I know the stories," Eric said. "Only part of it is true. I'll make sure that Von Eltz builds up your part in the film and in the end it will do you good."

"I wish I could believe that," she told him.

"Don't worry about it," the leading man said. "Just leave it in my hands."

"Why are you doing this for me?" she asked.

"It's quite simple," he said. "I'm in love with you."

She glanced to the table on the edge of the dance floor where Richard Wright was seated alone. She said, "What about Richard?"

Eric's face flamed red. He said nothing.

The dance ended and he took her back to Billy Bowers. The two men chatted for a few minutes and then Eric returned to Richard.

"What was that all about?" Billy asked her.

She told him, ending with, "He says he has influence with Von Eltz and he's going to help me get a good part."

"Maybe he has some plan," Billy agreed.

"He says so."

"Is Eric in love with you?"

"You know Eric."

"He had several interesting affairs with women before he married Barbara," the comedian said. "I think the right girl could change him."

"That's what he tells me," she said. "And he thinks I'm that girl."

Billy gave her a knowing glance. "That would be really paying Barbara back in spades!"

Classic Films was a larger company than Master. Nita reported for work at nine on Monday morning and waited in a studio until eleven when Rudolf Von Eltz arrived. He carried himself in arrogant style and his expression was surly. At his heels followed a small, dark man with thick glasses who apparently was his chief aide.

Nita was surrounded by a number of younger players whose names and faces were unfamiliar to her. It was typical of Von Eltz to use comparative unknowns with good looks and bodies. The director was the star of a Von Eltz film, with the actors playing only a secondary role. The top billing was always for the director, Rudolf Von Eltz.

Now he stood before the semi-circle of seated and standing actors and eyed them all with disdain. In his heavily accented English he told them the film was to be the story of a slave girl in ancient Arabia with a parallel story of modern New York where the same actress would play the office slave to a wicked financier. He indicated a pretty, dark-haired girl named Carol True, who would play the leading role. Nita found herself cast as the leading lady's jealous sister.

The surly director handed out copies of the script and told them all, "You will be here at seven tomorrow." Then he and his aide vanished.

There was much discussion and complaining among the actors. Carol True turned to Nita with a smile and said, "Is this your first Von Eltz film?"

"Yes," she said. "What about you?"

"I played a bit part in his last film," the dark-haired girl said. "It was an experience."

Shooting began the next morning. Nita was in only a few scenes at the opening of the film, so she sat much of the time on the sidelines waiting to be called. Von Eltz proved most demanding about the camera work, lighting and sets. If all did not suit him he would halt work until whatever bothered him was corrected. Nita spent several days waiting to be called to work.

His direction was precise and helpful, and Nita be-

172

gan to understand as the days went by why the Prussian was hailed by the critics as a genius. Nothing out of the way took place in the early stages of the film.

Then one afternoon he halted the filming to make an announcement. He tapped his whip against his puttees and, eyes fixed on the actors, his expression stolid, said, "Tomorrow we will shoot the orgy scene. It is the most important! But first, we much establish the proper moood. You will come prepared to remain in the studio as long as I deem necessary. The last time we worked around the clock for twenty-four hours. While this is in progress the set will be closed to outsiders. Those employed in the film will not be permitted to leave."

Discontented murmuring followed this announcement as Von Eltz made his usual strutting exit, after letting it be known that actors and extras would be paid double for the time they were involved in filming the orgy.

Nita arrived at the studio the next day filled with apprehension. She noticed that her nervousness was shared by most of the rest of the cast and began to understand why they had been chosen chiefly for their youth and physical good looks. She was one of the few better known players in the group.

Nita went to make-up and then donned the low-cut evening gown she was to wear in the party scene which Von Eltz had described as a bacchanal in a New York penthouse. The other girls and men arrived on the set, the women elegantly gowned and the men in full evening dress.

One of the men crossed the big studio floor to her and she was startled to see that it was none other than Eric Gray.

"What are you doing here?" she asked.

He smiled. "I told you I had a surprise for you. I'm playing a small role in the film."

"There was no mention of it."

"We decided to say nothing so Barbara wouldn't have a chance to complain to Lew Meyers. As it is, I have his permission."

"I'm glad you're here," she said. "There are a lot of rumors going the rounds and we're all more or less prisoners here until the orgy scene is completed."

Eric patted her arm. "Don't worry."

"Will I be working in the scene with you?"

"Not this one," Eric said. "But Von Eltz is considering adding another scene in which we will both appear. I'm going to speak to him about it now." After a moment more of conversation he left her to seek out the director.

A handsome young man whose face reminded Nita of Valentino came to her and said, "I see you and Eric Gray are friends."

"Yes," she said.

"Interesting man," the fellow said. "I'm new in Hollywood, but I've heard a lot about him."

She couldn't help wonder if the good-looking young man had ulterior motives. She said, "He has many friends."

"Of both sexes," he said knowingly. "Are you looking forward to the orgy?"

"Not really," she said.

"Might as well enjoy it," he told her cheerfully. "That's why most of us are here. To decorate the set with our bodies and provide Von Eltz with some really wild doings."

Von Eltz appeared shortly, also in evening dress, accompanied by Eric. The Prussian ordered the actors to give him their attention and a hush fell over the group.

"There are three scenes," he told them. "The first is in the banquet room where we will all gather to feast and drink fine champagne!" This brought a murmur of approval. He lifted a hand for silence and continued, "The next is the fountain scene in the courtyard of the millionaire's home and the third is the living room where the principal scene will be filmed. Now on to the banquet room!"

Nita followed the others onto a set representing a banquet hall with a huge table at which nearly a hundred people could be seated. It stretched the length of the room and was set with the finest china, silverware and crystal. Over heard, great chandeliers provided light. Camera men were located at all corners of the studio and two assistant directors were busily seating the actors.

She saw that Eric was at the head of the table with Von Eltz. Nita was seated between the handsome man with the Valentino face and a pretty ginger-haired girl who seemed excited and amused by it all. She was strikingly pretty and had a luscious figure much revealed by her scanty costume.

Von Eltz rose as waiters appeared to fill their wine glasses, and announced, "We will eat, drink and be merry!"

It was the beginning of a banquet which lasted more than two hours. Wines and liquors flowed extravagantly and there was squab, lobster, and a number of Continental delicacies to delight every taste. Nita tried to hold her drinking to a minimum but soon her head was reeling.

She gazed around her and saw that chaos was beginning to take over at the long table. A girl had leaped from her seat mid-way along the table and climbing into the table itself ahd torn off her dress and was now dancing wantonly in her filmy underthings. Men were rising and toasting her with champagne. Von Eltz watched it all quietly.

An arm encircled Nita and she turned to find the handsome man on her left leaning close. He kissed her and whispered an indecent suggestion.

She shook her head angrily and turned away from him in horror, his delighted laughter ringing in her ears. She gazed at the pretty girl next to her and saw that her dress had slipped from one shoulder so that one breast was entirely exposed.

More frightening than the noise, drunken laughter, and blatantly erotic actions going on around Nita was the relaxing of her own inhibitions. Feelings coursed through her which she had known before only in the most thrilling moments of passion. Vaguely she realized that she, like the others around her, was no longer in control of her emotions. She laughed raucously at a suggestive remark from the man across the table from her, and found herself eagerly returning a stranger's lascivious kiss.

Her head was growing lighter every moment and in her last few seconds of coherence thought she realized dimly what had happened. Von Eltz had put some subtle drug in all their drinks, some strong aphrodisiac which made them all his puppets. This was the secret of his great success as a director of powerfully erotic films.

Von Eltz rose in his place at the table and barked out orders in German. The assistant directors appeared again and now herded Nita and the others out of the banquet hall and on to the set representing a courtyard with a fountain at least fifteen feet tall and a wide pool around it. The young men and women were laughing and embracing. Then Von Eltz appeared on one of the several platforms above the fountain and lifted a megaphone to address them.

He shouted, "The fountain is flowing with champagne! You are to revel in the spray. You must tumble around and show boisterous amusement. Do not worry about ruining your costumes, that is expected and dressers will be waiting to look after them!"

The ginger-haired girl let out a cry of delight, kicked off her slippers and ran into the fountain, laughing under its spray. She was joined by dozens of others, men and women in elegant evening clothes, stumbling about in the water, lifting their lips to the spray as if drinking fine wine, embracing and kissing each other. Some of the men were ripping off the women's dresses, exposing their bodies. One of the assistant directors seized Nita and literally shoved her into the pool.

"Make something of the scene!" he shouted to her.

The scene proceeded and above the noise Von Eltz went on barking out further orders in German as the camera men on precarious perches above him continued to grind away.

Nita stumbled around, laughing young men propelling her one way and then the next. She felt she was in the midst of a madman's nightmare.

Now the assistant directors shouted at the actors in the pool, "Off with your clothes! The boss wants you all nude! Hurry it up!"

Nita listened in a daze and saw the boisterous, drugged crowd begin to disrobe. Suddenly a nude young man was tearing off her dress.

"No!" she cried, trying to push him away.

"Von Eltz ordered it!" The young man cried and laughingly tore away underclothing, leaving her stark naked along with all the others.

Now the uproar was greater than ever. The sight of so many naked bodies overwhelmed Nita. She knew it was only her drugged state which kept her from—

fainting. To her horror she was overwhelmed with erotic urges, as she watched the young men pairing off with the young women and carrying them away, their bodies dripping wet and shining, into secret corners of the studio.

Above it all, Von Eltz watched the carnival impassively. Nita was standing with her hands covering herself as best she could, when a handsome nude man came straight at her. It was Eric Gray and there was no mistaking his arousal.

He lifted her into his arms and amidst the bedlam carried her off to a small dark cubicle with a canvas cot behind the main set. He placed her on the cot and proceeded to take her greedily. Nita, overcome with passiong, was unable to resist, and abandoned herself to the fires of lust. The drink and the drugs had done their work.

Nita had no idea how long their love making went on, but she was amply convinced that Eric could satisfy a woman and enjoy it.

Eric told her, "I love you! I had to take this chance to prove it!"

She pressed close to him and whispered, "What now?"

"Von Eltz wants us back on the fountain set," he said. "It is most important!"

He led her to a large dressing room and a matronly woman at once handed her an evening gown to put on. Then she and the other girls made their way out to the fountain where the men were waiting in various stages of dress and undress. Eric was on hand in evening trousers and vest without a jacket. He led her over to the pool of water surrounding the fountain.

"We will do the fountain scene again!" Von Eltz cried out severely.

The benumbed revellers now replayed their tribute

to Bacchus, reproducing the orgy. They stumbled through the scene without the earlier boisterousness.

Von Eltz was now a cruel martinet. He wanted perfection and closeups of the exhausted, dissipated men and women. The assistant directors and cameramen worked from various angles for hours with only short rest periods to ease the actors' gruelling labors under the hot lights.

At last Von Eltz gave the order to end the day's shooting. Nita found her way to her dressing room, her head aching and her entire body exhausted and full of pain. She donned her own clothes and was about to leave for home when the door to her dressing room opened and Rudolf Von Eltz entered the room, a malevolent smile on his ugly face.

Chapter Nine

In his guttural manner of speech," he said, "You did very well indeed, Miss Nolan."

She gazed up at him fearfully and told him, "I do not like your methods. I have never been involved in anything like this before. How do you manage to get away with such actions?"

Von Eltz swaggered across the room. His monocle in his eye, he studied her. "You will find that silence concerning what went on in the studio today is written into your contract. It is the same with all the others."

"How wickedly clever of you," she said. "That is why one hears rumors about your filming but never the actual truth as I experienced it today."

He shrugged. "I must get certain results. It is the only way to know. Call it immoral or what you will, I can promise that it will bring good luck to you."

"What do you mean?" she asked sharply.

"I'm having an additional story line added to the film. You and Eric Gray will be featured. You will receive the script by messenger tomorrow morning, and tomorrow afternoon we begin shooting the scenes."

"Is there to be more of what went on today?" Nita asked.

The Prussian shook his shaven head. "That is over.

You need have no fear. And you will forgive me when you read the reviews of the film. I promise you it will be acclaimed as a classic."

Nita said grimly, "I know I shall never forget it."

He bowed. "Until tomorrow!" And he left.

Nita stumbled out of the parking lot and as she passed others of the cast, she noticed they were having the same reaction as herself. Now that the drug was clearing from their minds, their inhibitions were returning. They avoided looking at each other and hurried off singly or in couples, seemingly anxious not to remember what had gone on. And so another of the Von Eltz orgies would go down in Hollywood history to be secretly whispered about but never directly discussed.

For Nita, it had been both shocking and rewarding. She had the promise of the eccentric director that her role in the film was being made more important. And she had been made love to by Eric Gray. She could not deny that it had been a most satisfying interlude, and it made her feel that perhaps it was indeed the degenerate and cruel Barbara who had driven him to his sexual aberrations, as he had told her.

Though Barbara had arranged for Nita to be in the Von Eltz film to degrade her and set back her career, Eric had managed to turn the tables on his wife and now Nita would share a starring role in the film with him. Also, Nita now felt she could justly try to take Eric from his lesbian wife.

With Phillip Watters amrried to Sally Stark there was no true romantic interest left for her. She had been fond of the young doctor and would have married him, but he had fallen victim to the Hollywood poison and perhaps ruined his medical career as well. She would try to forget him.

As for Eric, his marriage was nothing but a sham.

181

It was true that Billy Bowers loved her, but Nita knew they were not right for each other. Even Billy admitted it.

She drove home still in a dazed state. It did not surprise her when Eric turned up at her cottage in Gardenia Court a little while later. He was dressed casually in sport clothes and the moment she opened the door to him he hungrily took her in his arms.

As they sat close together, his arm around her, he said, "After today there is no question in my mind. I must divorce Barbara and marry you."

"What about Lew Meyers?" she asked.

"He'll be afraid of a scandal and won't like it," Eric admitted.

"Worse than that, he'll try to stop you from making any change."

"I'll risk his anger," Eric said. "I love you and I want you to be my wife."

"Barbara will be venomous."

Eric sighed. "Isn't she always? But this time she won't succeed."

Nita gave him an anxious look. "I don't want to ruin your career."

"I'll manage," he said. "Meyers won't treat me the way he has Francis X. Bushman. I hear Bushman has been blacklisted at all the major studios and is taking any sort of cheap job."

"It should make a difference if the Von Eltz film is a success," she said.

"We'll wait until it's released before we do anything," he promised.

They talked for a while longer, then went to her bedroom and made love again. Eric was not as violent as he had been that afternoon, but the exchange left them both satisfied.

So began a period of ecstasy for Nita and Eric, a

time of secret trysts, intricate plotting in order to have time together, and working together in starring roles in the Von Eltz film, "Enslaved."

When the rushes came in, Von Eltz was pleased. It was obvious that the film was turning out as well as he'd hoped. After its completion Nita was put on the waiting list at Master again, so she had plenty of time to entertain Eric privately.

Eric had arranged for his Richard Wright to accompany Nita to social events while he escorted Barbara. When they reached the various parties they were able to be in each other's company part of the time without arousing suspicions. This, of course, meant that Wright was in on their secret.

Nita questioned Eric about him. "Wasn't he your lover? Surely he must resent me."

Eric smiled. "Not really. Richard is a friend and I have assured him that only you can make me happy. He is willing to help us."

So it was arranged. Thereafter, at many Hollywood parties Richard Wright, suave and smiling, escorted Nita. The gossip columnists noted this and speculated on a romance between them, which triggered a phone call from Billy Bowers.

Billy wanted to know, "What's going on with you and Wright?"

She laughed. "It's a trick. You should know that. It's to distract attention from Eric and me."

Billy grunted, indicating he wasn't too fond of that either. He said, "Be careful of Wright. I've heard some stories about him. He was close to Wally Reid."

"And you're a friend of Fatty Arbuckle," she reminded him. "You can't judge him because he and poor Wally were friendly."

"Maybe not," Billy conceded.

"What about your contract at MGM?" she asked him.

He hesitated. "That's off for the moment. Hammons and I are making a new batch of two-reelers. The demand is still strong for them and I'm getting good money."

"But I thought you wanted to do a major feature?"

"It can wait," Billy said. "I'll give you a call again and we'll go out."

"I'd love to," Nita replied, but she had little confidence that he would actually call. They had been drifting apart now that her own career was accelerating. She was worried about his change of attitude about making the feature film and guessed that he must have gone back to his heavy drinking.

"Enslaved" had a triumphant premiere at Grauman's Chinese Theatre. All the Hollywood greats and no-so-greats were there. As usual, it was Richard Wright who escorted Nita since Barbara had insisted on coming with Eric. Cecil B. DeMille was present and shook hands with Rudolf Von Eltz outside the theatre entrance. Irving Thalberg and Norma Shearer came, as did Mae Murray, one of Von Eltz's favorite stars and fading leading man Maurice Costello, now reduced to playing small character parts.

Nita watched tensely as the film began. When it came to the fountain scene she could not deny the genius of the Prussian director in creating an atmosphere of total depravity. It was more forceful than anything of its kind she had ever seen, and equally satisfying were the scenes with herself and Eric. Several times the audience applauded.

Beside her Richard Wright whispered, "Eric said this would make you a star and I think he was right."

She gave him a small smile and went back to watching the film. When it ended and the lights came up

184

there was loud applause and a standing ovation for Von Eltz.

Then invited guests moved on to the ballroom of the Beverly Wiltshire Hotel which Classic Films had engaged for a banquet. Eric managed to disengage himself from his wife and came over to Nita. He kissed her on the cheek and told her, "You were all that I hoped you would be!"

"Our night!" she said, her eyes bright.

He laughed. "Yes. And we owe it all to Barbara!"

"How is she taking it?"

"Furious," Eric said cheerfully. "I'd better get back to her before she makes a scene."

"Take no chances," Nita warned.

"I'll see you later tonight," he promised.

"Are you sure you can get away?"

He winked at her. "She'll think I have a date with Richard."

Eric had no sooner gone back along the crowded room to his wife than Lew Meyers appeared, resplendent in white tie and tails that nearly reached the ground.

The sour little man wore an unusual smile on his wizened face. "I was proud of you tonight," he told Nita.

Breathless at this unexpected praise, she said, "Thank you!"

"Von Eltz brought out your talent."

"He is a fine director."

"Master Films is not a company to waste talent," the little man went on. "From now on you have star status and you'll come to my office for a new contract."

"Do you really mean it?"

"I'm not in the habit of making statements I don't mean," Meyers said. "We've been trying to get Joan

Crawford to do a story called 'Bondage.' I'm going to test you for it instead."

"Thank you, Mr. Meyers," Nita said warmly.

He gave her a wise look. "Just keep out of trouble and you can go far."

She guessed that his statement could be interpreted as a warning for her not to cause a scandal with Eric Gray. She was sure the little man was not fooled by Richard Wright's being her continual companion. She would leave it in Eric's hands to sort out the difficult situation.

Richard had been standing in the background. Now he joined her with an amused look on his tanned face. "Good news?"

"Yes. Meyers liked my work. He's going to star me from now on."

Richard squeezed her arm. "Don't let him hire you cheaply. When you sign the new contract be sure it's for a decent salary."

"I should have you as a business agent," she said.

"You could do worse," he told her. And turning, he said, "I want you to meet two friends of mine, William Desmond Taylor and his brightest star, Mary Miles Minter."

"I hear she's after Mary Pickford's crown," Nita said.

"And she has a fair chance of getting it if she keeps on as she's been doing lately. Of course, she and Taylor are lovers. He's a womanizer. Mabel Normand is also one of his conquests and gossip has it she's terribly jealous of Mary and angry at Taylor for turning to her."

Nita smiled bleakly. "More Hollywood complications."

He said, "You can be broad-minded tonight. This is your big night!"

"All right, I'll meet them," she said. "How do you happen to know so many stars?"

"I get around," he replied with a wise smile.

Richard introduced her to the slender, middle-aged man and a petite, blonde girl. William Desmond Taylor was well known in Hollywood as a director, and the vivacious Mary Miles Minter was his favorite star. Taylor at once praised Nita's performance and spent all his time talking to her while Richard occupied himself with Mary Miles Minter.

"You showed true artistry tonight," Taylor said in his quiet, British-accented voice.

"I appreciate that a man of your reputation," said Nita.

He shrugged. "Anyone will tell you the same thing. I'd like to do a film with you. You must pay a visit to my place. Richard comes frequently."

"I'd love to," Nita said.

He lifted a sleeve and studied an expensive gold wristwatch with a diamond studded face. He said, "I must leave soon—we're working tomorrow."

"What a lovely watch!" she exclaimed.

The director smiled. "It was given to me by Mabel Normand. My initials are engraved on the back."

"You are close friends?"

"We were," he said. "We did several films together. But in Hollywood, people drift apart."

"I've learned that," she agreed. "I'm lucky to have Richard about."

Taylor glanced at the young man talking with Mary MIles Minter and said, "Richard is truly a vital part of the Hollywood social scene."

Nita then joined Richard and his companion for a few minutes and found the blonde star terribly nervous and rather dull in conversation. The young woman was

187

only interested in talking about her ambition to become America's Sweetheart in place of Mary Pickford.

"It's a matter of doing wholesome stories," the Minter girl told Nita earnestly. "And William knows how to select good scenarios."

Nita noted that Richard and the director had vanished somewhere. She attempted to keep up some small talk with the petite star, but it was a losing battle.

Then a voice at her elbow said, "Nita!"

She turned to confront Dr. Phillip Watters. "You!"

"Yes," he said with a somewhat guilty smile. "I'm still a member of the Hollywood community."

"I hadn't noticed," she said. "Sally is away on location filming so much. I expected you'd be with her."

He crimsoned. "I have been away with her several times. I'm proud of you tonight."

"Thank you," she said politely.

"I suppose you have someone to share your triumph?"

"Does it matter to you?"

"Very much," he said earnestly. "There'll soon be some interesting news in the papers."

"Really?"

"Yes," the young doctor said. "Even Lew Meyers now agrees that marriage was a mistake. Sally is going to Reno and taking up residence there to file suit for a divorce. It will be breaking in the newspapers in a few days."

"What about you?" she asked.

"I'm staying on in Hollywood for a while longer," the young doctor said. "I hope we can see each other when the smoke clears away."

Nita eyed him sadly. "You made your choice when you married Sally."

"Hardly of my own making," he protested.

"That could be argued," she said. "I also have my own life to lead."

"Is the gossip about you and Eric Gray true?"

"You should know better than to ask that," she said.

"Studio demands," Phillip said with a thin smile. "They rule our lives."

"If I had a degree in medicine they wouldn't rule mine," Nita said sharply. "I'd get away from this crazy town as soon as I could!"

"I'll gladly do that if you'll come with me!"

"Sorry," she said. "Your offer comes too late."

She was glad when the Rudolf Von Eltz interrupted them. He clicked his heels, bowed, took her hand and kissed it and, studying her with a sly look, asked, "Do you still think me a monster?"

Nita was forced to smile in return. "Yes. But let us say—a talented monster."

"That is all I ask," Von Eltz said. "I heard Meyers is at last aware of your possibilities. You'll be an international star when 'Enslaved' is distributed around the world. Eric is going to the New York area to make personal appearances."

Nita was surprised. "He didn't tell me."

"I have just arranged it with Meyers," Von Eltz said. "And I hear you are going into the new film, 'Bondage'."

"Slavery seems to pursue me," she agreed.

"I'd do it. A role like that could capitalize on your appearance in my film," Von Eltz said. "Who knows—we may work together again one day." And with another formal bow, he strode away.

Richard Wright saw her back to the cottage. Then she began the vigil of waiting for Eric to make his promised visit. It was after two-thirty in the morning when he arrived, still debonair but looking weary.

He kissed her and explained, "I have only just rid myself of Barbara."

"Do you want a drink?" she asked.

"No," he said. "How about some coffee?"

She kissed him again and smiling winsomely said, "We're getting so settled, just like two married folk."

He followed her into the small kitchen and sat at the table. "That's what we're going to be very soon."

As she went about making the coffee, she said, "Von Eltz told me you're going East on a personal appearance tour for the film."

"I promised," Eric said. "And Lew Meyers agreed. He's so impressed by your performance that he's agreed to let me ammounce that Barbara and I are separating while I'm in New York."

She crossed to him eagerly. "He's really agreed to that?"

"Yes," Eric smiled. "I told him I want to marry you. He suddenly seems to feel you're going to be more valuable to him than Barbara."

"He'd have to think so before he gave permission. He's a stern man. He enjoys the hold he has over all of us. By the way did you know that Dr. Phillip Watters and Sally Stark are also getting a divorce?" Nita asked.

"No. Are you sure?"

"Phillip told me so tonight."

Eric raised an eyebrow. "There are a lot of changes in the wind."

She brought him his coffee and poured for both of them. Then she sat with him again. "How long will you be gone in the East?"

"The tour will take about two months," he said. "And there's the journey there and back. Say close to ten weeks."

"I'll miss you," she said, smiling at him dreamily.

He leaned forward and kissed her. "I'll phone you every day."

They made love before he left at dawn. Two days later Eric left for New York on the publicity tour, and Nita was seated in Lew Meyers' office with Richard Wright, who was to act as her agent.

Lew Meyers glared at Nita and Richard across his desk. "You're trying to hold me up," he said angrily. "The money is too big. I can still keep Nita under her original contract."

Richard proved there was nothing weak about him in a business deal. He smiled suavely and shook his head. "You would be making a mistake, Mr. Meyers. Nita's original contract stipulates explicitly that it is only for bit roles and minor supporting parts. In the event that she stars, as you wish her to do now, the contract must be renegotiated."

Lew Meyers sat back in his chair and clasped his hands on his pot belly. "You've read all the fine print, young man."

"Whenever I do anything, I try to do it right," Richard said, his smile revealing pure white teeth in sharp contrast to his tanned face.

Nita spoke up. "I think the salary is fair, in view of what Master is paying Barbara Lamont and others."

The little film magnate sighed. "All right. Your terms, but I retain control of Nita's roles and an option on her services for the next six years."

Richard turned to her. "What do you say?"

"I'll go along with that," she said. "I trust Mr. Meyers when it comes to selecting stories and I've enjoyed working at Master."

"Then we'll sign," Richard Wright said.

When she and Richard had drinks together at the Beverly Wiltshire afterwards, he told her across the table, "You're going straight to the top and I'm going with you."

"I hope you're right."

"I am," he said confidently. "And there's no need to go on living in a cottage at Gardenia Court. You can buy yourself a real home in Beverly Hills and have it ready for Eric when he gets back. He won't be living with Barbara again."

"You think I dare go ahead and spend that kind of money?"

He nodded. "Your contract will cover whatever you spend."

"I think I'll stay on at Gardenia Court for a while," Nita said. "When Eric calls I'll mention the possibility of buying a house and see what he'd prefer."

Richard laughed. "I know Eric. He'll end up putting the choice right back on your shoulders."

"At least I'll discuss it with him," she said. "And I'll tell him what an excellent manager you've turned out to be."

"I'd like that," Richard said.

Eric called two or three times a week. "Enslaved" was going well and the public had received him with tremendous adulation. Nita told him about her new contract and he was jubilant. She also mentioned buying a house and he seemed to think that would be a good idea.

"Why not a place with a view of the ocean?" he asked.

"You'd like that?"

"Yes."

"I'll see what I can find," she said. "I haven't too much time now. I'm on the set of 'Bondage' from early morning to late afternoon, then when I return home I'm too tired for house hunting."

192

"Wait until I come back," he suggested. "I'll help you."

"I think that would be best," she agreed.

"I'm giving the story of Barbara's and my separation to the press on Monday next," Eric added.

"Does Barbara know?"

"Yes," Eric said. "Lew Meyers called her in and told her after I left. I love you, my darling! You've reshaped my life and I can't wait to begin the future with you!"

Nita was deliriously happy. Not only had she found a man who needed and appreciated her love, she was looked on as the brightest new star of Celluloid Town, and she had made new friends in Jack Steel, her new leading man, and his wife, Joyce. Jack Steel had been active in westerns until Lew Meyers had seen his potential and groomed him for society leading man parts. Joyce, his young red-haired wife, was almost a double for Clara Bow in looks and was just as much a playgirl.

The two had a fine home on Malibu Beach and they urged Nita to buy a house near them. She promised she would consider it as soon as Eric returned. The two held many parties which Nita attended whenever her strict work schedule would allow.

She returned home from the studio one night to find a taxi waiting outside her door. When she stepped out of her car a young woman got out of the car and came to greet her. It took her a moment to recognize the thin, shabby girl as Thelma Stone. Her face was pale and huge, sad eyes dominated her lovely face.

Nita embraced her and then said, "You've been ill!"

"Yes," Thelma said nervously. "Back East."

"You must stay with me for a few days," Nita said. "Send the taxi away."

"I can't," Thelma said in near panic. "Not now.

I can come back tomorrow. Right now I have to go back to my hotel. But I needed to see you first."

Nita was puzzled by the girl's nervous behavior and her shabby clothes. She said, "At least come inside for a moment. I have so many things to tell you."

She unlocked the door and they went inside. Thelma made no move to sit down but stood by the door in the same anxious manner.

Nita said, "What is wrong?"

"I need money! Cash! Right away! Please let me have two hundred dollars!" Thelma begged her.

She was shocked. "What do you need it for?"

"I can't tell you!" Thelma's voice broke on a sob.

Nita hesitated. "I may have that much here. I don't know. But I'll surely not let you leave here in this state without knowing what's wrong."

Thelma closed her eyes in despair and turned her back on her. "I'm hooked," she said in a choked voice.

"Hooked?"

"On heroin," the girl went on. "Alma Rubens and I have been shooting up together in New York. She went South and I ran out of money and work and came back here."

"Oh, no!" Nita cried, horrified.

Thelma turned to her, the once lovely face pathetically faded and thin. "It began with Wally Reid. I thought when I went East I'd break the habit. Then Alma came along and I mixed with her gang and soon I was hooked worse than ever."

"How could you do this to yourself?" Nita reproached her.

"I'm going to beat the habit," the girl protested. "I only need enough to pay my dealer and get a last fix! I swear I'll quit tomorrow!"

Nita stared at her. "I don't know what to say!"

"I can't wait," Thelma sobbed. She lifted the sleeve of her dress and revealed her bare, pitted arm, scarred hypodermic needles. "If I don't get a fix I'll go mad! I'll kill myself!"

Nita considered and said, "I'll give you the money on one condition only. That tomorrow you'll put yourself in the hands of a doctor."

"I will! I will!" the girl promised.

"A doctor of my choice," she insisted. "And that you go along with whatever treatment he suggests."

"Give me the money! I'll agree to anything!"

Nita was sick at the sight of the girl begging. She went to her room and found the money, then came back with the bills in her hand. Before she passed the money over, she said, "I have to know where you're staying."

"The Palm Court," Thelma said, her eyes on the bills. "Room 406."

Nita gave her the money. "I'll come to you with a doctor tomorrow. I'm working but I'll get off somehow!"

"Thank you, Nita!" The other girl said, tears in her eyes. "You look so well! I knew I could depend on you!" And she hurried out to the waiting taxi and was driven away.

It was the first time Nita had been brought face to face with the terrifying damage caused by drugs. She had heard stories but she had never seen anyone so ravaged as poor Thelma.

She searched the phone book and found Dr. Phillip Watters' private number. She tried it several times but received no reply.

Around eight o'clock she tried his number again and this time she reached him, "Phillip! I must talk to you!" she said urgently.

"I'll be there at once," he promised.

The very fact of his coming to see her and sharing the burden of her knowledge made Nita relax a little. She had a difficult day of filming ahead and the camera magnified every weary line in one's face. She lay down but could not sleep. Then the doorbell rang and it was Phillip.

She let him in and told him the story, ending with, "I must help her."

Phillip had listened gravely and now he said, "I can fully understand your being upset. But it's doubtful at this stage if anything can be done for the girl."

"You can't mean that!"

"I'm afraid it's all too true. From your description I'd say her health is probably already ruined. It is just a matter of how long it takes for her to die. People like her also lack the will to accept treatment. She'd have to be placed in a padded cell as Wally Reid was. And that means the risk of death during withdrawal."

"She must be helped!" Nita persisted.

"I'll do what I can for her," he said.

"I want to be with you, to persuade her to take treatment," Nita said. "I'll call the studio and say I'm ill."

"Wait!" Phillip objected. "You mustn't do that."

"Why not?"

"You're at a critical point in your career. You can't afford a set-back."

"It would only mean a few hours."

"I'm not thinking of that," Phillip told her. "I'm worrying that something might happen. Drug addicts are notoriously unstable. You might find yourself involved in a scandal which would cause bad publicity."

She eyed him in bewilderment. "Thelma is my friend! I can't desert her."

"I don't ask you to desert her," he said. "I say

leave it in my hands. As a doctor, I'm not taking the same chances as you. The newspapers have only a marginal interest in me, especially now that Sally is divorcing me. You'd better remain in the background and let me carry out your wishes."

"You honestly think that is best?"

"I do."

She sighed. "Very well. I want you to see her and send her to some good private hospital for treatment. I'll pay the bills."

"The one in the hills that Wally Reid went to is the best," he said.

"Then take her there," she said. "It's fitting! She told me he was the one who started her on drugs."

Phillip was frowning. He said, "I don't think I should wait until tomorrow. In cases like these time is vital."

"You think you ought to go to her now?"

"Yes," he said. "Let me make a phone call first."

She waited as he looked up the number of the hospital and dialled. He managed to get permission to take Thelma there at once.

He came back from the phone and said, "They'll take her. It'll be costly."

"I don't mind," she said.

"Where will I find her?"

"The Palm Court Hotel."

"That's a Skid Row place," he said grimly.

"I know," Nita agreed. "She said she was in room 406."

"Which may or may not be the truth," he warned her. "Drug addicts learn to lie and steal along with a lot of other nasty things."

Her eyes widened. "You mean she may not be there at all?"

"There's that chance."

"Can't I go along?" she pleaded.

"No. You have too much to lose," he said. "I'll call you as soon as I have word."

She followed him to the door and said, "Thank you, Phillip."

"It's all right," he said, and kissed her gently on the cheek. "Just don't upset yourself anymore."

His advice was good but Nita was unable to benefit by it. She had visions of Thelma, hiding from everyone, living desperately from day to day for the fix which now made her miserable existence possible, frantic to obtain the money she must have to pay the vicious ones supplying her with drugs. Nita could only hope that Phillip would reach her in time.

At last the phone rang. It was Phillip and he was clearly tense. He said, "I can only speak to you for a minute."

"How is she?"

"Dead."

"No!"

"I found her in her room. She'd taken an overdose. I had the desk clerk call the police. They're here now."

"What will happen?"

"Nothing much as long as you're not linked to it. She wasn't a big name or even working in movies now."

"How did you explain being there?"

"I said I was an old friend and I came to try and help her out," he said. "So far they've believed the story."

"Thank you, Phillip!"

"I'll see you later," he promised.

"The funeral arrangements. Do something about them," she pleaded.

"Something will be managed," he said. "If she

has no close relatives I'll ask to be given the body for burial.''

Thelma Stone had a sister in Ohio, but she could neither afford to take care of the burial nor come to her sister's funeral. Dr. Phillip Watters made arrangements for a simple funeral, which was attended only by Nita and himself.

Nita tried to force the tragedy from her mind by working harder than ever. The filming of ''Bondage'' was almost at an end and some of the scenes presented difficulties and had to be done over many times. Nita did not complain about the long hours or the retakes.

But Jack Steel did, and he insisted she join him and his wife at their Malibu place for the weekend. ''You can rest as much as you like,'' he promised her.

''You know how it will be!'' she protested. ''Drinking and doing the Charleston all night! I've been there before!''

''This week it will be different,'' he assured her. ''And we're having a guest I want you to meet. His name is Tommy Gallegher and he's everyone's idea of a handsome Irishman.''

She smiled. ''I wouldn't want Eric to hear about my meeting him.''

''Don't worry about that. Tommy is too busy to bother with females. He's the biggest bootleg operator on the Pacific Coast.''

''A rum-runner?'' she said.

''Yes,'' Jack Steel said, amused. ''He's the darling of all the best people and you're bound to like him.''

''I don't know,'' she said, thinking she might need protection. So she added, ''If I come, can I bring an escort?''

''Anyone you like,'' Jack said generously.

Nita asked Phillip to take her and he agreed, so on

199

Friday evening they arrived at the huge white mansion on the seashore. They were greeted by the Steels. Mary Miles Minter, Mabel Normand and William Desmond Taylor were among the guests, and Nita renewed her acquaintance with them.

William Desmond Taylor eyed Nita in friendly fashion and said, "Your face is so lovely I'm haunted by it. I wish I could direct you in a film."

"You'll have to talk to Lew Meyers," she warned him.

"I know," Taylor said. "And he's a tyrant."

"Don't you and he get along?"

"No," the famous director said. "He's offered me films but his offer has always been too small."

"One day, perhaps," she said.

He moved on to the next cluster of people. All at once in the doorway of the big room there appeared the magnificent figure of a man, broad-shouldered, large of frame and dressed in the best a London tailor could provide. He had curly hair of light brown and at some point in his career his nose had been broken, which gave him the look of a pirate. Nita was sure he was Tommy Gallegher, of whom Jack Steel had spoken.

Jack greeted the newcomer and brought him straight over to Nita. He said, "This is Tommy Gallegher whom I told you about."

The Irishman towered over her, his craggy face alight. He said, "Would you be interested to know I've had a likeness of you pinned up in my cabin for more than a year?"

Chapter Ten

"I'm very flattered," Nita said, amused by the intensity of the big Irishman.

"More than that," Tommy Gallegher declared, "I made up my mind I had to meet you. And now I have."

She laughed. "I wish I had more fans like you!"

The big man stared at her. "I don't want to be a fan!" he shouted. "I want to be your man!" And he kissed her.

This left her speechless and an embarrassed Jack Steele took the bootlegger by the arm and said, "Before you completely commit yourself, Tommy, come meet the rest of our guests."

"I'll be back," the Irishman promised her over his shoulder.

Phillip, who had been standing in the background, now came up to her to ask, "How well do you know that man?"

"I've never met him before," Nita confessed.

"He seemed a little familiar by my standards," the young doctor complained.

She took him by the arm. "He's a crazy Irishman! I know them well enough not to take him seriously. Don't forget I'm Irish myself."

Phillip continued to be worried. "I've heard stories about him," he said. "He has more money than he knows what to do with and the most successful bootleg operation anywhere. He has his pick of the loveliest Hollywood women and now he's reaching for the stars."

"He'll only get so far with this star," she promised.

"I'm your escort," he said. "I feel responsible."

"It will be all right," she said.

"Not judging by the way he's begun," Phillip said. "I say, make an excuse. Say you're tired and let's leave."

"I can't do that!"

"Why?"

"Jack and Joyce would be hurt. I can't let them down!"

"It's a weird collection of guests anyway," the young doctor said darkly. "I don't like Taylor, Mary Miles Minter seems on the idiotic side and Mabel Normand is getting a very bad reputation."

"I didn't know that."

"There are whispers of orgies at Taylor's place and I hear both Taylor and Normand are taking drugs. You saw what they did to Thelma Stone."

Nita stared across the room where the three actors were talking animatedly to some of the other guests. She said, "They all look so well I can't think it's more than gossip."

Phillip said, "There are times when I think I know the seamy side of this town better than you do."

She talked him out of his gloomy mood. Dinner was served on the patio outside, then as darkness fell the pool was spotlighted and Jack and Joyce invited everyone to swim.

"There are bathing suits in all your rooms," Joyce Steele told her guests gaily.

Within a short time all had changed and were back at the pool. Jack Steel was the first one in, followed by Mabel Normand and Desmond Taylor. Next Tommy Gallegher arrived carrying in his arms a slender young girl who was playing a bit part in "Bondage." Tommy held the girl close to him and then as he reached the pool side, let her down beside him.

As the girl stood laughing with the bootlegger, the others at the pool saw with carying reactions that she wore only a small pair of briefs and her shapely breasts were completely naked. She and Tommy both jumped into the pool and swam together.

Phillip, in bathing trunks, a towel in his hand, stood by Nita at the end of the pool and said, "What sort of a party is this turning out to be?"

"I don't know," she confessed. "Jack will take charge and see it doesn't go too far."

"It's gone too far for decency now," Phillip said.

She gave him a glance. "For someone who's been married to Sally Stark you're easily shocked."

She'd barely said this when Tommy's hand pawed at her ankle from the pool. His wet hair was plastered down on his forehead he grinned boyishly up at her and said, "Come on in! Let's be buddies!"

Nita drew back. "In a minute," she said.

Tommy guffawed and swam back to join the topless bathing beauty, and groped at her making her scream, gasp and submerge. He submerged along with her.

Phillip's face was dark with outrage. "Are you enjoying this?"

"Not much," Nita admitted. "And especially not with you complaining every minute!"

"Do you expect me to stand by and watch Jack Steel let his pet bootlegger maul the women guests?"

"It's hardly come to that!"

"Look!" he declared. And he pointed to the far end

of the pool where the screaming starlet had retreated with Tommy still fondling her breasts.

Nita glanced around desperately to find their host and hostess. Joyce had vanished with William Desmond Taylor. Jack and Mabel Normand were stretched out beside the pool together in their wet bathing suits, and it appeared Jack was showing her how to kiss properly for close-ups.

"We can go inside," she suggested.

Phillip looked grim. "I know what I'm going to do. I'm going upstairs and dress. I'll be ready to leave in ten minutes and if you're not ready to join me I'm leaving alone."

"Phil!" she pleaded.

"I mean it," he said, striding off into the house.

Nita watched after him worriedly, torn between wanting to leave with him and feeling she should remain at the party. If she left with him there might be gossip which would reach Eric and would be unpleasant. If she remained she was sure the party would soon calm down a good deal . . . At least, she hoped so.

The thing which weighed most in her decision to remain was that she didn't want to create a bad situation between herself and her co-star and his wife. The previous times they had entertained her had been wild and drunken but never as abandoned as this! Nita believed and hoped that the wild Irishman would calm down and the rest of the party follow suit.

She stood back from the pool for a few minutes thinking that Phillip might come to her before he left and she might talk him out of going. But as she waited the likelihood of this seemed to vanish.

When Joyce returned to the poolside with William Desmond Taylor on her arm, she announced, "We've been wading in the ocean. We loved it!"

Taylor looked amused. "We saw your doctor friend

driving away, looking very angry. Did you two quarrel?"

"No," she said. "He had leave. A call from a patient. He was sorry to leave."

"Too bad!" Joyce said. "But at least you'll be able to stay."

"Perhaps I should go as well," she said. "I'm rather tired."

Joyce saw Tommy Gallegher and the half-nude girl climbing out of the pool and go away hand in hand together. The hostess shrugged. "I'd be more upset if I didn't know she's been sleeping with him for months."

"She isn't very discreet," Nita said.

"Nor is the charming Mabel, stretched out there with your husband," Taylor said to Joyce. "I'll just go and break up that little love match before it goes further." He went on to join the two.

Joyce turned to Nita. "I'm sorry. I guess things are a little out of hand. We offended the doctor."

"Yes."

"Is there anything I can do?"

"Not now," she said.

Joyce turned her attention to Mabel Normand and her husband who were now sitting up and talking to Taylor. She said, "Mabel is out to take Jack from me. She's not satisfied with having Taylor and a lot of other men."

"Is she that wild?"

"She has been since she began using cocaine," Joyce said significantly. "She's not the same girl at all. They say Taylor started her on drugs."

This confirmed what Phillip Watters had earlier told Nita. She was stunned to discover that his suspicions were true. She said, "How do they get these drugs?"

"It's easy if you have the money," Joyce Steel

assured her. "I have to keep a close eye on Jack. Luckily his weakness seems only to be women. It could be worse!"

They went inside and dressed. Nita felt troubled and lost without her escort. Taylor sat at the piano and he proved to be a clever musician and singer. He seemed to excel at all things.

More drinks were served and everyone gathered around the piano as Taylor sang witty and dirty parodies on a number of popular songs. Mabel Normand sat on the piano bench beside him and howled with laughter whenever he came up with an especially suggestive line.

Jack Steel came to hwere Nita was seated on a large pillow a little distance away from the piano. He sat down on the carpet beside her, his drink in his hand and said, "You don't look as if you're having a good time."

She managed a smile. "I'm doing well enough."

"I think not," Jack said contritely. "Joyce told me about the doctor leaving."

"We'll just forget about it," she suggested.

"I invited the wrong people," he apologized. "I wanted Tommy to be at ease. The only one he insisted I have was you. I ought not to have had Taylor, Mabel and the others. They're a different lot of people."

"So it seems," she said.

"Tommy wants to take us out on his boat," Jack said as he got up to cross the room and refill his glass.

Then Tommy returned to the living room in slacks and a colorful open-necked shirt. The starlet was with him, smirking a little, and wearing a clinging dress with an unusually short skirt. The bootlegger took the girl over to the bar and poured drinks for her and for himself. Then he left her flirting with Jack Steel as he came back to Nita.

He sat down on the carpet beside her as Jack had, smiled at her over his drink and said, "Hello, dream girl!"

She gave him a cool look. "I saw you cavorting with your dream girl in the pool."

Tommy's craggy face showed annoyance. "Trouble with you is, you have two many fairies around you!"

Her eyebrows raised. "What?"

"Come on, now!" the big Irishman said. "People know about you. That you've been sleeping around with that pansy, Eric Gray, and you've taken on his boyfriend, Richard Wright, as your manager. You can't be too fussy!"

Nita at once jumped up and ignoring the singing of Taylor told Tommy in a low, angry voice, "I will not take that from you or anyone!"

She at once dashed out of the room and ran through the doorway in the adjoining room which led to the swimming pool. She dropped into a canvas chair and began to weep.

"I'm sorry." It was Tommy Gallegher, who had followed her out and was standing by her chair.

"Go away!"

"I said I was sorry!"

"You said far too much," she told him.

"How did I know what kind of girl you were?" he asked. "Most of the broads here only want a good time and a good lay. I thought I'd be a nice change for you from those fairies. We'd have a fun weekend and get to know each other."

She stared up at him and saw the puzzled look on his face and heard the desolate note in his voice, and it suddenly occurred to her that he was talking like this because he thought it was the norm. That he actually didn't know any better.

She stood up and faced him. "I was brought up

with ignorant Irish. I happen to be one myself. But I never expected to meet the likes of you.''

He stared at her. Then he said again, ''I'm sorry.''

''You think that makes everything right?'' she asked incredulously.

''I mean it,'' he said. ''I see I was wrong. You're not an easy lay. So I'll have to wait a little to sleep with you.''

''A longer time than you'd ever guess,'' she said, her voice hard.

''Okay! So I blew it!'' the big man with the broken nose said contritely. ''I didn't act right.''

''Act right!'' she echoed in disgusted disbelief.

''So I'm a big ape,'' Tommy Gallegher went on. ''It takes a decent Irish girl to spot it.''

She said, ''At least you now know what I am.''

''So I'll treat you like my sister, Mamie, back in Illinois. Don't you think that even an ape like me has a family, a sister and a mother?''

''I don't dare think of how you must treat them!''

''They manage all right,'' he said grimly. ''And so will you if you forget what happened and let me start over again.''

''I'll be satisfied if you just leave me alone for the rest of the weekend,'' she shot back.

''All right,'' the big man said. ''I'll leave you alone.'' And he went back inside.

Nita remained by the floodlit swimming pool. After a little William Desmond Taylor came out. He said, ''I couldn't have entertained you very well. You walked out in the middle of my act.''

Nita turned to him. ''I had my reasons.''

''Tommy?''

''Yes.''

The director asked, ''What did you say to him?''

"I'm not sure that I remember," Nita replied. "At any rate, he left me."

"Must have been something drastic," Taylor said. "He came back to the living room and spoke to no one. He took a whiskey bottle into a corner with him and he's sitting alone there getting drunk."

Nita said, "It can't be that I hurt his feelings. He has a hide like an elephant."

"I think he's also sensitive in a strange way," Taylor told her. "I take it you rejected him. That hasn't happened in a long while. He's absolute ruler here! He names his price for his booze and gets it! He takes his risks and laughs at them! If he has rivals he has them killed, or does it himself. And women are a sort of commodity which he expects to buy and discard as it pleases him."

"He explained that and I told him my opinion of it," she said. "And of him!"

Taylor smiled at her knowingly. "You're quite a girl, Nita," he said. "I'd have liked to have had you come my way."

She gave him a cool look. "From all I hear you do very well!"

"You have rather special tastes in men, I'm told," he went on easily. "I have some experience in that direction. Perhaps we can still get together."

"Don't count on it," she snapped.

Nita had had enough. In a dark mood she left him and went up to her own room, locking the door. The weekend had turned out to be sheer disaster. It would have been bad enough with only Tommy Gallegher and the girl he'd dragged along, but William Desmond Taylor and his harem completed the chaos. She did not blame Phillip for leaving and she decided that in the morning she would call a taxi and leave on her own.

Eric had promised to call her from New York or Philadelphia. He hadn't been sure where he'd be for the weekend. He had been moving back and forth between the big Eastern cities promoting "Enslaved." Nita had given him the Steels' beach house number but so far there had been no word from him. This also was worrying her. She would be glad when the tour was over and he'd be back in Hollywood.

Richard Wright was supportive, but aside from being astute in business, he gave much of his energy to his life in the underground homosexual world of Hollywood. He was still a mystery to her and not much comfort. It was for this reason she'd invited Phillip with her on the weekend.

She went to bed in a very upset state. Listening to the wash of the waves on the nearby beach, she tried to think things through. It was hard to say which troubled her most—Phillip's leaving in ager, or not hearing from Eric. She realized how much both men meant to her.

It was Eric who needed her most and whom she had come to care for deeply. He had won her heart. There had been a time when she might have married Phillip, but he had chosen to marry Sally Stark, and now that the marriage was breaking up, Nita was no longer interested. She still valued him as a close friend and did not want to lose him.

She went to sleep eventually as she dwelt on the devious ways of the Hollywood film colony, and awakened to the morning sunshine pouring in her windows. When she went down for breakfast only Jack Steel, looking pale and wan, was there.

With a sheepish smile he seated her at the dining room table and said, "I guess everybody knocked themselves out last night."

"So it seems," she agreed, taking her napkin.

"You feeling better?"

"No."

"That's too bad," he said.

"I shouldn't have come," she told him. "We have a busy shooting schedule tomorrow and the rest of the week. I should have conserved my strength by remaining home. I'll pack after breakfast."

"You should stay," he urged her. "Tommy wants to take us all out in his new yacht. They say it's armed like a light cruiser."

She smiled bleakly. "I don't think he'll miss me."

"He drank himself into a stupor last night," Jack said. "It was a job getting him upstairs. It's not often he drinks his own bootleg booze."

"He's badly short on manners," she said.

"I know," Jack agreed as the maid came to serve them. "He was just a kind of gangster before Prohibition elevated him to his present power."

"His new prominence hasn't worked any wonders in him. He's a very rough diamond," was Nita's opinion.

She and Jack continued to talk over the breakfast table and afterwards she went to stand in the sunshine by the pool. He continued to try to persuade her to remain but she was anxious to leave.

"I'm worried about Eric," she said. "He was to call me and he never breaks his promises. Perhaps there is a message waiting for me at home."

She was about to go inside and upstairs to pack when an unexpected visitor came out through the French doors leading to the poolside. The moment Nita saw his grave face she knew he was bringing her bad news.

Richard was wearing a white summer suit and carrying a Panama hat in his hand as he came slowly towards her.

211

She took a faltering step towards him. "What is wrong?" she asked softly.

Richard stood before her a moment. Then in a taut voice he said, "I don't know how to begin."

"What has happened?" Her voice was raised in fear.

"It's Eric," he said.

"Go on!"

"He was returning from Philadelphia in a private plane and it crashed."

Nita stood there stunned, not wanting to understand his words. She said dazedly, "Crashed! Was he hurt badly?"

There was great pain in Richard's eyes. "He's dead," he said in a choked voice. "Eric is dead! It's already in the headlines of the Eastern papers. Lew Meyers located me and broke the news."

Nita made no reply because she had fainted as soon as Richard's words registered in her brain. She felt something cold and wet touching her lips and opened her eyes to see that Jack Steel was offering her a drink.

"This will help," he said tensely.

She obeyed him and as the burning liquid trickled down her throat and awareness returned, she realized that she was lying on one of the poolside couches. With awareness came a crushing sense of sorrow and loss.

Looking up at Richard who was standing beside her, she whispered, "There's no doubt at all? It's not just some dreadful mistake?"

"I'm afraid not," Richard said sadly. "I'm sorry I had to break the news, Nita."

"What about Barbara?" she asked.

"Lew Meyers told her. She'd been expecting an announcement of his divorcing her and Lew claims she was almost pleased to hear that Eric was killed before he could return to you. Lew thinks it best that nothing be released about his intentions now," Richard went on, "So Barbara can play the role of grieving widow to the hilt."

"It will be as honest as anything else she has done," was Nita's bitter comment.

"Poor Eric!" Jack Steel said. And he asked her, "Do you want another drink?"

"Not yet," she said.

Richard sat by her on an adjoining couch and said, "Lew is going to have production on your new film delayed for a week to give you time to recover."

Jack nodded. "That was wise, I didn't think Meyers had that much heart."

"It's partly heart and partly cunning," Richard said. "He's afraid that Nita might collapse on the set and the news hens would sniff out the story of her romance with Eric all over again. He wants the scandal kept to a minimum and he wants Nita hidden away somewhere until after the funeral."

Nita stared unseeing at the sunlight sparkling on the blue ripples of the pool. "Eric and I had so many plans."

Jack Steel said, "There's no question he was in love with you."

Richard Wright's fine-featured face showed chagrin. He said, "The question is, where to take Nita to keep her away from the press?"

"Why not let her remain here?" Jack wanted to know.

"No good!" Richard said. "As soon as they hear that production is halted they'll be out here looking for you."

Jack knelt by her and said urgently, "I think I have the solution, if you'll listen."

Lost in her dismal thoughts, Nita asked bleakly

without paying much attention, "What do you have to suggest?"

"The yacht," he said. "Gallegher's yacht! He wants to take us all out for a cruise. I call it an ideal place for you to rest in privacy."

She said wearily, "You know how I feel about Gallegher."

"He'll behave, I give you my word," Jack said. "He'll be as shocked as the rest of us to hear what happened to Eric."

"He'll probably say it's just one less fairy left in the world!" was her caustic reply.

Richard spoke up impatiently, "You don't have to like him! Jack's offering you a chance to recuperate and get away from Hollywood."

She glanced at the young man and said, "I'll go if you'll come along."

"Give me a couple of hours and I'll be back, ready to leave," Richard promised. "I'll have to let Lew know where you're going to be."

She said, "See that flowers are sent . . ."

"I'll look after everything before I leave," the young man promised.

Nita went up to her room and lay on the bed and sobbed for hours. She couldn't collect her thoughts or make any plans. She knew that for the moment she would have to simply drift along and let others do her thinking for her.

Joyce Steel came up and offered her sympathy as well as the concern of William Desmond Taylor and his women friends. From what Nita gathered they would all be going on the cruise. She wondered if she could stand their company in the close quarters of Gallegher's yacht.

She was dozing fitfully when she heard a knock at her door. When she opened it she saw the big man with the broken nose standing there. His battered Irish face showed a good deal of compassion.

"I'm sorry," he managed awkwardly.

"Thank you," she said.

"I hear you're coming on the boat."

"Yes."

"You'll be safe on board," he promised.

"It's kind of you," she said listlessly, turning her back to him and staring out the window at the beach.

"I owe Lew Meyers a favor," he said, and vanished down the hall.

Richard Wright returned and drove her to the dock in his long, cream convertible. He said little to her on the drive. She could see that he as well was badly shaken by Eric's death.

The yacht was waiting for them. It was larger than Nita had expected, gleaming white, with shining brass and graceful lines. A curt man in a white uniform welcomed them aboard and introduced himself as Captain Navarro. They explained that the others were on their way.

"Let me show you to your cabin, Miss Nolan," the Captain requested. Followed by a sailor who carried her bags, he led her below and down a long corridor which was extremely narrow to a small but elegant cabin with a porthole looking out on the ocean.

"I'll be most comfortable here," she said as the sailor put her bags down.

"We'll talk later," Richard Wright said. He left with the Captain and the steward to be shown to his own quarters.

Nita remained in her cabin. Through the open porthole she heard cars arrive and the voices of the others as they boarded the craft. Tommy Gallegher's rough-edged voice was louder than any of the others as he barked out order.

She remained in her tiny cabin, unable to face the others yet. The yacht put out to sea and she had her evening meal brought down to her. Jack Steel came to see how she was but staye donly a short time.

Then Richard Wright came to sit and talk with her for a little. He said, "You'll have to get over this. Maybe it was best, after all."

"How can you say that?" she demanded in rage.

He shrugged. "Suppose Eric had failed you as a husband."

"He wouldn't have!"

"It would have been all right at first," the man across from her said smoothly. "But be realistic. He had strong ties among the underground community in Hollywood. I think he would sooner or later have been drawn back."

"Like you?"

Richard stated, "I've never left it."

"He was also your lover."

"Yes."

"Would you have tried to take him away from me?"

"I don't know," the young man said. "I'm your agent because Eric wanted it. And I happen to be fond of you as well."

"Not as Eric was."

"Not as Eric was," he agreed. "But I can supply a lot of things for which you might have looked to him. I can be your escort, your advisor, and I'm already your business manager."

Nita looked up at him. "You should hate me for coming between you."

Richard stood with his back to her as he gazed out the porthole. "I did for a while."

"But that's over?"

Richard turned to her. "Of course! We're partners now. As your agent I must do my best for you."

She stared at him. "You've always been a mystery to me—and to many other people."

"How so?"

"You live well and dress well. How have you managed?"

"I've managed and I will," he told her. "You are my first agency client. I intend to build up a list until I'm making all the money I need."

"That doesn't explain the past or now," she persisted.

"No need for you to worry," he told her. "You're looking better already." And he went back above without answering her question.

The evening wore on and turned into night. The yacht began to sway more as they moved out into rougher waters. As darkness came it brought with it thoughts of death, and of Eric lost in that great black void, lost to her as Marty had been lost to her.

For all the triumph Hollywood had brought her she had paid a bitter price. And she had seen others pay for their faith in the celluloid dream, Thelma Stone among them.

At last she could not stand being alone in the cabin any longer. She made her way along the narrow corridor to the steps leading above and emerged on the fore deck. She walked to the bow and stood clinging to the railing as the yacht nosed forward amid the heavy waves. Its slight heaving made the stars seem to tilt in rhythm to the yacht's movements. She clung to the rail and stared into the darkness ahead.

From aft there came the sounds of revelry in the lounge. Nita knew that this room which served as dining hall and common room was surely the scene of another drunken orgy, and prayed that she would not be bothered by any of them while she remained out there alone with her sorrow.

All at once she was aware of someone coming up behind her. She turned and saw that it was Tommy Gallegher. The big man was casually dressed in trousers and shirt which seemed to be what he usually wore. He came and stood beside her. There was liquor on his breath but he was not drunk.

He said, "You don't want to join the others?"

"No."

"You're missing something," he said. "Your friend, Richard, is making a play for William Desmond Taylor. Mabel Normand is furious!"

"I'd rather not hear about it," she said.

"Sure." He was silent for a moment. Then he said, "I know what it's like."

She glanced at him. "What?"

"Death," he said. "Maybe I'm the big ape you think. But I've looked into the face of death more than once."

"Have you?" she said, trying to be sarcastic but failing.

"My brother died on this ship."

This caught her attention. She stared at him. "How?"

"Shot down," the big man said in a casual tone. "This is no pleasure yacht. It's a rum-runner!"

"You'd never think it!"

"We're on our way now to pick up a load," he assured her. "When we take on the cargo we'll sail back to port."

"And your brother was shot down defending the ship from the coast patrol?"

"From hijackers," Gallegher said. "They're all along the coast. Wolf ships looking for easy marks. They've never found me an easy mark!"

"I'm sure they haven't," she said.

"My brother was up above, fighting off a pirate

218

trying to board us. A stray shot got him before the pirate retreated under our fire. There are cannon hidden along the deck, ready to use. I left my place down here and went up to him. He was bleeding bad. He looked up at me and smiled and then he coughed up some blood and he died. Died with me holding him!''

She was studying him. ''You can't forget it, can you?''

''I'm a stupid Irishman. Why should I feel anything?''

''I'm sorry,'' she said. ''But you gave me that impression yourself.''

''So I'm no gentlemen,'' he said. ''And I play rough. I have no time to play games like your Hollywood friends. I've got my own date.''

''Your own date?''

''With death!'' he said almost angrily. ''Death that frightens you so much! I'm overdue now. One night I'll get it and you know what?''

''Go on,'' she said.

''It'll just be another ape out of the way. No one will care. Another gang will take over this boat and my load of booze!''

''You don't really believe that?''

''Maybe my mother will shed a tear, and my sister, Mamie,'' he said. ''But there's money put by for them. They'll say a mass and forget me. And so they should.''

She shook her head. ''Your Irish gloom helps me, oddly enough.''

The big man put an arm around her and said earnestly, ''We don't look alike and we don't talk alike. But we're the same sort of mad Micks! If we'd met somewhere else we'd have got along better.''

The warmth and shelter of his arms made her press against him and sob, ''What has happened to me?''

"You're lost in the damned Hollywood bog!" he said with fury. "And so am I, in my own way!"

"What will happen to us?" she moaned.

"We'll go our way and we'll do what we mean to do and in the end we'll maybe be lost like the others. But ill-matched as we are, we speak the same brogue!"

She looked up into his rough hewn face in wonder. She had not expected this understanding from Tommy. But she knew he spoke the truth and he was the only one on board who could help her in her grief.

Phillip had been shocked by the Irishman and had deserted her. But Tommy Gallegher satisfied an inner need in her at this awful time. It was as if the folk back in Lynn were reaching out and offering their clumsy sympathies and joining her in her lone wake.

Tommy held her close and told her, "If I hadn't spoiled it all I could have told you I loved you. And you might have seen something besides the ape in me!"

"You're near, I need you," she said. "Don't talk!"

The big Irishman let his lips caress hers, and all at once there was a passionate explosion between them. He held her tightly to him and she responded, clinging to him as he lifted her in his arms and carried her down to her cabin.

Nita was nude and ready as soon as he was, and when he pressed his great, manly body to hers she lost herself in the comfort of his embrace. He caressed her gently and murmured low words she did not hear or even care about. Their union was as rewarding and joyous as her grief and despair had been a short while ago.

Their love making went on until they were both exhausted. Then they lay naked and breathing heavily and let the ecstasy they had known withdraw slowly, leaving them facing reality again.

She stared up at the cabin ceiling and in a dull voice said, "You wanted. Now you've had me."

Tommy leaned on his elbow and gazed down at her. "It was no conquest! I wanted to give you something! Irish comfort, if you like. It's the only sort most of my people ever knew!"

Nita smiled up at him gently. "Irish comfort! I like that! Is that what you really wanted to do? Help me?"

"God strike me if I've lied!"

She reached up and stroked his cheek. "I believe you. And I thank you."

"I've served me purpose, I'll be moving on," he said almost gruffly, and quickly dressed.

She watched him from her tiny bed. "I think I know you better now, Tommy Gallegher," she said.

He stood over her, fully clothed. His face stern, he said, "You need not fear there will be any word of this said. What happened was between us alone."

"The Irish in exile," she said. "Thank you."

He looked at her for a long moment, then turned and made his way out. She pulled the bedclothes up over her naked body and closed her eyes. She knew now that she could manage. She would go on.

Her love making with Tommy had not dissolved the bond between herself and her lost love, Eric. In a way it had been a celebration of life in the face of death. And it had given her the strength she needed. Two of the lost Irish had reached out to comfort one another in the darkness of the night.

Chapter Eleven

Next morning Nita came up on deck for a stroll after breakfast and was almost immediately greeted by a dapper William Desmond Taylor in blue blazer and white flannels. He studied her with a quizzical smile.

"You look much better already," he said. "The voyage seems to be doing you good."

"I feel better," she said, wondering if Taylor guessed that Gallegher had visited her cabin.

"We saw little of you last night."

"I preferred to keep to myself," she said.

His eyes held a taunting gleam. "It seems to have agreed with you."

Her urge was to get away from the slim, older man but he had managed to position himself between her and the only route of escape along the narrow deck.

To change the subject, she asked, "Have you any idea where we are bound?"

"Only Gallegher knows that," Taylor said. "And he won't tell us. But I'd judge we are at least twenty miles offshore."

"I could be a thousand since you can see no sign of land," she said, gazing out across the water.

"I imagine he has a rendezvous with some craft

loaded with liquor," Taylor said. "Then he'll head back to Los Angeles."

Richard Wright joined them. "Good to see youa round again," he said to Nita.

"I'm in a better frame of mind," she said.

Taylor eyed them with grim amusement. "I know you two have private matters to discuss so I won't remain to eavesdrop." With that he walked on to the bow of the ship where Mabel Normand, Mary Miles Minter and Tommy's starlet were all stretched out sunning in deck chairs.

Nita looked after the director. "I don't like him! He's a poisonous type."

"Sly and clever," Richard Wright said. "Not a good person to do business with."

"I'd imagine not," she said angrily. "I can't think why someone as bright as Mabel Normand lets him rule her so."

"She's infatuated with him, my dear," Richard said in his extravagant fashion.

"Have you heard any further word about Eric?" she asked.

"I have a report from the wireless operator. He picked up some news from the press agency. Eric's body is being returned to Los Angeles for a public funeral on Saturday. The casket will be closed and Barbara is arranging a memorial service. The chief speaker will be Thomas Meighan."

"That's a good choice," she said. "They always got along well."

"The papers must be full of the tragedy. They expect a great crowd at the funeral."

Nita stared out at the ocean. "I'm glad I won't be there. Eric and I had great happiness together. Now it's over. One has to accept that."

Richard studied her in wonder. "You've changed

223

a great deal since yesterday. You've found your strength again.''

She turned to him and nodded wordlessly.

''And be sure Lew Meyers will want to push you. Eric's death will make the Von Eltz film all the bigger! And you played opposite him in it, so it will help your career.''

''Do you think this will establish me as a star?''

''It's bound to,'' Richard said. ''And when option time comes around, I'll be able to get you much more money.''

''Just be careful of the type of films Meyers wants me to do,'' she said. ''The wrong behicles could harm me.''

''I'll be careful,'' Richard promised.

Later she met Tommy Gallegher and the starlet on deck. The starlet was wearing the tiniest bathing suit possible and Tommy was paying his usual attentions to her. As they passed Nita, he gave her a brief, meaningful look and then returned to the pert redhead on his arm.

As they sailed on she became familiar with Gallegher's way of managing things. He paid no attention to her at all and when he wasn't involved with the starlet, spent his time chatting casually with the other women or Taylor. He was determined that no one would guess that for a brief moment they had been lovers.

By the end of the fifth day Nita was beginning to be weary of the confinement of the sleek yacht. And then just at dusk the excitement began.

The lights of a tramp steamer showed on the horizon. Tommy Gallegher alerted his crew and they lined up on deck, waiting.

He ordered his guests, ''I ask you to keep out of the way until our business is finished.''

"Not very hospitable!" Mabel Normand said with disdain as he walked away.

Taylor gave her a dark look. "You talk too much, Mabel. It is going to get you in trouble one day."

"And I've plenty to tell," she snapped back. But she joined the others on the side of the yacht away from Gallegher and his crew.

As the tramp steamer came close Richard Wright smiled at Nita and drawled, "This is where we take on merchandise."

"You think so?"

"Sure," he said. "That's how it's done. The steamer probably supplies a half-dozen operators like Gallegher and then goes back for further supplies. This one probably came down the coast from Canada."

The tramp blew its horn and pulled close to the yacht. Gallegher ordered two large lifeboats to be lowered to make their way across to the steamship. The boats were manned and when they reached the side of the tramp they were loaded with cases of bootleg whiskey.

"A fortune in that cargo," Taylor said, a greedy look on his thin face as the cases of whiskey were brought back and lifted up into the ship. Waiting crewmen stowed them below at once.

Nita could not help but be thrilled as she watched the illegal operation. She knew that both ships were in peril from the coast guard and from the pirates who preyed on the bootleg ships to hijack their cargoes. Tommy Gallegher shouted out commands and the men obeyed. He was a figure of strength as the operation continued long after dark. Torches were set out on the steamship and on the yacht to make the work easier.

"Come on, men! We're taking too long!" Tommy shouted as the returning boats lagged.

"The oars are getting heavy, boss," one of the men

panted as he carried up another case and heaved it onto the deck.

"Then let me take a hand!" The big man exclaimed. And he went down to the first boat and replaced one of the men.

Nita made no comment but she marvelled at Gallegher's great strength and determination. He kept up a pace that even the youngest among his crew found it hard to match.

"You still think he's an ape?" It was Jack Steel at her elbow.

She turned to the actor, "He's many things. But one can't deny he has energy and courage."

"Not many of his sort around," Jack said, watching grimly.

Nita began to wonder where all the cases were being stored, when the operation suddenly ended. There were shouts from the steamship and answering cries from the crew of the yacht. Then the big tramp steamer sailed off into the night and soon her lights disappeared from view.

Once again Gallegher's guests were allowed the freedom of the ship. He was now below, working feverishly at storing the cases of whiskey. He came up once and stood perspiring in the light of the torches. Nita watched him from the shadows and saw him return below to the gurelling task.

There was a party that night. Both crew and passengers celebrated, the crew in their own quarters and the passengers in the lounge. Nita joined the group for a little while but as the night went on everyone became more drunken and she was anxious to escape.

Richard, who'd been drinking less than the others, came to her rescue, saying, "Would you like to leave?"

"Please," she agreed, rising.

"Let me escort you to your cabin then," he said.

He walked with her along the deck and down to her cabin. At the door he gave her a goodnight peck on the cheek, telling her, "We should make port by tomorrow night."

"That soon?"

"It's been a week. Gallegher won't dally now that he is loaded with booze. He'll want to be rid of it."

"I'm sure that's true," she agreed.

She said goodnight and went into her cabin. When she turned on the light, she found William Desmond Taylor standing there in dressing gown and pajamas. He smiled at her in his sly way.

"It struck me you might be lonely," he said.

She was shocked and frightened. "How dare you come in here?"

The older man's thin face continued to show a smile. He said, "You don't have to pretend with me. You're not all that virtuous. You like a man now and then."

"Get out!" she said, opening the door.

"I'll tell them you lured me here and then changed your mind," he warned her.

"You wouldn't!"

"Try me!"

"Please go," she begged him. "I'm in no mood for this sort of thing!"

The director came towards her and reaching out for her said, "Funny, it happens that I am."

But just as he reached for her something entirely unexpected happened. The yacht gave a dreadful lurch and seemed suddenly to spin around. Both she and Taylor lost their balance and fell to the floor of the cabin. Now the engines were roaring at full speed and the ship had changed direction.

Taylor stumbled across to the porthole and looked

227

out. Then he cried, "Someone is bearing down on us!" He ran out the door.

Nita followed him along the corridor and up the stairway to the deck. Most of the others were already there, as well as Gallegher and some of his crew.

Coming close to them was a yacht similar to the one they were on. The lights from Gallegher's yacht were directed at the other craft, keeping it spotlighted against the night.. At the same time the other yacht's lights were flooding Gallegher's.

A man appeared on the deck of the other craft and using a megaphone, called out, "Stand by for boarding!"

"Go to hell!" Gallegher called to him, shaking a fist.

The two boats raced on, Gallegher's in an effort to escape and the other ship following it closely. The man with the megaphone shouted, "Stop or we'll open fire!"

"Open fire and you'll get more of the same yourself!" Tommy Gallegher cried defiantly, his fist in the air.

The other yacht moved closer and Nita could see the machine guns on its deck, the operators crouched over them. At a given signal the machine guns rattled out their deadly fire.

"Down on the deck!" Gallegher cried in warning for them to follow his example.

The yacht opened fire on the pursuing craft and now loud clatters of machine gun fire roared in the night. Nita and the others remained pressed to the deck as the exchange between the two craft went on.

Suddenly there was a bright flash from the other craft and a direct strike on the railing above. Part of the cabin was splintered and smoking.

"Shells!" Tommy Gallegher roared. "They're really asking for it, boys!"

Jadck Steel crouched down on the deck with Nita and in a quavering voice said, "I hope we make it to shore alive!"

There was another blast and now the damage was lower and near the bow of the sleek yacht. The smoke and acrid powder smell filled Nita's lungs and blinded her. The other passengers were coughing and crying out in fear.

Nita heard Gallegher give a wild shout and she looked up to see him on the upper deck, preparing something in his hand. He hurled it across to the other yacht as it made an attempt to come up broadside to his yacht.

"Drive her ahead like hell!" The big man shouted.

The yacht spurted forward and at the same instant there was a huge explosion on the other craft. Only then did Nita realize that Gallegher had thrown a powerful high explosive onto the deck of the hijacker.

The black night was filled with an angry glow and clouds of gray smoke as a second explosion rocked the other craft. By this time they were a good distance away and it seemed clear the hijacker was doomed to sink.

Nita and the others were struggling to their feet, dirty from smoke and terrified. Gallegher came striding down the steps to their level, his face smeared with black powder dust and perspiration.

"Now you know it's not all drinking and proft!" he said belligerently, then moved away to direct his crew in repairing of the damage.

Nita and Richard stood in the bow gazing back at the distant red glow of the hijacker still ablaze. Richard said, "We'll get no more interference from that quarter."

"I thought they were going to sink us and we'd all be drowned," she said.

"Gallegher was too much for them," he said.

There was no celebration that night. Two of the crew had suffered minor wounds, and Gallegher had vanished with his starlet, presumably for a final night of loving before they docked.

Nita was not bothered again by William Desmond Taylor. The battle at sea seemed to have thrown him off his stride. He kept away from her, not even looking in her direction when they did happen to be in close proximity. For her part, she said nothing about his visit. She knew the voyage was almost at an end and she couldn't wait to return to the seclusion of her cottage.

They docked the following morning. Gallegher did not say goodbye to her. As Nita was getting into the car with Richard she looked back. He was standing on the upper deck of the yacht watching her and he waved. She waved back. It was enough. They understood each other.

Nita rested and read the back newspapers with their many photos of Eric. The sight of his smiling face gazing at her from the front pages made her break into tears once more but she forced them back. She remained a recluse in the cottage. The press did not bother her as the funeral was over and they were now pursuing other stories.

Two days later Nita was called to the huge office of Lew Meyers. The little man actually rose from behind his desk and came forward to greet her warmly. He placed an arm around her and escorted her to a chair.

"You're a smart girl, Nita," he said, pleased. "Taking that cruise was a good move."

"It gave me a chance to collect myself," she said.

He stood behind his desk, noticing her smart gray frock and said, "None of that black nonsense like Barbara! You are worth two of her."

"Eric is gone," she said. "No amount of mourning can bring him back."

The little man pointed a stubby forefinger at her. "So true! Tears will only mar your lovely face, and a sad heart makes for a sad expression. The cameras don't like sad expressions."

"I understand," she said.

"We will resume 'Bondage' tomorrow," Meyers said. "When it's finished I want you to step into a new film right away."

"Without any break?"

"You've had a rest," the little man protested.

"I earned it in a painful way," she said. "It wasn't so much a rest as it was coming to terms with grief."

"I know," Meyers said sadly as he paced back and forth. "But maybe it is just as well. It might not have turned out so good."

"I think we'd have been ideally happy," she said.

"So!" The little man sighed. "Live long enough and you'll be happy again."

"Perhaps," Nita said wryly.

"We need to get a couple of good films starring you out at once," Lew Meyers went. "Work hard until they are done and I'll give you a vacation. I'll send you to New York for a few days."

Nita rose. "I'll do it if Richard agrees and approves of the scripts."

Meyers looked upset. "Do I have to keep on dealing with him?"

"He's my agent."

"And he's one of those pansies," Lew Meyers complained. "You ought to try and get rid of him."

231

"Eric chose him for my agent."

"Eric was his boyfriend," Lew Meyers said with disgust. "*You* ain't sleeping with the guy, are you?"

"No. We are very close, but not in that way."

"So try and get rid of him before your stock shoots higher. He'll try to take all he can from you."

"I have complete confidence in Richard," Nita replied.

"I hope it doesn't cost you too much," the little man told her.

Nita left the producer's office in a depressed state. She wished that Meyers could see her as a human being and not merely as a commodity for him to manipulate. But it was stupid to hope for that. Lew Meyers was one of the original pioneers in the film industry. These men would always be tight-fisted and crass, it was bred in their bones.

She was crossing the parking lot to her car when Phillip Watters drove up. When he saw her he got out of his roadster and came to where she sat behind the wheel of her own vehicle.

"I'm sorry about Eric," he said.

"Thank you," she said, coldly polite.

"I felt like a heel when I read the headlines. I went back to Malibu but you and all that crowd had left on Gallegher's boat."

"It doesn't matter," she said.

"I hope I can see you more often," he said.

She started her engine. "I expect to be very busy. I'm beginning a new film as soon as I complete the one I'm on."

Phillip reproached her, "You can always find time for those you want to see. Like William Desmond Taylor and his crowd. Or Tommy Gallegher!"

"I choose my own company as I like, remember

232

that," she said. And she drove away leaving him frowning after her.

Nita returned to work on "Bondage," which was finished in a record four days. Then she at once moved on to another set to film "Dancing Girl," the story of life in a small vaudeville troupe. She was glad to be doing a movie which would give her a chance to show her talents. She had worked hard to learn to sing and dance and she didn't want to be restricted to only dramatic roles.

Richard Wright wasn't pleased. He told her, "The part is good for you but I don't like the story. It's too late to do anything about it now. Meyers has everything set, including the director and dance director."

At night Nita spent her time studying the script for each new day's production, and each morning she spent an hour on her dance routines. The director was an elderly Austrian who had a bad speech problem. His English was extremely limited and it was hard for him to explain anything to his cast. As a result many of them did as they liked and just walked through their roles.

This angered Nita since the production meant a great deal to her. Then she had an inspiration. She went to Lew Meyers and told him her problem.

He was sympathetic but he explained, "Getting an assistant director won't be easy. The Austrian won't share any credits. And it's impossible to hire a good assistant without giving him credit."

She said, "I think I know someone who could do a fine job and who wouldn't expect or even desire any credit."

"Who have you in mind?" the studio head asked.

"I have a friend who knows Roscoe Arbuckle and he's taking on any kind of work. He's very competent as a director."

The little man looked as if he might burst with indignation. "Fatty Arbuckle!" he exclaimed. "I wouldn't have him inside Master Studios. He's still an untouchable! You should know better!"

"I'm sorry," she said.

"You'll have to get along with the man we have," Lew Meyers said. "I'll get an interpreter on the set. He knows his work. It's only the language problem that's holding him up."

The next day the interpreter was on hand and the tempo of work picked up. A studio orchestra supplied moood music and also the music for the vaudeville numbers. A great many extras had been engaged and one day Nita noticed a figure large, floppy hat which looked familiar to her.

She went over to the woman and was delighted and astonished to see that it was none other than Madame Irma. The elderly singer had taken on a few more pounds but she looked much like her old self.

"Madame Irma!" Nita cried, hugging her. "Why didn't you let me know you were on the set?"

The big woman was pleased. "I know my place," she said. "It's not like the old days. You're a star now."

"I haven't changed a bit," she said. "Nor have you! How long have you been in Hollywood?"

"Almost a year," Madame Irma said.

"You know Marty was killed," Nita told her old friend.

"It was in *Billboard*," the veteran singer said, naming the national theatrical weekly. "Poor lad!"

"And the others?" Nita asked. "What about them?"

Madame Irma chuckled. "Pontiface stopped his drinking and was taken back by the brothers. They allowed him to bring Percy with him and they're now both at a monastery somewhere in Michigan!''

"And Belle?''

"She's singing and dancing in Earl Carroll Revues,'' Madame Irma said. "I expect you'll see her out here one day.''

"And the magician? He was best man when I married Marty.''

"Still playing the small time the last I heard of him,'' the big woman said. "He was never very good.''

"Where is Sherman Kress?''

Madame Irma rolled her eyes Heavenwards. "Up there—I hope. He died during a Saturday night performance in Omaha. That's when the unit broke up and I decided to try my luck here.''

"Poor man!''

"He had his good points,'' the big woman agreed. "It was a heart attack and all over in a few minutes. I was with him at the end.''

"Have you had any real acting parts since you've been here?''

"Not yet. I've been lucky to get extra work,'' Madame Irma said. "There are a lot of people looking for jobs.''

"But you are especially talented,'' Nita insisted. "I'm going to speak to Mr. Meyers about you.''

True to her word, Nita saw Meyers in his office the next day and told him, "Madame Irma is an old friend of mine and has lots of experience and talent. I've seen her work magic with the worst kind of audiences.''

"So what do you want?'' Lew Meyers groaned. "As soon as you're stars, all you people get to be headaches!''

"I'm trying to help you. This woman is great,'' she

said. "I've been talking to the writers on the set and they can use her for a small scene and develop it if we have your permission. When you see her work you'll know what I mean."

He waved her off. "All right! Tell them it's okay! I have troubles enough as it is! Did you know that Barbara Lamont is moving to Paramount?"

She smiled cynically at Meyers. "And you're letting her go because you know she's passed her peak at the box-office."

He chuckled. "Nita, you have too good a head to be an actress! You oughta be my assistant!"

"One more thing," she said. "Until you make a decision about giving Madame Irma a contract for character parts, I'd like to have her used as an extra on all my films."

"I'll see to it," Lew Meyers said. "But don't ask me for the studio. I'm leaving it to my sons!"

Once Nita had established all this she arranged with the writers to build up Madame Irma's scene. Then she sought out the old woman on the set. "I'm sure you'll get a contract for character roles after Lew Meyers sees you," she promised.

Madame Irma shook her head. "I can't believe it!"

"Where are you living?" she asked the veteran actress.

"I have a room downtown. It's not much but I'm not used to any frills," Madame Irma said.

"We must find you a better place," said Nita.

Only a day later, Richard Wright came to Nita with what he declared was the chance of a lifetime.

"There's a Malibu Beach house available, just down the road from where Jack and Joyce Steel are," he said with more excitement than she had ever seen in him. "It's a fine property with a main house and a guest house fifty yeards or so away. The grounds are gorgeous and if we take it right away we can get it at a rock bottom price.''

"Do I need it?'' she wanted to know.

Richard grimaced. "How many stars life in Gardenia Court, darling?''

"Can I afford it?''

"You can,'' he said. "I have it all worked out. And I can help you.''

"How?''

"I'll share the purhcase price. I want to buy the cottage for myself. It will ease the burden on you financially and you don't really need the guest house. The main building will house a dozen guests.''

"You really think I should take it?''

"At the price it is being offered furnished, you can't lose,'' her agent said.

"I'll speak to Lew Meyers about it,'' she said.

Lew Meyers surprised her by approving. "Real estate is always a good investment in Hollywood. This place hasn't grown at all by Eastern standards. Those who get in early will profit. The studio will advance you cash for a down payment if you need it and take the mortgage.''

She shook her head. "That won't be necessary. Richard says I have enough. And he wants to share in the purchase by buying the guest cottage.''

"That's a mistake!'' the producer said sharply.

"What can I do? He found the place.''

Lew Meyers leaned across his desk and said, "He's no good. One day you'll want to get rid of him. You shouldn't tie yourself to him further by having him share a property with you.''

"I'm in the middle of a picture,'' she lamented. "I don't want to be put through a quarrel.''

Meyers sighed. "All right. If you have to go along with him, do this. Include a clause which gives you the right to buy back the property at the price he paid for it plus any improvements at any time you wish.''

"Do you think he'll agree to that?''

"Try him,'' he said.

After some argument, Richard Wright agreed. Nita visited the Spanish style house with its fine furnishings and liked it. By the end of the week the contract was signed. By the middle of the week she had moved in, and Richard had taken over the guest house.

It was then that Nita sought out Madame Irma on the set and told her, "I've just moved to Malibu Beach. I've bought a place there.''

Madame Irma looked pleased. "You deserve it. I've seen how hard you're working here. And you're really good. They all think so.''

"I've hired a housekeeper,'' Nita went on. "And I want you to come and live with me and be my companion in exchange for your accomodation.''

The old woman gasped. "I couldn't do that!''

"Why not?''

"For one thing, I'm not grand enough for Malibu Beach!''

"The young girl you looked after long ago is grand enough for it and so are you. I need you,'' Nita told her.

"You really mean that?''

"I do,'' she said. "And I'm certain in a short while you're going to be a big name out here. I think the part we've created for you in this picture shows you at your best.''

Madame Irma laughed. "I'm playing a broken-down star reduced to playing in small time vaudeville. It's the real me!''

The character woman's moving into the house at Malibu Beach made life much more pleasant for Nita. They drove to work together in the morning and they talked a good deal when they came home. Also the Madame Irma gave Nita diction lessons and advice about her singing, in anticipation that one day the movies would learn to talk.

Nita was especially grateful for the woman's presence since the moment Richard Wright took over the guest house he became much more difficult. He had guests coming and going at the place at all hours of the night, and she knew the cottage was often the scene of orgies in which slender, young males from the extra ranks played prominent roles.

Madame Irma sniffed her displeasure at his actions. "You may have to get rid of him," she warned Nita. "The way he's acting can only lead to trouble."

"I had no idea he'd be so brazen."

"I don't like him at all," the old woman said, confirming what everyone else was telling her.

But Nita was working desperately hard and was in no mood for a legal and personal battle. She knew Richard Wright was doing too well as her agent to give up without making it as hard for her as he could. On the strength of his connection with her he had picked up several other big names as clients. It was his personal life style which she objected to, but he became coldly uncommunicative whenever she tried to broach the subject.

"Dancing Girl" was completed and Lew Meyers moved her to the second, a comedy of marriage in which she was able to get Madame Irma a small role with several good scenes as a society matron. In the middle of the filming of the marriage comedy a private showing was held of the roughly cut version of "Dancing Girl."

Nita, Madame Irma and Richard Wright were all in attendance at the screening. Lew Meyers was there along with all the studio top brass. The reaction to the

239

story was good, Nita's performance was praised, but the big excitement of the evening was Madame Irma. In her several scenes the weary-faced big woman literally stole the show. There was spontaneous applause from all over the crowded screening room.

Lew Meyers came to them after the screening and told Nita, "You were right again, baby." To Madame Irma he added, "Come to my office tomorrow morning at ten. I want to talk to you about a contract."

There were tears in Madame Irma's eyes as she promised, "I'll be there!"

"You know, you could be another Marie Dressler," Lew Meyers informed her before he rejoined his associates.

Richard Wright offered the old woman one of his urbane smiles. "I'd better go with you, darling. We don't want Father Meyers to cheat you."

"I'll take my chances," Madame Irma said at once. "I'm not important enought to need an agent." Despite Richard's protests she was staunch in her decision.

The next morning Nita waited tensely as she went about working on the set with David Torrence and Jack Steel, who was rapidly being regarded as her idea leading man. She tried to keep her mind on her work but she couldn't help wondering how Madame Irma was faring.

It was close to noon during a break while Nita was in her dressing room having coffee when Madame Irma arrived.

Nita jumped up and asked, "Well?"

The old woman chuckled. "I have it. A contract for seven years with options along the way."

"You're wonderful!" Nita said hugging her. "You'll be a star one day."

"Only if pictures start to talk," the actress said. "I'd have more to offer then."

"But your pantomime and comedy timing is excellent," Nita insisted.

Madame Irma said, "The main thing is that now I can pay you for my board and lodging!"

"There's no need!"

"What else have I to do with the money?" Madame Irma wanted to know.

They had coffee together and then the old woman left to shop as she wasn't in the scenes which were being shot that day. Nita felt tremendously happy at having been able to help her friend and went out to begin the afternoon's scenes with more than usual enthusiasm.

The stern David Torrence, playing her father-in-law in the film, was already on the set waiting for her. The elegant old Scotchman gave her one of his sour smiles and said, "I've seldom seen you so glowing."

"I've had a good day," she said.

He raised his eyebrows. "You're probably one of the few women in Hollywood who has."

She stared at him as the crew worked at lighting the scene for the waiting cameramen. "What do you mean?" she asked.

"Another terrible scandal has broken," he said. "And the papers say that a number of famous stars may be involved."

"Tell me about it."

"Someone murdered William Desmond Taylor," David Torrence said, a grim look on his patrician face. "It may be the worst Hollywood scandal since the Arbuckle affair."

Chapter Twelve

Nita gasped. "I knew him!"

"I wouldn't admit it if I were you," the character actor cautioned. "The news is spreading like wildfire. Everyone in the studio is talking about it."

Still shocked, she asked, "Where did it happen?"

"In his house. Someone entered his Westlake place in the night and shot him. A servant found him and sounded the alarm."

"Why would anyone want to kill him?"

The elderly actor gave her a wise look. "I can think of a few jealous husbands who could be guilty. And some jealous women as well. Taylor also was mixed up with drugs and homosexuals."

"He was mysterious and rather unpleasant," she recalled.

"You describe him well," David Torrence said.

The lights were ready and they went on with the scene but Nita had a hard time concentrating. She couldn't forget her meetings with the suave, menacing director, especially the time he had made his way to the cabin of Gallegher's yacht and tried to force her to go to bed with him. She recalled that Phillip Watters had violently disliked Taylor and his crowd, though Richard Wright had been friendly with the slain man.

She finished her scenes for the day and was in her dressing room changing into her street clothes when a distraught Richard Wright arrived.

He burst in, the tension showing on his face, and said, "You've heard about Taylor?"

"Yes," she said, turning to face him.

He removed his hat and sank limply into the dressing room's single easy chair. He said, "There's hell to pay! I can tell you that."

"Do the police know who did it?"

"They don't seem to," he said sourly. "And the reporters are making a sideshow of it."

"I can imagine."

Richard suddenly gave her a penetrating glance. "Did you, by any chance, write him any letters?"

"Never."

"Good. You're one of the lucky ones."

"In what way?"

He explained, "A lot of the women he was involved with sent him incriminating letters. As soon as word reached Mary Miles Minter and Mabel Normand, they were there searching for their letters."

"Did they succeed before the police intervened?" Nita asked.

"Yes, but they were still there when the police and press arrived. Mabel Normand had retrieved some letters and Mary Miles Minter was stumbling around in a stupor."

"How dreadful!" Nita exclaimed.

"You're sure there's nothing to connect you with Taylor?" Richard probed.

"Only that I met him a few times socially. So did you."

He groaned and held his head in his hands. "The weekend at the Steels and then the cruise!" Richard's face was dark with apprehension. "If Lew Meyers

243

gets wind of that he'll fire you from the studio as quick as a wink!''

''That's silly,'' she protested. ''A great many people must have known Taylor.''

''We were on a private party with him, on the yacht of that bootlegger.''

''I'm sure it will be all right,'' she said.

''Don't talk to anyone,'' he warned her.

''I won't.''

He was on his feet, his hat held nervously in his hand. ''Maybe we can bluff things through. But there's no telling what revelations this may lead to.''

''He was with Paramount, wasn't he?''

''Yes. Adolph Zukor sent someone out to get rid of the bootleg booze. The place was loaded with it.''

She said, ''If everyone in Hollywood who had bootleg booze was murdered there wouldn't be anyone left alive in the entire city.''

Richard gave her an angry look. ''This is no laughing matter!''

Nita got to her feet. She said, ''Actually, you knew Taylor better than I did.''

Richard's eyes narrowed. ''Why do you say that?''

''I remember when you saw him at Steel's place, after you brought word of Eric's death. He greeted you like an old friend.''

''You're wrong! I'd never met him before that day!'' her agent protested.

Nita sensed he was lying and she also knew he was most unlikely to admit it. She said, ''It wasn't that long ago!''

''I don't know how you got this silly idea into your head,'' he decalred, his voice high-pitched with anger. ''But I swear you're wrong. Don't tell anyone that story,'' he warned her. ''I promise you I'll deny it if you do. We should be sticking together at a time like this instead of trying to hurt each other.''

''I had no intention of hurting you!''

''Saying a thing like that? You must be joking!''

''I'm sorry. I must have made a mistake.''

''It seems to me you've made a series of mistakes lately,'' he raged. ''One of them being taking that old has-been to live with you!''

''I like Irma and she's company for me,'' Nita said.

''She hates me and you must be aware of that,'' Richard raged.

Nita tried to placate him. ''She's a little strange in some ways. She's used to being on her own.''

''Ever since she's been living with you I've seen a great change in your attitude towards me,'' he ranted on.

''I have a dreadful headache,'' she said, putting her hands to her temples. ''I can't remain in this stuffy dressing room arguing with you any longer!''

He backed down a little saying, ''I simply wanted to warn you that Taylor's name is on everybody's lips.''

''Well, you've done that,'' she said. ''Now I'm going home.''

She left him outside the lot. He told her he was going to stop by the Beverly Wiltshire to see a client and find out any other information he could about the murder. Nita was relieved to be free of him and drove to Malibu as quickly as she could. When she arrived, Madame Irma was waiting for her with a selection of newspapers.

''The *Los Angeles Times* has the most pictures,'' the old woman told her. ''And a diagram of where Taylor was found. He was on his back on the floor as if he were in a trance, with his arms held straight out. A chair had fallen over his legs.''

"It could have been robbery," Nita said, scanning the tabloid which was next on the heap.

"No!" Madame Irma said. "It couldn't have been. He was still wearing that big diamond. And no money was taken either."

Nita was reading another paper. "It says here that the Studio and Mary Miles Minter's mother, Mrs. Charlotte Shelby, were notified before the police. And they didn't let the police know but rushed to the Westlake house and tried to collect any letters or papers which might connect them with Taylor. The police arrived later and caught them in the midst of ransacking the place."

"The Arbuckle scandal is barely settled," Madame Irma sighed, "and now this!"

"He's still waiting for another trial, though it won't do him any good," Nita said. "I tried to get him a temporary job with the studio but Lew Meyers wouldn't hear of it."

"I should think not," the older woman said. "How do you happen to know such a man?"

"He's a friend of Billy Bowers. You'll remember Marty worked with Billy in the old days. When I first came out here Billy was very kind to me. Billy, along with Buster Keaton, have been friendly with Arbuckle."

"It's a strange place, this Hollywood," Madame Irma reflected.

"I haven't heard from Billy in a long while," Nita said. "I must phone him. He always has good adivce."

"You could use some now and you won't get it from Richard Wright," Madame Irma warned her.

Nita went to the phone in the sunken living room and called Billy Bowers. It was Murphy who answered.

She said, "This is Nita Nolan. May I speak with Billy?"

There was a moment's hesitation at the other end of the line and then Murphy said in a surprised tone, "Didn't you hear the news, Miss?"

"What news?"

"Billy collapsed on the set last week. He's been in the hospital ever since."

"What's wrong?"

Murphy said bitterly, "The old trouble. He's been boozing like mad since he lost his chance with Metro."

"Oh, no," she said in dismay.

"It was that and some other things," Murphy said. "I think he missed you when you left."

"I couldn't stay on there, Murphy," she pointed out.

"I understand," he said. "But you know how he is."

"Is he in bad shape?"

"Bad enough to be kept in the hospital. But I think he'll come around all right."

"Let me know if there's any change," she told him.

"I will. Try and get around to see him if you can."

"Depend on it," she promised.

"I'll tell him you called," Murphy said.

She had barely put the phone down when it rang. This time it was Jack Steel, clearly distraught. He said, "You've heard what's happened?"

"I know," she said grimly. "I don't think there's anyone in Hollywood who doesn't."

"The police have just been here asking questions," Jack warned her. "An Inspector Moore. They're questioning everyone, so they'll likely get around to you."

She said, "They know about the party on the yacht?"

"Yes," Jack said. "If any of us are tied to this

thing in the press we'll be finished. You know what Lew Meyers is like."

"I know."

"I'm in debt up to my neck," Jack went on. "I don't know what I'd do if he cancelled my contract. There's a morals clause in it."

Nita said, "We haven't reached that point yet."

"With the police calling, the newspapers may not be far behind," Jack warned her. "Good luck!"

She thanked him and hung up. Then she tried to reach Richard Wright in his bungalow, feeling certain that if the police questioned her they would also question him, since he had also been a member of the party. Besides, contrary to what he had sworn, she was sure he knew Taylor fairly well.

She kept ringing his number with no success. Still holding the phone she asked Irma, "Can you see any lights down at the cottage?"

The old woman went to the windows which overlooked the guest house and peered out. "No lights at all. He can't be home."

Over a light dinner Nita told the character actress how Richard had behaved earlier in the afternoon when he'd visited her in her dressing room, that he'd protested she was wrong when she'd suggested he'd known Taylor before she introduced them.

Madame Irma scowled. "That young man is trouble! Believe me!"

"I'm beginning to," she worried. "Eric didn't realize how unstable Richard is or he wouldn't have suggested I use him as my agent. Now it's difficult to get rid of him."

They were finishing their coffee when a car drove up and the doorbell rang. The housekeeper answered it and showed in a man in a shabby gray suit, a crushed felt hat in his hand, and a grim expression on his lined, thin face.

He introduced himself to Nita, showing his detective's badge. He said in a raspy voice, "I'm Moore. I've been assigned to the Taylor case."

She said, "Do sit down, Inspector Moore."

He shook his head, his sharp eyes on her. "I'd just as soon stand."

"What do you want?"

He said, "I've been told you knew Taylor."

"Very slightly."

The lined face looked bored. "I have sworn statements to the effect that you were a member of a small party at the Steel house and that you went on a week's cruise on the yacht of a well-known bootlegger."

Feeling weak, Nita sat down and said, "None of that has anything to do with Taylor's murder."

"How do you know?"

Her cheeks flushed. "I don't!"

"I'd say it was up to the police to find out," Inspector Moore said dryly.

"Without question," she agreed.

"Did you and Taylor ever have an argument?" he wanted to know.

She shook her head. "No."

"Did you ever visit his house?"

"No."

He gave her a look that suggested he didn't believe her. "A photo of yours was found there, a five by seven glossy print."

"That's a publicity still," she protested. "There are hundreds of them around. He could have picked one up anywhere."

"You didn't give it to him? Write anything on it?"

"No! Never!" she exclaimed.

The Inspector stared at her. "Well, at least you're

right in that. There wasn't anything written on your photo. But there were some sweet things on those of the other women. Now, tell me all that was said between you and Taylor the week you were a member of the party.''

She repeated all she could remember including the story of his coming to her cabin and trying to force himself on her. ''After that he kept away from me,'' she said.

''You showed good taste,'' Inspector Moore declared as he made some notes in a small book. ''From what we've discovered, about half the female population of Hollywood have had affairs with him and it looks as if some jealous woman killed him.''

''Why do you say that?'' Nita asked.

''There's the testimony of a neighbor,'' he told her. ''She heard a loud noise late at night. She thought it might have been a tire blowing, but it was probably the shot. As she looked out into the darkness she saw a figure running down the walk from Taylor's house. It looked like a woman dressed in man's clothing, with a muffler around her chin and a cap pulled down over her eyes. The figure was thin and walked with quick little steps like a woman.''

Madame Irma spoke up for the first time, saying, ''You'll need a lot more evidence than that to convict anyone.''

''That's right,'' Inspector Moore said sourly. Then he asked Nita, ''Do you happen to own a .38 gun?''

''No! Never!''

Ne nodded. ''That'll be all for now. I may have to come back if the department wants any more information.''

''I understand,'' she said.

''Does Richard Wright live here?'' the Inspector asked.

"No."

"We have this address listed for him."

"He owns the guest house on this land," Nita explained.

The detective raised an eyebrow. "You involved with him in some way?"

"He's my agent," she said faintly.

His hard eyes were studying her. "Your agent," he repeated in his rasping voice. "Interesting! I'd like to speak with him."

"He's not home," Madame Irma told the detective, her tone angry. "And I don't understand why you should interrogate this poor child as if she were a criminal!"

"I have a job to do, madam," Inspector Moore said. And he asked Nita, "Is it the house down near the beach?"

"Yes. But I'm sure he's not there."

"I'll check anyway," the Inspector said. "Good night, and thank you."

The two women faced each other after he left. Nita asked Irma, "What do you make of it?"

"I'd call him a terribly rude man!"

"He is investigating a murder. But he can't think I had anything to do with it."

Madame Irma reminded her, "He wants to question Richard also."

"That really doesn't mean much," Nita said. "He'll be questioning everyone who was at the party or on the yacht. Though I doubt if he'll catch up with Tommy Gallegher."

"Who's Gallegher?" the older woman wanted to know.

Nita told her and they sat discussing the entire unfortunate mess. They were still talking when another car arrived and the doorbell rang a second time. Nita

251

answered it herself, thinking it might be Richard back from the Beverly Wiltshire at last.

But it wasn't Richard. It was Phillip Watters. He stood waiting to be invited in, his face shadowed with concern. He said, "Can I talk to you, Nita?"

"If you like," she said. She brought him in and introduced him to Madame Irma and then asked, "What is it?"

He sighed and then asked, "May I speak freely?"

"Madame Irma is my trusted friend," she told him.

He nodded. "All right. You know what happened to Taylor."

"I've been hearing nothing else," she said. "I just had a police inspector here questioning me."

"About the Steel party?" he said.

"Yes."

He paced nervously before them. "I guessed they would be here. What about Wright? Did they question him?"

"They're going to," Nita said. "He wasn't in when they came. He lives in the guest cottage."

Phillip came up to her. "Nita, you've got to rid yourself of that man."

"Why?"

"He's going to be on all the front pages in connection with the Taylor case if he isn't careful!"

"Go on!"

"I have confidential information," he told her. "A friend of mine has been treating Mabel Normand for cocaine addiction and she's not responding. Her friends are desperate. Mack Sennett is trying to sell a feature she's made and no one dares take it knowing the scandal over her head. She has a two thousand dollar a month habit!"

"So drugs are behind all this, too," Nita said.

"Drugs and perversion," Phillip went on. "Taylor

was also on cocaine and so were some of the others. They'd been going to a place where effeminate men and masculine women in kimonos used marijauna, opium and heroin.''

Madame Irma spoke up. "Does Richard Wright have anything to do with this place?''

"He's a co-partner in it, according to what my friend has been able to," Phillip said. "Everyone knows that Richard is queer, and it now seems he's also the most notorious dope peddler in the area. He's been supplying most of the stars who are hooked.''

"So that is where he got his money!'' Nita gasped. "And that's why he denied ever having previously seen Taylor.''

"Without a doubt,'' the young doctor said. "And there's more. The police found a locked closet in Taylor's bungalow with a collection of lingerie belonging to a number of stars, each tagged with initials and a date. Taylor kept them as souvenirs of his various conquests. And there was a nightgown embroidered with the initials M.M.M., which means that Mary Miles Minter will be through as Mary Pickford's virtuous rival on the screen.''

"Is she also on drugs?'' Nita asked.

"Not according to my friend. But she's been foolish enough to let Taylor rule her life.''

"What now?'' she asked.

"The scandal will grow. Each day new facts and new names will be revealed.''

"Do you think Taylor's killer is likely to be found?'' she asked. "The police think it was a woman dressed like a man, if Inspector Moore was truthful.''

Phillip said, "It could well be. The suspicion seems to fall chiefly on Mabel Normand. She's been frantic and they had a quarrel. She has often dressed in men's clothing for a joke at parties. In her drug-crazed state she might have decided to wear that disguise to cover up a murder."

"Then she may be charged and proven guilty."

"I doubt it," Phillip said grimly. "There's too little evidence against her and too many suspects."

Madame Irma agreed. "It would seem most of the film colony wanted to do him in."

Phillip turned to Nita again and said, "Has Richard ever tried to sell dope to you?"

"No. Not yet."

"You're lucky," he said. "Get rid of him. You can't afford to be linked to him."

"I'll try!"

"You must," the young doctor said firmly. "For the sake of your career. I want to prevent your being dragged into the case. Wright is bound to be charged with drug peddling and as he's your agent it is sure to reflect on you."

"I'll do what I can," she said weakly.

Phillip nodded. "It's late. I must go. You'll need your rest if you have to be at the studio in the morning." He said goodnight to Madame Irma and then Nita saw him outside.

On the dark steps she said, "Thank you for taking the trouble to warn me, Phillip."

He looked at her earnestly. "I couldn't do less. I've been half mad with worry about you ever since I heard about Richard."

She looked up at him. "We shouldn't have drifted apart. I ought not to have quarreled with you. You've always been my good friend."

"I want to be more than that," he said, taking her in his arms.

"Please, Phillip," she protested. "This is neither the time nor the place."

"Still, I want you to know how I feel," he said. "I love you. I always have, and I always will!"

With that he drew her close and kissed her tenderly. He held her in his arms for a long few moments and she realized how much she'd missed this kind of unselfish affection. She'd not known such comfort since the night Tommy Gallegher had come to her in her misery at Eric's death.

He let her go and said, "You must phone me if you need any help. And be careful with Wright."

"I will," she promised.

"I'll keep in close touch," he said as he opened his car door to get in and drive away.

Nita and Madame Irma had a drink and talked for a while longer. Then Nita got up and went to the window. At once she turned to the older woman and said, "Richard's back! He must have returned while we were having our drink."

Madame Irma rose and joined her. She said, "I see two cars out there. Someone must have come with him."

"Maybe that's why he didn't stop by," she guessed. "He should have come to keep me informed."

"What are you going to do?"

Nita said, "I'm going over there and face him. I'll tell him I've heard things which I cannot tolerate, that I want him off this property and I want to replace him as my agent."

Madame Irma's faces h owed cynicism. "You think he will listen to you?"

"If he doesn't I'll go to Lew Meyers. He'll help me."

"He might also want to drop you if he thinks you're going to be caught up in a scandal," the older woman reminded her.

"I'll have to take that chance," Nita said.

"Do you want me to go along?"

"No," she said. "You'll only annoy him. I think I can do better alone."

Madame Irma pointed out, "But he isn't alone."

"He can surely get rid of whoever is there," she said.

"If he wants to."

Nita had found her courage again. She knew she was right and she meant to have a showdown with Richard Wright. She said, "I'll soon find out."

Nita walked along the roadway to the guest house in the cool darkness. Lights shone brightly through the window and Richard's cream convertible was parked by the door with a small red roadster behind it. As she reached the house she heard a phonograph playing "Lonesome and Sorry."

She knocked on the door, but there was no answer. She tried the knob. It turned and she stepped into the room. She had barely entered when Richard in slacks and singlet came out of the bedroom. When he saw her his tanned, handsome face was angry.

"Have you forgotten this is my house?" he demanded.

"It won't be for long, Richard," she said quietly. "I'm going to buy it back as the lease allows."

"The hell you are!" he said angrily. "What are you doing pussyfooting in here at this hour?"

She faced him defiantly. "I've come to tell you it's all over, Richard. I know what you are and what you've been doing. The police know as well and they were here tonight looking for you."

"I don't believe it!"

"I know about Mabel Normand and her cocaine habit which you're supplying at thousands of dollars a month! How many others are there besides her and Taylor?"

"You vixen!" he cried and stepping forward, he slapped her hard across the face.

She reeled from the blow and told him, "Madame Irma knows where I am and she's waiting with the phone in her hand to call the police if I don't return immediately."

The threat made him hesitate, then he sneered at her, "You don't dare make a move. You're involved with me and you are bound to suffer if I do."

"Perhaps I'm willing to take that chance," she said. "I want you to see a lawyer tomorrow and dissolve our agency agreement."

"Likely I will!" he said derisively. "I have you exactly where I want. You can't make a move!"

As he finished speaking a younger man with blue eyes and curly blond hair came out of the bedroom, dressed in extremely tight fitting silken black trousers, and a gold lamé jacket. His shirt was open at the neck and he came over to Richard.

"I'm going," the youth said quietly. "I'll see you tomorrow."

Richard did not look at him but kept glaring at Nita. He said, "All right! Get out!"

Nita was suddenly frozen with fear, not by Richard's words or actions, but because of what she had just seen. The blond youth was wearing the gold watch studded with diamonds which she had last seen on William Desmond Taylor's wrist.

The door closed behind the blond boy and a few seconds later she heard his car start and drive off. She gazed at Richard with horror. In a husky voice, she whispered, *"You did it!"*

"What are you talking about?" he demanded, but his tone was unsure.

"The watch!" she cried. "I recognized Taylor's watch. Either you killed Taylor and took it, or the boy

257

was an accomplice and took it from the body while you were doing something else!''

''Shut up!'' Richard screamed. He seized her wrist in a vise-like grip. ''Now listen to me! By tomorrow that watch won't be anywhere it can be found. No one will believe your story. But if you dare to repeat it to a living soul I give you my word I'll kill you!''

''You wouldn't dare!'' she cried.

He intensified the pressure on her wrist. ''I promise you I will. If the police catch on I haven't a chance anyway. I'll at least have the pleasure of taking you with me!''

''*Let me go!*''

''Not before you understand that I *will* go on living here and I *will* continue to be your agent, and you *will* keep that mouth of yours shut!''

Nita began to sob and he released her and hurled her towards the door. She groped for the handle and let herself out then ran all the way back to the house, sobbing.

Madame Irma was waiting anxiously for her. ''What happened?''

Nita sank into a chair and said, ''I can't get anywhere with him. He promises to kill me if I take any action against him.''

''I was afraid of something like that,'' Madame Irma said. ''You should call the police.''

''No,'' she said. ''I must think. Perhaps Mr. Meyers can work it out.''

Madame Irma said, ''While you were out some man phoned you. I told him you'd be back soon. He said he'd call again.''

''Phillip?'' she asked hopefully.

''The doctor? I don't think so,'' the older woman said.

Just then the phone rang again. A thoroughly shaken Nita answered it and a male voice at the other end asked, "Are you all right?"

She recognized the voice and exclaimed, "Tommy! Tommy Gallegher!"

"I knew they might be making it tough for you," he said.

"It's worse than you think," she said with a sob. "Richard Wright is involved!"

"And?"

"He's been selling dope and I think he killed Taylor. He's threatened to kill me if I don't go along with him and keep quiet."

"Are you surprised?" Tommy asked.

"I shouldn't be, but I am."

"Where's your Irish fight?"

She smiled through her tears. "I guess I've lost it."

"Not you," he said. "Don't worry!"

"How can I not?"

"It's easy once you learn," the Irishman said. "We're shipping out at dawn. I want to be away from the police for a little. I promise you, things will work out."

"I hope so," she said wearily. "Good luck, Tommy."

"The same to you, Nita Nolan!" And he hung up.

Nita slept little that night. When she joined Madame Irma early the next morning she found the old woman staring out the window at the cottage.

Madame Irma turned to her and said, "Wright's convertible is gone."

Nita saw this was true. "It's too much to hope that he's run off somewhere."

"Let's pray he has," the older woman said.

They had breakfast and were getting ready to leave for their early studio call when a car drove up. It was Inspector Moore again, wearing the same shabby suit and with the same grim expression on his lined face.

He said, "I'd like your permission to search the guest house, Miss Nolan."

She said, "It's rented by Mr. Wright."

He nodded. "I know. I don't think he'll object. Richard Wright is dead."

Nita couldn't believe what she was hearing. *"Dead?"*

"Yes," the Inspector said in his rasping voice. "His car was found down by the docks. He was shot to death in his car. There was money on the floor and packets of cocaine in several of his pockets. These drug boys play rough, especially when someone like Wright moves into their territory."

"I see," she said in a whisper, and hoped she wouldn't faint. It all fit—Tommy Gallegher's call, the car down at the docks with Richard's body in it. She had no doubt that Tommy or one of his men had lured Richard to the docks and murdered him there. That explained why Tommy had been so cool about it all, why he had assured her that things would "work out."

"On your way to the studio, Miss Nolan?" The Inspector asked, breaking into her reverie.

"Yes," she said in a small voice. "I'm on my way to the studio."

But there was no filming that day. Instead Lew Meyers called Nita into his office for an urgent conference. The little man paced up and down in a trouble state.

"I warned you about that fellow," he said.

"At least now I'm rid of him."

"But he was your agent and he was killed peddling dope," Lew Meyers said. "The papers are coming

260

out with it all today. You'll be tainted with the story.''

She protested, ''But I had nothing to do with the drug thing!''

''I believe you, Nita,'' the little man said sadly. ''But will my stockholders and the Will Hays censor office want you on the screen?''

''I suppose not.''

''We'll try to sell the pictures you've made. We'll finish this one. We may be barred from all the best bookings. We'll take a big loss. The best I can do is put you on suspension after you finish this feature. Then we'll wait and see. If the scandal dies down and your pictures are marketable, we can start again.''

Nita rose slowly from her chair. ''Don't count on it, Mr. Meyers. I'm leaving Hollywood.''

He stared at her. ''Where will you go? Your friends are all here.''

''I have no friends in this town,'' she told him.

The scandal was as bad as Lew Meyers had feared. The press openly questioned whether or not Nita was a ''dope fiend.'' There were pictures of herself and Taylor in the papers, along with photos of Mable Normand and Mary Miles Minter. Both the other young women were banned from the nation's silver screens just as Nita was.

She made arrangements to sell the Malibu house and Madame Irma, who was set to star in a feature of her own, took over the cottage. When Phillip Watters came back again, he remained until Nita consented to marry him. Then he told her he had an immediate opportunity to join the staff of a New York Hospital. Needless to say she agreed to go with him.

It was Nita's final day in Hollywood. That night she and Phillip would be taking the train to New York where they planned to be quietly married. She was packing her bag when she was interrupted by the phone.

It was Murphy on the line. There was a break in his voice as he said, "Billy's dead, Miss Nolan! He died this morning."

"And I didn't see him," she said, tears filling her eyes.

"I was with him last night," Murphy said. "He talked about what he should have done and he said that he should have made you marry him. He thought it night all have worked out if he had."

"I doubt that, Murph," she said. "I won't be at the funeral. I'm leaving Hollywood tonight. I'll send flowers."

"It won't be the same without him," Murphy said.

It seemed oddly appropriate to Nita that Billy should have died at this time. He had played a part in her coming to Hollywood and now again in her leaving. Like Marty and herself and all the others, Billy Bowers had lived in a world of hopes, dreams, and illusions. Their struggles had been ignored in their fierce devotion to make-believe. Theirs was a make-believe world, and Hollywood was the capital city of a make-believe kingdom.

But Nita wanted no more make-believe. She bent to close her suitcase, her eyes still blurred by tears. The last thing she had packed was her old good luck charm, the doll she'd taken with her a few short years ago when she'd run off to join Marty, full of excitement and plans for a glorious future. Once again she was making a new start, setting out on a new adventure. After a moment's hesitation, she took the doll out of the suitcase and set it on the bed. What would the new tenant think of it, she wondered. Would some other star-struck young woman claim the battered toy as a token of luck? Resolutely she closed the suitcase. No time to think about that now. After all, Phillip was waiting. It was time to leave make-believe behind, and join the real world of true love and devotion!

GENTLE TIGRESS
C. O. Lamp

PRICE: $2.25   LB727
CATEGORY: Non-fiction (Original)

The true story of Dorothy Yuen, an American girl
of Swedish-Chinese descent, who becomes the
sweetheart of the Fourteenth Air Force, the Flying Tigers who were stationed in China during
World War II. Dorothy and her family come to
war-torn Shanghai to claim her father's
birthright. They are plunged into the thick of the
fighting between the Chinese and Japanese.
Dorothy becomes an unwitting courier for Chinese Intelligence and later a CIA agent as a
member of the Flying Tigers. She was decorated
for bravery by the American government.

MOTHERS AND LOVERS
By Jeannie Sakol
Best selling author of "Hot 30" and "Flora Sweet"

PRICE: $2.25 LB743
CATEGORY: Novel

A witty, romantic novel of the intricate rela-
tionships between mother and daughter, husband
and wife, man and woman. Stephanie, twenty-
four, pregnant and on the verge of a divorce,
blames her mother Melissa for the mess she's in.
But Melissa's life has been no bed of roses either.
Stephanie finally realizes that no one is responsible for another's mistakes. She must solve her
own problems and fulfill her own destiny.

TRAVELIN' WOMAN
Katherine Gibbs

PRICE: $1.95 LB728
CATEGORY: Historical Romance (original)

Lovely young Samantha Houston lived on a small
farm in Alabama with her loving husband Josh
and their three small children. When Josh mys-
teriously disappeared, Samantha was forced to
flee with the children to the bustling port of
Savannah. But Samantha's struggles had only
begun. In her desperation to make a new life, she
became an uncompromising frontier business-
woman. But, when the suave, handsome Wade
McCain entered her life, Samantha wondered if
she could still be tender.

MOMENT OF THE PREDATOR
George Bernard

Author of "Inside the National Enquirer" and "Confessions of an Undercover Reporter".

PRICE: $2.25 LB807
CATEGORY: Novel (original)

A shocking and suspenseful novel of a vendetta against America by the PLO. Supermodel Dianne Spain—daughter of a prominent Nazi scientist entrusted with the heinous mission of murder and mayhem—is earmarked for destruction by the PLO. The plan is for Yasir Arafat to blow up the World Trade Center by pushing the detonator button while he is making a speech at the United Nations! The author actually went inside the PLO to write this work of fiction that is steeped in frightening reality.

Mr. Bernard is a frequent contributor to the National Star.

ALLEGRA
By Rosemary Winfield

PRICE: $1.95 LB720
CATEGORY: Historical Romance (Original)

Allegra Fontana, unhappy with her guardian's choice of a husband for her, is delighted to receive an invitation to attend the wedding of a distant relative, the Prince Raimundo de Lisi, in Southern Italy. Amid the lush palazzos of the Italian aristocracy, she succumbs to a forbidden love and falls hopelessly in love with Prince Raimundo. But the Prince is soon to be married. Then Laura, who has also been in love with Raimundo, is found dead, and Allegra realizes her life may be in danger, too. When Allegra learns the secret of her birth, it promises to unlock the door to a life of boundless happiness.

IN LOVE AND WAR
By Lorinda Hagen

PRICE: $2.25 LB719
CATEGORY: Novel (Original)

Esther, a minister's daughter from a small town, goes to Cincinnati to seek her fortune. She is discovered singing in a night club and is signed for a national tour and an opportunity for a movie test. She meets Neil Patterson, an aspiring novelist, who sells his first book to Hollywood. Esther gets the lead in his film at Neil's insistence. Esther Eden becomes a star and marries Neil. But they are soon separated when Neil signs on as a war correspondent after the attack on Pearl Harbor. Their world is torn apart, not only by the war, but by rumors of Esther's infidelity. Esther wages a passionate battle to hold onto the only man she has ever really loved.

LOUISIANA LIL
Donald McGregor

PRICE: $1.95 LB737
CATEGORY: Historical Novel

When Lamey arrives in Frenchtown looking for hi
long-lost sister, he runs into trouble with th
ruthless Donovan gang. It doesn't take him long t
discover that the gang is after the nearby tungste
mines—and that the town's notorious madam, Dia
mond-Stacked Lil, is really his sister. Encountering
treachery and violence at every turn, Lamey fight
the Donovans, reforms his sister, and wins the lov
of the beautiful Irene Randolph, the richest lady i
town!

ALABAMA BROWN
By Lorinda Hagen

PRICE: $2.25 LB753
CATEGORY: Historical Romance (Original)

When Rebecca Pearson first met handsome Steve
Mourgan, a scout for the wagon train bearing her
westward, she fell instantly in love. Joined by
passion yet separated by disaster, they vowed to
overcome the barriers that kept them apart!

SEND TO: LEISURE BOOKS
            P.O. Box 270
            Norwalk, Connecticut 06852

Please send me the following titles:

Quantity	Book Number	Price
_____	_____	_____
_____	_____	_____
_____	_____	_____
_____	_____	_____
_____	_____	_____

In the event we are out of stock on any of your selections, please list alternate titles below.

_____	_____	_____
_____	_____	_____
_____	_____	_____
_____	_____	_____

Postage/Handling _____

I enclose..... _____

FOR U.S. ORDERS, add 50¢ for the first book and 10¢ for each additional book to cover cost of postage and handling. Buy five or more copies and we will pay for shipping. Sorry, no C.O.D.'s.

FOR ORDERS SENT OUTSIDE THE U.S.A.
Add $1.00 for the first book and 25¢ for each additional book. PAY BY foreign draft or money order drawn on a U.S. bank, payable in U.S. ($) dollars.
☐Please send me a free catalog.

NAME _____
                    (Please print)

ADDRESS _____

CITY _____ **STATE**_____ **ZIP** _____
        Allow Four Weeks for Delivery